WHEN WE FELL

Machado Family Series
Book 1

CRISTINA SANTOS

Paperback: 978-1-7390407-6-5

E-book: 978-1-7390407-7-2

Cover Design: Kateryna Meleshchuk

Developmental Editing: Kristen at Kristen's Red Pen

Line Editing: Katie at Spice Me Up Editing

I'm dedicating this one to myself because this book was really freaking hard to write.

But also, if you've ever done something difficult even though you didn't think you could, this is for you, too. You did that shit. Own it!

Contents

Glossary

Because there are a lot of nicknames and animals in this book, here's a little guide to the ones you're about to meet.

NICKNAMES:

- Arthur Machado - Boss, Boss man
- Alice Preece - Whinny
- Rosemary - Ro, Rooster
- Paige - Gear
- Sam - Mouse
- Corey - Pop

ANIMALS:

- Horses already at the ranch:
  - Scout
  - Billy
  - Jasper
- New therapy horses:
  - Moose

- - Buttercup
  - Winston
- Dog:
  - Luther
- Goat:
  - Goaton Ramsey (Winston's companion)

THE MACHADOS (in order of oldest to youngest):

- Ana Maria - Bisa (Great-Grandma), Vó (Grandma)
- Ivan - Pai (Dad), Vô (Grandpa)
- Andrea - Mãe (Mom), Vó (Grandma)
- Arthur - Tio (Uncle), Mano (brother)
- Rafael - Tio (Uncle), main character in Out of Focus
- Gabriel - main character in the next Machado book!
- Marcelo - Tio (Uncle)
- Gustavo - Tio (Uncle)
- Daniela - Dani, Tia (Aunt)

Playlist

If you want to listen as you read, here's the playlist I curated for Arthur and Alice.

1. "Treasure" - Bruno Mars
2. "Wanna Be That Song" - Brett Eldredge
3. "You're On Your Own, Kid" - Taylor Swift
4. "I Can Do It With a Broken Heart" - Taylor Swift
5. "August" - Taylor Swift
6. "Beautiful Things" - Benson Boone
7. "First Time" - Hozier
8. "Say Don't Go" - Taylor Swift
9. "Breathe Me" - Sia
10. "Heaven" - Niall Horan
11. "Curls In the Wind" - Mark Amber
12. "Golden" - Harry Styles
13. "How Do I Love You" - Ashley Kutcher
14. "Cowboys Cry Too" - Kelsey Ballerini, Noah Kahan
15. "Don't Fade" - Vance Joy
16. "The Only Exception" - Paramore
17. "Klonopin" - Caleb Hearn

18. "Sink" - Noah Kahan
19. "Falling" - Harry Styles
20. "Vienna" - Billy Joel
21. "Don't Forget Me" - Maggie Rogers
22. "Paperweight" - Joshua Radin, Schuyler Fisk
23. "If We Were Vampires" - Noah Kahan, Wesley Schultz
24. "Death by a Thousand Cuts" - Taylor Swift
25. "Someone You Loved" - Lewis Capaldi
26. "Cardigan" - Taylor Swift
27. "Everywhere, Everything" - Noah Kahan, Gracie Abrams
28. "Safe With Me" - Ike Dweck
29. "Work Song" - Hozier
30. "Speechless" - Dan + Shay

A little note...

First of all, thank you.

I will never get over the fact that people want to read the stories I've written, and I appreciate you so, so much!

That being said, parts of this book may be triggering to you. I always want you to go into my stories knowing what to expect, but if you don't have any particular triggers and don't want any potential spoilers, skip the 'Content Warnings' page.

This is an 'open door' book, and that means that my characters have sex on the page, and things are described in detail. If that's not for you (or you're related to me), the chapters you should skip are in the 'Dicktionary.'

I hope Arthur and Alice remind you that you are not your past, you are not your circumstances, and you do, in fact, deserve all the love in the world.

xoxo,

-Cristina

Content Warnings

Please note that this book contains the following:

- Main character with a past struggling with addiction
- Mention of a parent's death
- Strained family relationships
- Character who is orphaned
- Chronic pain, specifically cervicogenic headaches
- Character taking care of family member with Alzheimer's
- Mention of a car accident
- Character in hospital
- Mention of pregnancy
- Open-door scenes of the couple being intimate

Reading this book might make you feel things, yes, but I never want to trigger negative thoughts or feelings, so please be kind to yourself.

Dicktionary

Whether you want to skip it, or skip *to* it, here's where you can find the spice and whose POV it's in:

Chapter 25: Alice
Chapter 28: Arthur
Chapter 29: Alice
Chapter 32: Alice
Epilogue: Alice

Enjoy! (Or don't…)

sounded like she was auditioning for a 1990's porno

Arthur

It's a Wednesday night, and while the bar is a little more lively than I'd like, it's still pretty quiet compared to the weekends. I prefer when it's just me and a few other regulars here. I come in, I sit alone, and no one bothers me. I drink my coffee while occasionally chatting with the owners, Beau and Josie. It's nice. I like it. Exactly the way it is.

But despite tonight not being a busy one, there's an extra buzz in the air, and the music is just a touch louder than usual. The lights seem a little lower, too.

I've been sitting here for an hour when a flash of light pulls my attention to the dance floor, where a blonde woman is attempting to dance with someone who is clearly not into it. The guy is so drunk, he's barely holding himself up, let alone her.

I shake my head and bring my gaze back to the shiny wooden bar top.

"For a guy who doesn't drink, you sure spend a lot of

time here." Jo rounds the corner of the bar and sets a fresh cup in front of me, a small smile causing her eyes to crinkle. "I'm gonna guess that coffee is ice cold by now and probably tastes like piss. I brewed you a fresh pot."

"Thanks, Josie Posie. Beau's good at a lot of things, but coffee-making is nowhere close to being one of them. You're an angel." I wink at her and bring the freshly made coffee to my lips, breathing in the scent.

"You know, Arthur, that lopsided smile and wink of yours are nothing but trouble." She waves a finger at me, taking the cold coffee cup and spinning on her heel to dump its contents in the sink and place it on a rack of dirty glasses. The familiar clinking of glasses momentarily drowns out the terrible pop song currently playing. When she turns back toward me, she begins to wipe the bar top, but stops when something catches her eye. "Hmm…"

As the song changes to "Treasure" by Bruno Mars, I follow her gaze to the other end of the bar, where a woman has just sat on a stool, elbows propped on the bar with her head in her hands. The same blonde from the dance floor—the one with a sparkly belt that she seems to be trying to pass off as a shirt—is next to her, rolling her eyes, oblivious to or uncaring of her friend's feelings. The brunette looks up, trying to get Beau's attention behind the bar, but he's deep into some inventory and either doesn't see her or is ignoring her. Waving, the blonde girl walks away with her dance partner, who's easily three sheets to the wind. His scrawny, tattooed arm goes around her shoulder as they leave the bar and he gives her a sloppy kiss I wish I hadn't witnessed.

Josie makes a sound of disgust next to me before whistling, making the brunette with slick, straight hair look in our direction. Her eyes practically glow in the dimly lit bar, the golden color drawing me in as her gaze roams my face, then swings to Jo, where it softens as she takes in the tall woman with a kind smile.

"Come on over here, sweetie." Jo waves a hand to the empty stool next to me, and I stiffen. What the fuck is she doing? She might not always be running the bar with Beau, but she knows I don't come here to socialize.

I silently glare at the woman I thought was my friend as her grin widens. "You look like you need something to take your woes away. My husband is in his own world counting bottles, so he might be a while. What can I get you?"

Without hesitation, the smooth-as-silk voice next to me says, "Two shots of tequila, please." She sits on the backless wooden stool next to mine and her scent—something soft and fresh—floats over, and I instinctively inhale. Coconut and something flowery. Pretty. Like her.

I force my focus back to my cup and keep my body as still as a statue. Without another word, two shot glasses are set in front of her. "Thank you," the newcomer says softly to Jo, but makes no move to drink the alcohol.

"Just holler if you need me. My name's Josie. Or Jo. I'll answer to both." She knocks on the bar top twice and takes a nearly empty rack of dirty glasses to the back. It's completely unnecessary. Beau would never bother to run those through the dishwasher without the rack being full, he'd call it a waste of resources.

But Meddling Josie here has an ulterior motive. She thinks I'm going to strike up a conversation with a stranger. She's wrong.

Looking around the room, I take in the details I've already memorized. Pictures behind the bar of Josie and Beau growing up together. Their families. Places they've visited. Friends who have visited the bar. The walls are olive green with exposed wooden beams on the ceiling and along some of the walls as shelves. Everything here has a history, and though most people don't know that when they walk in, it's what makes this place so special. You can feel the familiarity in the space even without understanding why. It always makes me think of the TV show *Cheers*. I'd hate for everyone to know my name, but I like knowing all our troubles are the same when we walk in.

"Your coffee smells good." Speaking a little louder than before, her voice startles me, and I turn quickly toward her, making the mistake of meeting her eyes. She averts my gaze just as fast as I do hers, but it's too late. I saw their amber glow, and now I know she's not just pretty, she's fucking gorgeous. "Your day must be going as well as mine if you're at a bar on a Wednesday night drinking coffee alone."

Ouch. Okay, yeah, I get what this looks like, but it's just part of my routine, really. A routine almost no one knows about.

She winces. "Sorry. That wasn't—I didn't mean it like that. I didn't mean to assume what your day was like or why you're here. I'm just grumpy because my life has been turned upside down. Now, the person I was supposed to room with just told me her new boyfriend is moving in, so I have no place to live. I was supposed to move in tomorrow, but apparently, buddy-with-the-terrible-tats needs the room that would have been mine for his doll collection. I'm not even kidding. That's the real reason. He collects porcelain dolls, and as desperate as I am for a place to live, I'm not *that* desperate, you know? I mean, could you imagine waking up in the middle of the night with all those beady, glass eyes staring at you?" She shivers dramatically, and I bite my lip to keep from smiling.

I make no other move to indicate I'm listening to her.

I'm hanging on every word, though, for some weird reason.

Her adorable tangent doesn't stop there. "Those two were practically dry-humping at our table earlier, not caring whether anyone could see them. But that's not even the actual issue. It was the noises. Kit sounded like she was auditioning for a 1990s porno, and Doll Boy kisses *loudly*, you know? Like not the hot kind of kissing noises, the sloppy kind that sounds like slurping soup. Ugh, gosh, just thinking about it is making me a little nauseous." She brings a hand to her stomach, her eyes taking in the same details I had just been cataloging.

I can't help the chuckle that comes out of me, then.

Tilting her face toward me, her eyes widen, her pouty peach lips forming an 'O.' I hope she doesn't think I'm laughing at her expense. There's just something about the way she's been rambling, the way she uses her hands when she's speaking, like she needs to physically punctuate certain parts of her story. Even her voice has me strangely captivated.

"I'm sorry," I mumble, clearing my throat. "I'm not laughing at you, I swear." I spin my coffee cup slowly on the bar, noting that she's dressed far more casually than her blonde friend was. Her jeans have big tears at the knees and they're loose around her legs, but they cinch in perfectly at her waist, where her cropped pink T-shirt leaves just a small sliver of bronze skin exposed. The sneakers on her feet are white, and it's clear they're well-loved based on the scuff marks. She has gold jewelry on, which makes me think of the color of her eyes, and there's an odd dichotomy to her baggy, ripped jeans and the pretty jewelry, but somehow, she makes it work. She tilts her head again, and I'm reminded to continue what I had started saying. "But I do agree that you're better off not sleeping with some dude's creepy-ass dolls. There'd be no recovering from those nightmares."

It's her turn to laugh. It starts small, then expands into a sound that has her eyes clamping shut as she throws her head back. She brings a hand to her chest, like she can't control the feeling, and something like pride blooms inside me for making someone who was clearly having a shitty time feel joy. I'm not usually that guy. My brothers Raf, Marcelo, and Gus? Sure. They're effortlessly hilarious, but Gabriel and I didn't get the funny traits.

When she finally settles down, a rogue giggle slipping out as she shakes her head, she spins in her stool to face me. "Thanks for that. I needed someone to not sugarcoat the situation for me and tell it like it is." After crossing her legs, she leans forward with her elbow on her knee. "I just shared more information than is appropriate with a perfect stranger. Care to tell me why you're having coffee at a bar in the middle of the week?" Resting her cheek on her fist, she smiles, a little dimple popping on her cheek. "I mean, you don't have to, but it only seems fair." Her shoulders lift in a shrug as her lips turn down into a pout that disappears too quickly for me to memorize.

I blow out a loud breath, having an answer for her question that is a distant version of the truth at the ready, because it's not the first time I've been asked. "Well, it's a very interesting story, really. All the good coffee shops in town close early, and I like it here. Even if Beau, the owner, is grumpy as hell and can't make coffee taste like anything other than rat piss. But Josie made this one, and it's delicious." I punctuate my point by taking a sip, and her amber eyes track my every movement as she pulls her lips between her teeth.

"That's… the least interesting thing I've ever heard." She purses her lips, holding back a smile. "Wow. I mean, did I fall asleep for a second there? I think I might have." She fakes a loud yawn, and what I know is a pathetically goofy smile on my face only grows as she continues, "You owe me a better story. I gave you porn noises and haunted dolls, man. This isn't even close to fair." She sighs, feigning exasperation as her dimple gives her away. She doesn't seem capable of fighting off her smile any more than I am, and I really like that.

I've never met a woman at Beau's Bar before. Never wanted to. I come here for peace and quiet, and if I want someone to hook up with, I head to the touristy places in town. It doesn't normally take more than an hour before someone is eyeing my muddy boots, asking what I do for a living, and wondering just how well I know how to ride. It's always some version of the same lame innuendo, but I like the predictability of it all. They want to save a horse and ride a cowboy—which I most certainly am not, but don't bother to correct—and I want... well... sex. Specifically, with someone I don't have to see ever again. Someone who doesn't have to carry any of my burdens, because no one should have to.

I focus back on the surprisingly enticing woman next to me, whose sparkling eyes look like golden coins. "Hate to break it to you, tesouro." The nickname slips out, either because of the song or those damn eyes I'm fascinated by. Thankfully, they're not so distracting that I can't finish my thought. "But I'm a pretty boring guy." Not a lie. I don't do much outside of work and this. Occasionally, I might see one of my siblings, but the guilt, shame, and fear of letting more people down mostly keeps me away from my family—they don't deserve any of my bullshit either. My friend and sponsor would vehemently disagree with me, but he's been trying to convince me to make amends with my family for years, and I haven't budged yet.

"Is that so?" she asks, eyes squinting with disbelief.

Clearing my throat as I force myself not to dwell on the things I can't fix right now, I go on, "I like having a simple life. Simple routines. And I'm not ashamed to admit that curling up with my dog at the end of the day with a good book is an ideal night for me." More truths I don't normally share, because if you tell a woman you have a pet, they'll want to meet it. I don't bring anyone to the farmhouse. Ever. For a multitude of reasons. Though I'm sure Luther would love a new friend to play with.

"What kinds of books?" Her eyes light up, and the question takes me by surprise. I expected her to ask about the dog, and since I never get to talk about books with anyone, my answer slips out easily.

"Thrillers, mostly." I scratch the back of my neck, leaving out the fact that occasionally I borrow one of Raf's romance novels. The mystery woman next to me raises her brows, silently asking me to elaborate. "But sometimes it's nice to read something lighter, I guess, you know?" At the unsure tone in my voice, Josie, who's been pretending not to listen as she putters around behind the bar, covers up a laugh with a cough. She's a menace.

Biting her lip thoughtfully, my new companion shakes her head. "Well, not really, no. I don't even remember the last time I read something that wasn't educational or self-help or something." Coming out of most people, that sentence might sound condescending or judgmental, but she says it almost like she's upset at the fact she just stated about herself. Her lips momentarily turn into a frown. "I wouldn't even know what I like to read when it comes to fiction, to be honest, but I think I'd like to find out." A small smile tugs at one side of her mouth as her eyes meet mine again, hope written across what is probably the prettiest face I've ever seen. "Can you recommend anything?"

I don't even hesitate. I say the first thing that comes to my mind, which isn't usually the best choice. "Karina Halle has a great dark, sort of gothic, and paranormal book called Grave Matter. It's a little science-y, and there's a great twist. It takes place in British Columbia." Fuck. That book is also technically a romance. It definitely has explicit sex scenes.

Shit.

I just recommended smut to a woman whose first name I don't know.

Is that inappropriate? I don't know what the etiquette on stuff like this is.

Without questioning anything else about the book, because why would she, she slides her phone out of her back pocket and mouths the title as she types. The way her lips move is distractingly sexy. And adorable. "Got it." Her tone is triumphant. "I wonder if that cool outdoor bookstore will have it," she says mostly to herself. "Anyway, thanks…"

"Arthur," I finish. Again, my mouth works faster than my brain, and before I know it, so does my hand, because it's outstretched.

She places her small, delicate hand in my callused one, and I hold my breath as the simple touch travels from the tips of my fingers and straight to my chest like a bolt of lightning on a skyscraper.

"Alice," she says softly, and only then do I exhale.

Alice, I repeat in my mind.

"It's nice to meet you, Arthur."

it has my mind—and my dick—reeling

Arthur

With her hand still in mine and a bright smile on her face, she stands. "Wanna dance with me?" Her question takes me entirely by surprise.

I don't move, but then it registers that there's a slow country song is playing. Beau usually puts shit like this on when it's dead in here, so I recognize it almost immediately.

Alice's grin slips when I take too long to respond, and as she starts to retrieve her hand, I squeeze a little tighter. I'm on my feet before I let go, flexing my fingers as if that will get rid of the tingling sensation. I don't know what the fuck has gotten into me, but apparently, I'm going to dance with her, so I nod and we make our way slowly to the dimly lit dance floor.

We get into position silently, her hands resting on my shoulders before wrapping gently around my neck as mine settle low on her back. We start out like two awkward teenagers at a middle school dance—bodies a little stiff and averting our eyes to look at everything but each other. But as the seconds tick by, we relax, and as her sweet scent fills my lungs, I close my eyes just long enough to take the deepest breath, as if it may be my last. When I let it out, her feet shift closer, or maybe it's mine that move first. I can't be bothered to care that we're cheek to cheek, shifting so slowly in the nearly empty room that I'm not even sure this counts as dancing. When my hands shift along her back, my fingers graze the space between her shirt and the waistband of her jeans, and she melts a little deeper into me. She's so soft, and the sweet humming noise she makes when I draw little circles on her skin has my mind—and my dick—reeling.

I've never danced with anyone at Beau's Bar. I've never wanted to. Maybe it was the way her shoulders were slumped when her friend left, or the way her dimple popped when she smiled, or how hopeful she sounded at the simple prospect of a new book to read. Let's go with that. Let's go with the fact that whatever her troubles are, she's here because she needs a pick-me-up, and if I can help to give her that, then I will. Vó always says we're born with two hands for a reason: one to give and one to receive.

The song ends, and there are a couple of seconds of silence before the next one starts up. I say a silent prayer for another ballad. Something that will keep us here. But nope. Fucking "Chattahoochee" starts to play, and Alice's forehead comes to rest on my shoulder as her body shakes with laughter. She steps back, taking all the warmth in the room with her when she turns to walk back to our stools. As much as I dislike that we've lost our physical connection, I'm not mad about the view. The way her jeans hug her hips and ass is sinful, and I wouldn't change a damn thing about it.

We take our seats, her body still turned toward mine when she says, "Thank you for the dance." Her focus drops to the two shots still on the bar. "Well, I guess I should drink these, huh? I thought they might improve my day, but sitting here with you has already taken care of that." Her cheeks turn a shade of pink I'd definitely like to see again, but she pushes through her embarrassment and meets my eyes. "I suppose they can't make the day worse, though, right?" She doesn't wait for an answer. "Would you like to join me?" Her bright eyes widen as she waits for my answer.

After a long silence, I glance at the shot glass that's been pushed closer to me while my body remains perfectly still. I smell the alcohol, but I'm not tempted by it. I never am.

"I'm good," I respond, not chancing a look at her face again. Like Beau, I don't have a problem being near alcohol, but I won't drink it. We also choose not to surround ourselves with people who drink excessively, who lose control. He's always had strict rules about how much he serves his patrons, and if they don't like it, they can leave.

It confused me at first, a Narcotics Anonymous sponsor who owned a bar, but it makes sense now. Beau likes to take care of people, and he feels he can do that by ensuring everyone is safe in his bar.

Alice shrugs, seemingly unaffected by my refusal. "More for me, then." She clinks her glass with the one on the bar and takes the shot. The empty glass has barely touched the shiny wood before she's downed the second shot glass and thrown its contents back, too, without so much as a wince. She might as well be taking shots of apple juice, not tequila.

Something awfully close to disappointment twists in my gut as I look at the empty glasses. It doesn't normally bother me to see people drinking, though I suppose I was hoping for a completely sober interaction tonight. Especially after that dance.

"Hey, Jo, can I get a glass of water, please?" I'd get it myself, but Beau hates it when I go behind the bar, and I don't feel like getting a lecture from him today when I'm actually enjoying a conversation with someone other than him or his wife.

"Thank you," she whispers to Josie when the glass of water is placed in front of her. Alice looks at me while she takes several sips of water, and as she sets the glass down, those golden eyes hold mine. Time comes to a standstill as we sit and stare at each other, until movement catches my eye, and I look down to where she's pulled her full lower lip into her mouth.

Before I can form any other thoughts or make an excuse to leave, she releases her lip. "All right." She clears her throat. "Two truths and a lie. Go. And try not to put me to sleep this time with your fun facts, 'kay?" That cute dimple taunts me again, and I wonder how exactly this happened. We've only just met, and she already knows more about me than most people I have conversations with. I'm about to share more, and I don't mind one bit. Not with her.

I scratch my jaw, thinking about what on Earth could be interesting enough to share. She watches my every move, and it's hard to think with her eyes on me. "Um, well, let's see. I lost my virginity when I was fourteen—she was seventeen. I'm dangerously allergic to mushrooms. I've jumped out of an airplane twelve times." It's the best I can do under pressure.

She squints while she thinks over my answers. "I could totally see you being a heartbreaker, even at fourteen, so I believe that." Josie snorts from somewhere close-by, not even pretending not to listen anymore. "But there's no way you've done anything as wild as jumping out of an airplane, let alone twelve times. Not Mr. Snuggles-up-with-his-dog-and-a-book."

The smile that takes over my face is triumphant. She's so confident, yet she got it wrong. "My brother is allergic to mushrooms," I state as she gasps and mutters something under her breath that sounds like *son of a biscuit*, and I chuckle. "Your turn."

"Fine," she huffs. "I'm terrified of spiders, but I work with twelve-hundred-pound animals all day. I have five siblings. I've never been to a bar before tonight." After clasping her hands together on her lap, she waits for me to study her the way she did me, but I don't have to. She gives herself away with her facial expressions. It's like she's incapable of telling a lie.

"You don't have any siblings, do you?" Her face falls immediately, and I know I have her pegged. She tucks a stray hair behind her ear and sets her hand on the bar, looking at the floor with the saddest expression. "Hey," I say gently, reaching for her fingers. "I didn't mean to upset you." We're barely touching, but every nerve ending in my body is aware of the small connection. Every inch of my skin feels suddenly charged, like her touch is awakening some hibernating part of me. She doesn't pull away, and neither do I.

"It's okay," she replies. "I just didn't think it would be so obvious that I'm an only child." Her small smile is forced this time, and my favorite dimple stays hidden.

"It's not that," I start to explain. "You just have a really expressive face. There was no emotion when you told me the lie." She meets my gaze again, curiosity painted beautifully on her bronze skin. "But you lit up when you mentioned your work, like it makes you happy, and there was a tiny shrug when you said you've never been to a bar, like that fact doesn't bother you one bit."

It happens again. We sit, eyes locked, fingertips touching, and this bar could be packed full of people and I wouldn't know it. There's only her. Though I know this won't go any further tonight because I'm not here for a hook-up, and—more importantly—because the way she's throwing back shots tells me it absolutely can't, I let myself continue to touch her anyway. Just for now.

After taking a shaky breath, she pulls away, and I sip my coffee as Alice fans herself and reaches back to where I hadn't noticed a small purse was hanging on the back of the stool. She pulls out a clip and twists her hair up effortlessly. Her cheeks are no longer rosy, but now a deep shade of crimson, and I wonder if it's the alcohol or if I've made her uncomfortable.

"Excuse me, I'll be right back." She shoots out of her stool and heads toward the restrooms, practically breaking into a jog. Gulping down my coffee, I try to shake off whatever this feeling is. She's beautiful, yes, but the short conversation we've had has been far more enjoyable than any interaction I've had with a woman in a very long time. There's been none of my usual transactional flirting—the kind where I know the witty comments and playful touches will lead somewhere. That somewhere starts with a touch here, a wink there, and we both get what we're after, then leave without ever expecting to see one another again.

But this isn't that. Sure, she might be flirting, but it feels like more. It feels like she's sharing herself with me in the same unexpected way that I'm sharing myself with her.

Other than telling me that my presence has helped her take her mind off her shitty day, she's given me no impression that she's interested in me, but I feel it the same way I feel my fingertips drumming on the bar top.

Several minutes pass as I replay the last hour. For a moment, I wonder if she has left, but then worry hits me that maybe something is wrong. If there's one thing my grandmother always drilled into me, it was to always listen to my gut. Vó is one of the wisest, feistiest women I've ever met. I probably like Josie so much because in the next few decades, she'll be just like Vó. I look around for my friend, wondering if she can go check on Alice, but she's not around, and Beau has his nose in a calculator I won't dare pull him away from. I learned my lesson after the first mistake, and I don't want to do his inventory ever again.

Fuck it.

I head for the small hallway at the back of the bar. After knocking lightly on the closed bathroom door, I wait a few seconds for a response, but I don't get one. Then I hear it. The telltale wretch of someone being sick.

For reasons I might never be able to explain, I try to open the door, expecting to find it locked. It opens instantly, and there she is, on her knees, face in the toilet bowl. There's a bottle of disinfectant and a wad of paper towels next to her, which is odd, but I don't have time to question it.

She hasn't heard me come in, so I kneel next to her, placing my hand on her back. "Hey, hey, it's okay. You're gonna be all right," I soothe. She must have had more to drink tonight if those two shots did her in like that, but she didn't look drunk at all. I know appearances don't mean anything, though. It's amazing how good people can get at hiding just how fucked up they are. I would know.

She flushes the toilet and reaches for the roll of paper towel on the floor. I grab it for her, ripping a piece and handing it over. She doesn't say anything as she wipes at her teary cheeks and mouth. I give her a moment, heading to the sink to run some more paper towels under cold water, wringing them out carefully, then kneeling behind her, placing the cool paper on the back of her neck. She sighs and relaxes, sitting on her feet.

Taking deep breaths, she closes her eyes then whispers, "Oh no," before leaning forward again to heave into the toilet. I rub her back as she successfully empties her stomach. Again and again, her body convulses as she sobs, and I feel completely helpless.

When she finally stops, slumping on the floor, I pull her back to lean on me, and she rests her head on my shoulder, her face turned away. "I'm so sorry," she mumbles through soft sobs, and I wonder if she has someone, anyone, who can help her. I've been at rock bottom, so I know what it looks like. If I had to guess, she's either there now or close to it.

Eventually, Josie appears at the door. "Oh shit." Her eyes widen as she takes in the nearly passed-out woman and me on the bathroom floor.

"Yeah," I whisper. "She's conscious, but barely. I'm not sure what to do." Especially since I don't think she has a place to stay.

"Bring her upstairs. I'll take care of her tonight and see what she needs in the morning. Won't be the first time, and certainly not the last that someone drinks too much and needs a safe space to wake up in." No-nonsense Josie starts to walk away, then turns back. "You gonna need my help?"

"No, I got her." As I start to move, Alice remains mostly limp in my arms, and as I carry her up the stairs to set her on Josie and Beau's couch, I wonder how I didn't see that she was under the influence while we were talking. I should know better, damn it.

what did i tell you about smacking my ass outside of the bedroom?

Alice

I wake abruptly, but don't open my eyes. The pounding inside my skull is severe, and after the violent way my stomach emptied its contents, I don't trust myself to make any sudden movements. I need to see where I am, though, because it's surely not in the bar bathroom anymore. I'm warm, there's a blanket covering me up, and it smells faintly of honey in here.

"You're all right," a gentle voice says somewhere in the room. "You're safe. When you're ready to open your eyes, there's some water and a painkiller next to you." Something creaks over and over, and I wince at the sound. If there's a light on, I know it'll hurt like hell when I open my eyes, but I have to do it.

With a deep breath and placing a hand on my stomach, I squint, taking in the cozy living room. The lights are dim, and it's still dark out. Across from me is the woman from the bar, Josie, in a rocking chair. She's focused on whatever is resting on her lap, so I take the opportunity to slowly sit up, gauging my nausea. It's still lingering, but mostly gone. Once I've taken the pill and set the glass down, I look up to find Josie peering at me.

"Just how much did you have to drink before you went to the bar?" The concern in her voice makes my chest hurt. It's been so long since anyone has worried about me, and part of me wants to ask her why she cares.

Instead, I answer her plainly, "I—I didn't. I didn't drink anything." Her brows shoot up in surprise, or maybe disbelief. "I swear, I didn't. I've never even had alcohol before. That was the first time I drank anything. Ever." I sniffle, looking around for a box of tissues, and thankfully finding one on a nearby side table.

Josie walks to where I am, sitting on the coffee table and eyeing me curiously. "Your cheeks are very red," she notes. "And you're stuffed up." She nods, looking in my eyes in the dim light. "Hmm. How are you feeling right now?" She places the back of her hand on my clammy forehead, and I close my eyes for a second, leaning into her cool touch.

Catching myself, I sit up a little straighter. "My head really hurts, but I have chronic headaches, so that's not very unusual for me. I'm still a little nauseous, which also isn't uncommon with the headaches. I'm stuffed up, like you said, and my skin feels a little hot. I'm tired, but that's it." I sniffle again, reaching for another tissue.

"No shortness of breath? Stomach pain? Itching or hives anywhere?" She takes my chin, inspecting each side of my face. "You don't have any swelling, so that's a good sign."

"Um, none of that other stuff, either." It's strange that this woman I met mere hours ago seems so invested in my well-being. What could she want with me? "Anyway, I can get going. I'm sure I'll be fine. But thank you for letting me stay here. That was very nice of you. Can I pay you? Shoot. I haven't even paid for my drinks yet." I reach behind me, hoping to find my purse, and when it's not there, my eyes roam the space, hoping to see it somewhere. Josie just continues to watch me carefully. "I'm sorry. You have no reason to be this nice to me. I can just get my stuff and go, I—"

Before I can go on with my rambling apology and try to leave, she interrupts me, "I think you have alcohol intolerance. Probably not an allergy, because you don't seem to be having any other major reactions, unless you have rashes we can't see. You said earlier that your roommate just invited her boyfriend to move in, so you don't have a place to go, do you?"

After a brief pause, she lays a hand on my knee, and I flinch, but she doesn't let up. "It's okay. I don't need you to pay me for anything. I was a nurse for years, and my husband has owned that bar for a very long time. Between the two of us, we've seen it all, believe me. I've taken care of a lot of people over the years. I own the store next to the bar and stick to honey and baked goods since stepping away from healthcare, but once a nurse, always a nurse." As she gives my knee a squeeze, I look at her. She has a kind face, but people can seem one way and then turn out to be another. I know this. It's a fact. "I still think you should get a test to make sure it's not an allergy, but either way, it's probably best to keep away from alcohol. You can stay here. No need to rush out. If you don't feel safe, by all means, go, but I'm offering you a pretty comfortable couch and some fresh bread in the morning. Are you new in town?"

Given the way the pounding in my head has just escalated from a single drum to an entire marching band, this couch is looking better by the second. And fresh bread? Is she kidding me? Bread is my weakness. How does she know?

"Uh, sort of, yes. I'm looking after my grandmother, and I just got a job here." That's as much as she's getting out of me regarding my personal life.

"I already knew you were a good egg. You don't have to try to prove it to me. I'm an excellent judge of character. Why do you think I called you over at the bar?" She chuckles, like what she said is humorous in any way. She can't be more than a decade older than me. She doesn't look a day over forty, and yet she knits on a rocking chair and says things like *good egg*. "Anyway, get some rest. Holler if you start to feel any worse. We'll be down the hall. Beau sleeps like the dead, but I'll wake up if you need me."

I lay back and close my eyes, willing the tears building behind my eyelids not to fall. That would be embarrassing. But her words play on a loop until sleep takes over.

If you need me.

When was the last time I needed anyone? Better yet, when was the last time I needed anyone and could count on them to actually take care of me?

I MUST BE in heaven because the air is thick with the scent of fresh bread.

Geez, that smells amazing.

There's a faint aroma of coffee, too, and I know I'm either dead or dreaming because when have I ever woken up anywhere that smelled this good? That felt this cozy?

"Shh. I told you not to use that stupid kettle, didn't I? Why can't you just drink coffee in the morning like a normal person?" The hushed voice is followed by a deep sigh.

"Darlin', you know there's nothing normal about me. You've known that since we were twelve years old. I like what I like." The deep male voice is kind, and is followed by a faint thud, then a hiss.

"Beau James Michaelson. What did I tell you about smacking my ass outside of the bedroom?"

The man chuckles. "I don't remember. Want me to take you in there and you can remind me?"

"Honestly, you are still as insatiable as you were when we married. Get it together. We have a guest." Through the whispering, I make out that it's Josie's voice.

Josie. The bar. Tequila. Vomit.

It all comes back to me as I try to remain perfectly still, keeping my breathing even.

"She's sleeping. And it's no secret to anyone in this town that I can't keep my hands off my beautiful wife." There's a loud kissing sound and another smack.

"She's awake, you fool." Her tone is nowhere near as harsh as her words, and a low laugh follows. "Now, be a good host and get that bread on the table. Butter, too."

Well, I guess I've been found out, but between not knowing where I was at first and kind of wanting to see how this little scene played out, pretending to be asleep seemed like the right choice.

Ignoring the pang in my chest at how sweet their entire interaction was, I clear my throat. "Morning." Opening my eyes, I pull in a long breath, noting that my nausea is gone and my headache is nothing but an annoying twinge now.

"Hey, you." Josie's already smiling when I look up at her across the room to the open kitchen. "Feeling better?"

Sitting up slowly, I nod. "Yes, thank you."

"Good. Now, are you normal, or do you drink herbal tea in the mornings, too?" Shoot. I guess she knows I heard the whole conversation.

"I'd love a coffee, please." I stand and tidy the blanket and pillows I slept with, and when I approach the kitchen, there's a hot cup in front of the vacant chair at the table, a steaming loaf of bread and some butter in the middle, sugar, cream, and milk sitting out. It looks like something I've seen in movies, with the soft sunlight pouring through the sheer curtains and a nice-looking couple sitting together for breakfast.

"Good morning. We weren't properly introduced yesterday. I'm Beau." The gentleman with sky-blue eyes and patches of gray hair around his temples smiles up at me.

"Nice to meet you, Beau. I'm Alice. Thank you so much for letting me stay here." At that, Josie taps the table, nodding to the empty seat.

"Alice. That's a lovely name." She reaches for a slice of bread and bites into it without any butter. "Eat up," Jo says around her mouthful as Beau chuckles into his coffee mug, eyes never leaving his wife.

I guess I might as well enjoy this before facing the realities of being homeless, starting a new job, and figuring out what to do with my sick grandmother and her uninhabitable house.

ask for forgiveness, not for permission, right?

Alice

Beau and Josie asked surprisingly few questions, other than where I'd be working and what I do. The look they exchanged when I mentioned the ranch was quick but pointed. I don't know what it meant, and I didn't bother asking. I need the job, and I'm not going to give myself any reason not to take it when the owners seem like they're decent people.

Not wanting to overstay my welcome, I thanked Josie and Beau again and promised I had a place to stay. I didn't tell them that place would be a hotel thirty minutes outside of town because everything in Ojai is overpriced. They're on a need-to-know basis, considering they're practically strangers.

After a hot shower, a long stretching session, and another painkiller to make sure this headache doesn't make a comeback, I check over the folder I put together with everything I need for my new job. I was nervous about taking this because, being an occupational therapist, I don't always get to choose the patients I'll work with, but Owen and Maeve have decided to offer hippotherapy at their ranch, and it was always my dream to help people and be around horses all day. Once I discovered the peace that horses brought me, I had to pursue a career where I'd get to be around them.

I'd been at my last job for six months when I got the call that Gran had nearly burned her house down and would likely need to be moved into an assisted-living facility. It was impossible to make that happen from hours away, so here I am. Everything happened so fast, I hardly had time to register that in the two weeks since that call, I had emptied my apartment, quit my job, gotten a new one, and found a new roommate. Well, until last night, that is.

Regardless of yesterday's drama, I'm glad I'll see some horses today and set foot in a stable again. It is my happy place, after all.

I'm on my way there now, to sign paperwork and meet everyone in person. I've had a few calls with Rosemary, the Certified Therapeutic Riding Instructor in charge of hiring me and Owen, one of the owners. His wife will also be there to meet me today, along with most of the staff. It's a small team for now, which I'm kind of excited about. As excited as I'll allow myself to get for this temporary position, anyway.

As I pull in, I take in the field of wildflowers to one side, a farmhouse in the distance with what must be an amazing view of the sunset over the mountains, and finally, the main barn.

I take in a deep breath the second I step out of my Jeep, allowing myself a moment to appreciate the sun on my face and the fresh air.

The crunch of gravel snaps me out of it, and I exhale slowly before facing whoever is headed toward me. Thank goodness for video calls to prepare me for this moment, because the very tall, very blond man walking over here is drop-dead gorgeous. I knew he had a nice face, but whoa. This is… a lot. And he has a baby attached to him.

Goodness gracious.

My brain chooses this moment to remember strong arms and gentle brown eyes. The warm, spicy scent that enveloped me when I sat next to the man who managed to turn my day around with easy conversation and a slow dance. Until I went and messed it all up, anyway.

I shake myself out of my stupor and refocus on my new boss.

"Alice, hey!" He waves, and as he gets closer, stretches out a hand. "It's so nice to finally meet you in person."

Giving him a firm handshake, I smile at him and the adorable baby blowing raspberries on his chest. "Hi, Owen. Great to meet you as well. And who is this?"

"This is Douglas, our youngest." His eyes soften as he gazes down at his son before looking up at me. "You ready to meet the crew? Maeve's been very excited to meet you." I swear his eyes sparkle when he says his wife's name. What is in the water here, with all these couples happily in love? "Our head honcho isn't here today. He has some training to attend and we're looking to acquire some more horses and expand the stables, so he's going to be working unusual hours for the next week or so."

"No problem. I'm looking forward to meeting everyone." We make our way to the barn, where the sound of happy chatter greets us. The horses are quiet, looking quite content as they listen in.

"Alice?" A gorgeous blonde woman who seems vaguely familiar smiles brightly at me, and I smile back, confirming her assumption of who I am. "Wonderful to meet you! We're thrilled to have you here and to get started with these new programs." Her British accent is strong, and that's when recognition slams into me like a transport truck.

"Oh, wow, you're Maeve Howard," I breathe out, slightly star-struck, having never met a celebrity before. Maybe I should have done more research on my new employers, but I was just so happy to find a job, I didn't bother in case I found something I didn't like. I can't be looking for reasons not to accept the opportunities that come my way. Not right now.

"Owen didn't tell you?" She glowers at her husband, but the look almost immediately softens when he winks at her and then kisses their baby's head. "Well, yes. I hope that's not a problem for you. We live at the property next door, but I'll be sure to let you know when I want to come by to see my girls. I'd hate to disrupt any of your work." She looks over at the young woman to her right, who's had a friendly smile on her face this entire time.

"N-no, it's not a problem. Of course not." I'll just be working for the most beautiful people I've ever met, and one of them is a major celebrity. It's fine.

"Brilliant. Well, this is Paige. She's in charge while boss-man is out and about. She's in training to take over once Arty moves into Rosemary's position. Corey is another of our team members," she says, patting a middle-aged man on the shoulder who nods at me, "and Sam is around here somewhere, too. Probably on the move since they can't ever sit still." She looks around, and not seeing Sam, turns back to me. "It's a great team, and we think you'll be a valuable addition here." She nods, eyes bright and hopeful.

"I hope I am," I say, bottling down the urge to add that I won't be in Ojai forever. I'll still work as hard as I can while I'm here, so it doesn't matter. "It's great to meet you,

Paige and Corey." We shake hands, and we all turn to the shuffling sound coming from the other side of the barn.

"I think Polly is back. Made another mess." The tall, lanky individual brushes their hands on their worn jeans. "All cleaned up now, but I set another trap for that little jerk." Walking over to where we are, a hand is stretched toward me. "Hey, I'm Sam. Nice to meet ya."

My face must be doing something strange, because as I shake Sam's hand and say my name, Maeve and Owen both laugh.

"Polly is an opossum. And don't worry, it's a live trap, so Polly won't be hurt," my new coworker reassures me.

I let out a relieved breath, and we all laugh. Paige, Corey, and Sam show me around the stables, and we meet up with Rosemary at the clinic a few yards away. I get to meet the friendlier horses—two of them are a little on the unruly side, thanks to a bad experience at their last stable, so the crew is working with them. It's nice that they care so much about their animals here. I also come to find out that everyone has nicknames, which they normally go by around here. Paige's nickname is Gear, Corey's is Pop, and Sam's is Mouse. They tell me I have to figure out the reason by myself. Apparently, when the time is right, I'll get my own. Rosemary's nickname is Rooster, and I'd bet it's because she's clearly in charge and not afraid to make some noise when needed. I like that it also sort of sounds like her name.

"All right, Alice, if you still want to work here, we'd love to make it official with some signatures." Rosemary's statement is no nonsense, while Maeve smiles hopefully at me, with her hands framing her face, fingers crossed. I immediately nod my agreement. "Great!" Rosemary passes over the tablet she's been holding. "We need some standard information, your address, where to send payment, you know, all the boring but important stuff." As she waves her hand dismissively, my entire body stiffens.

My address. Shit.

"Um. Could I send you my address at a, uh, later date?" I keep my eyes on the form I'm filling out, not willing to see the potential judgment on her face.

"Oh. During our last call you said you'd found a place. Did something happen?" The genuine concern in Rosemary's voice only makes me more embarrassed. I should have my shit together enough to be able to provide an address. Except I don't.

"Yes," I answer honestly. "There was an issue with my roommate, and I no longer have one, so I need to find something else close by." Saying it out loud has my blood running so hot, sweat starts to build on the tip of my nose. Yep. My nose. That's where I sweat first.

It's not easy to find somewhere to rent in Ojai that doesn't cost a small fortune, but I want to stay close to Gran. "I've started looking in Fillmore. I know rentals in Ojai are a dime a dozen." Especially on my practically non-existent budget. I leave that part out and keep a smile on my face, but it's so forced, my cheeks ache.

"That's quite far away, isn't it?" Maeve's question is innocent enough, but as I bite the inside of my cheek, it's becoming harder to pretend like I have any of this figured out.

"And you'll be visiting your grandmother's assisted-living facility often as well, won't you? I mean, Rosemary mentioned it to me——" She breaks off when I take in a sharp, albeit shaky breath. "I'm sorry, Alice. I don't mean to pry." Her gentle hand lands on my forearm, and I'm the closest I've been to breaking down since the call that turned my life inside out a few short weeks ago.

The shuffle of feet behind us is my saving grace, and I

recover as best as I can. Owen appears next to his wife with a now-sleeping baby in his arms. They exchange a look, though Owen seems as confused as I am by whatever is transpiring.

"If you don't mind a male roommate, there is an extra room at the farmhouse. It's quite literally on the property, so you can walk over here. I'm sure you saw it on your way in. Our head of operations lives there, and while he is arguably a bit quiet and rather boring, he's absolutely wonderful." She squeezes my arm before bringing it back to her side.

"Maevey, what are you—" Owen is shushed by his wife.

"Ask for forgiveness, not for permission, right? He'll be fine. He's hardly even home anyway." She does a silent clap, looking excitedly over at me, then Owen. "You'll talk to him, darling? Please?" This woman is obviously a mastermind, and it's one thousand percent clear that Owen will absolutely do whatever she asks. I, however, am not sure how to feel about this new development. Sure, living so close to work that I can walk here every day would be amazing. Yeah, not worrying about whether or not my old-as-dirt Jeep will break down at any given moment would be lovely. But can I accept this? I should be able to handle something as simple as finding a place to live on my own. Without any help. The way I've done just about everything else in my life.

Right?

Never look a gift horse in the mouth. That's what my mom used to say, but she's not exactly the kind of person I strive to emulate. In fact, she's the last person I want to turn out like, but she said that it was actually an old teacher who always said that to her, so… maybe it has some merit.

Rosemary stays quiet during our interaction, but

there's a small, approving smile on her face. If two people don't see a problem with this, maybe I shouldn't either.

"It doesn't have to be permanent. I'll keep looking for a place close by, I promise. And of course, I'll pay rent for however long I'm there." My insides are vibrating with the possibility that I might actually have a place to live. It means I can go visit Gran instead of spending all my time looking at ads for places I can't afford.

"You can sort that out later with your new roomie." Maeve remains calm as I frantically finish up the forms. "O can speak with him tonight, and you can move in tomorrow. I figure your first few days will be a bit shorter than normal anyway, so you can get settled in, right, Rosie?" Owen shifts uncomfortably, as do I. Not sure whether I should be comforted or concerned by the fact that he's as wary as I am about this situation.

Rosemary, however, gives nothing away. In fact, she looks pleased as punch. "Absolutely. I think you're going to really like it here, Alice. We'll get started with getting you acquainted with Scout, who's already gone through all the physical health assessments." She smiles warmly at me, and I nod. How can I not? This is literally the best-case scenario. I met Scout today and pretty much fell in love with the sweet mare, so of course I *want* to stay here.

"Thank you, Maeve. And Owen, if it doesn't work out, it's okay. I'll figure it out." Somehow...

"I'm sure it'll be fine, Alice. We take care of each other here. You'll see." I almost believe Owen's words.

We say our goodbyes, and I agree to meet Rosemary tomorrow morning at nine o'clock. As I drive toward the assisted-living facility Gran is in, I make a mental to-do list of everything I need to take care of tonight before putting the things I unpacked at the hotel back in my car.

Starting over is exhausting.

the fuck? you're joking

Arthur

"Heyyyy, buddy." Owen's jovial tone as he walks into my house immediately throws me off. He's up to something and I'm probably not gonna like it.

"Whoa. Stop. Who are you? What did you do to Owen?" He responds to that with a glare, and all is well with the world. "What do you need, old friend?" We're nearly the same age, but I love riling him up by calling him old. It's something my siblings have always done to me since I'm the firstborn, and it gets under Owen's skin way more than it ever got under mine.

"Shut up," he mumbles. "I'm about to make your day."

"Oh?" He's full of shit, and I know it. But I'll humor him, nonetheless. "And is this your doing or your wife's?" I love them both, but I like to pretend they're pains in my ass. Truth is, without Owen, I might not be doing as well as I have been for the last couple of years. Might not finally own the farmhouse that felt like home from the moment I set foot in it.

We made it official a few weeks back. Owen and Maeve agreed to split the land, so I get a couple of acres out of their forty or so, and now I have my little house on my own slice of Ojai soil. Sometimes I still can't believe it, and I owe them—Owen especially—a hell of a lot, even if they vehemently disagree with that statement.

"I'm not at liberty to say." His pointed stare makes me chuckle. Just as I thought. Maeve had an idea, and he's here to present it to me. The last time this happened was when they decided to bring on the occupational therapist, and I was all for that. So much so that it inspired an expansion plan. In preparation, I've been attending seminars, training, looking for new horses, and updating all of my first aid certifications so the OT isn't the only one who can help in case of a medical emergency. All of that on top of having Rosemary guide me in becoming a certified trainer while showing Gear the ins and outs of managing the ranch.

"All right. Out with it." Luther, my rowdy but extremely loveable dog, curls up on top of my feet as Owen and I sit around the kitchen table. It's one of the few places in this house that would be considered large. The kitchen is roomy, but so is the back porch, which also happens to be my favorite place, thanks to the mountain views.

"So the OT starts tomorrow. We met her earlier. She's great. Paige, Corey, and Sam really liked her. They're already toying with her nickname being Whinny." He shoves a handful of chips in his mouth, and I bite my tongue to hold back my laugh. As he coughs and sputters profanities, reaching for my untouched glass of water, I let my laugh out. Dummy had no idea they were the Marmite flavor that only Maeve and I like. She shares her British snacks with me, and it's no secret that Owen thinks these are vile. "Fucker," he whispers before continuing, "Anyway, she's your new roommate since Maeve offered her a place to stay with you to be closer to work. There. How do you like them apples?"

"The fuck? You're joking." The smile has completely vanished from my face. I'm the oldest of six kids, and my grandmother has lived with us my entire life. I have relished in living alone. The silence. The lack of needing to give a shit about what I do and when… It's a kind of freedom that once got me into big trouble, but now one that I deem priceless and very much necessary. Owen's stoic and slightly apologetic face tells me that he is not, in fact, joking.

"She said it's temporary, just until she finds another place close by, and she wants to pay you rent." His knowing look says it all. When Owen came to Ojai, we were roommates. He's richer than rich, so I know us living together was entirely for my sake. When he bought this property and I moved into the farmhouse, it was supposed to be temporary, too. I paid Owen whatever I could for rent while fixing up the old house, making it what it is now. When I asked him if they'd sell it to me once I had enough saved for a down payment, he showed me a number on his phone. He had saved all of my rent payments. For years. He cashed every check and kept the money aside, with the intention of giving it back to me so I could buy my own place. That's just the kind of guy he is.

"Fine," is the only response I can give.

I never stood a chance anyway. If I said no, Maeve would come over here and give me hell. Rosemary would probably kill me. But I can't say no. I wouldn't. I don't know what the new OT's situation is, and I'm hoping it's nothing like mine was back then, but it doesn't matter. If someone needs help, you help them. Like the beautiful stranger at the bar last night.

Better not let my thoughts run away with that, though. I scratch the stubble on my chin and look up at Owen. "I've only ever lived with women I'm related to, though, so I don't know what this is gonna be like."

Owen's deep laugh rouses Luther from his nap, and the dog lets out a loud sigh of annoyance before tucking his snout back under his leg. "I'm sure you'll be just fine. Your family prepared you well." After a short pause, he adds, "She moves in tomorrow." My eyes grow wide at this previously unmentioned detail. "Which means I should get going. Don't stay up too late. Better yet, just get some rest. The place looks great, and with the way you've been going lately, you probably won't even see her for another week."

He's not wrong about that. I'm trying to keep up with everything, and it's led to a string of very long days. Who knew expanding was going to be so much work?

Owen knocks on the table twice as he stands, and Luther barks out loudly, just once. I snap my finger before he can continue making noise and throw my friend a scolding glance as he winces apologetically. This dog has more baggage than I do, which is maybe why we get along so well. He's still learning how to deal with triggers and past trauma, so sudden noises aren't welcome.

With a pat on my shoulder, Owen says bye, gives Luther some ear scratches, and is on his way. I start on getting the bedroom set up before I give the whole house a clean, like Owen knew I would. He lived with me long enough to know that the need for a clean and tidy space was always important to me. I hope my new roommate is as understanding as Owen.

a Sam Elliot look-alike, complete with the scruffy mustache and everything

Alice

This morning, I came straight to the stable. I thought I'd get here early enough to meet the guy everyone simply refers to as 'the boss,' but he was already gone when I arrived at eight. I did end up staying and helping the team for the day. I wanted to get a feel for their routines and how they do things. I don't want to step on anyone's toes—literally and figuratively—and I'd like my focus to be on the patients rather than on whether or not I'm doing something right or pissing someone off by putting things away incorrectly.

The anxiety I'd been feeling about meeting my new boss and roommate was settled by everyone having nothing but nice things to say about him whenever I asked. Between that and how easy today felt, the day flew by.

Gosh, it feels good to be around horses again. I missed the peace that comes from their steady presence. I needed it after showing up to see Gran yesterday and having her throw a pudding cup at me. She's been angry and confused because of the move, but I know this is for the best.

For both of us.

Her Alzheimer's diagnosis surprised me, but only because I haven't been around for the last decade to catch any sign of it. We had barely spoken on the phone in the last few years, and I've had so many mixed feelings about that. There's been no time to process all of the changes, and as I breathe in the familiar scent of pine air freshener in my Jeep, I'm thankful I have at least this old hunk of metal to call my own and offer me some comfort.

Settling into the driver's seat, I take notice of how my body aches. I'm less anxious, but still wholly unprepared for meeting my new roommate tonight. As I make the short drive up to the farmhouse, I note the massive wraparound porch. It's what dreams are made of. The house itself isn't huge, but the porch makes it seem bigger. It's either new or has been majorly updated. Even the planters by the garage look pristine.

Owen has assured me the front door would be unlocked, so I grab a suitcase and make my way up the steps. When I open the door, I'm immediately greeted by deep barking. Oh no. No one said anything about a dog! Whatever and wherever it is, it sounds humongous, and I'm not prepared to meet my maker, so I turn to head right back out the door I came in from, but the barking never gets closer. The beast is contained somewhere, and that has my racing heart slowing significantly.

On the table by the front door, there's a spiral notebook open with neat printing on a clean page.

Make yourself at home. Your room is the second door on the left upstairs. Luther (my dog) will be in the room down the hall. He's friendly, but has a mean bark. Feel free to let him out, but not outside unless it's through the back door into his dog run. He might keep making noise if he knows you're in the house, but I promise, he just wants to lick your face and get belly rubs.

Help yourself to anything in the kitchen.

See you soon,

-A.M.

It's a kind note, but it would have been nicer to get a warning about the dog. Memories of being chased by one of my mom's boyfriend's rottweiler make me shudder. I have zero intentions of letting the pup out of whatever room he's safely being kept in. And he's given me one more reason to look for a new place to live ASAP!

After three trips to my car, I have all of my belongings in my new bedroom. It's surprisingly cozy, with an antique-looking four-poster bed in the middle, mismatched nightstands that somehow work, and a chair, with a floor lamp and small footstool in the corner. The dresser is empty, so I intend to fill it immediately. I hate living out of a suitcase. Before all of that, though, I need a shower.

After moving through the house as quietly as I can, I have an extra-long, extra-hot shower in the gloriously large bathroom. It's a work of art, this room, with its massive soaker tub in the center, flanked by the biggest shower I've ever been in and two wooden vanities. The shower walls are a soft blue, and the gold fixtures make everything look so rich and fancy. It's in total opposition to what I would have imagined the inside of this house to look like, but also, it works. It's warm, functional, and the vintage-looking faucets fit the vibe perfectly.

The water pressure also doesn't hurt.

My thick, curly hair hasn't been properly washed since I got to Ojai, but the water pressure here is magnificent. I washed my hair twice. It felt incredible.

Now I'm lying in bed, wearing nothing but my towel, eating the snacks I bought for the hotel, and my eyes are growing heavy. It's warm, the mattress is soft, and I had the most relaxing shower maybe ever. I could just…

MY ALARM BLARES, startling me awake. After fumbling for my phone in the covers, I finally find it and silence the darn thing. It's seven o'clock in the morning, which means I slept for twelve hours.

Wow. I don't remember the last time that happened.

I slide out of bed and wrap an oversized sweater around me then head straight for the door as my bladder screams at me. I peek into the hallway, looking and listening for the signs of life from the beast that barked at me yesterday or my new roommate. Hearing nothing but the faint humming of a fan nearby, I tiptoe to the bathroom.

After washing and drying my hands, I step back into the hallway only to trip over an animal. No, not any animal. A dog. He's not as huge as he sounded yesterday, but he's sturdy and doesn't budge, despite the fact that I tried to walk right through him. As he sits at my feet, his tail wags across the floor, a soft whooshing sound meeting my ears as he begins to pant and squirm with his tongue hanging out of his open mouth.

"Uh… hi," I mumble, and his tail wags harder, making me wonder if the way it loudly thumps against the wall is hurting him at all. His ears wiggle, and his wide brown eyes study mine as he brings his wet nose to my hand, nudging it enough to force my palm to land on top of his head. "Oh, you want some scratches?" The thumping of his tail gets louder, and I laugh as the pup—Luther, according to the note—makes a grunting sound. The moment my fingers reach his ear, he melts into me, falling over onto my feet, belly up, tongue still hanging out. I laugh harder, disbelief washing over me that this was the terrifying beast barking at me when I arrived last night.

After a minute of petting this now-limp dog, I gently pat his belly. "Okay, buddy. I gotta get ready for work." I straighten to make my way back to my room, but the dog is fast, and when he stands, he's immediately pawing at me, jumping up to get my attention. "No!" I huff, but he jumps again, causing me to yelp and scurry into my room, shutting the door before he can come in with me. He scratches at the door for a few seconds, then whines. "No way, dude. You're not coming in here! Especially if you're gonna jump me like that," I yell through the safety of my door, which I locked. Just in case.

With a few sniffs and a loud huff, the door rattles again, this time from the weight of his body leaning against it as he either sits or lays down out there, waiting for me. Well, shoot. How am I going to leave?

I vow to figure it out after I'm dressed for work, with my snacks packed in my bag for the day. A few granola bars and the quickly browning banana I had left over will have to do for breakfast and lunch today. Maybe I'll have time for a grocery run afterward. I can properly contribute to the food supply once I get my first paycheck. I wonder if this guy will be the kind of roommate who's okay with splitting things like condiments, or if we'll need to keep everything separate. I wonder how many rules he'll have about things like when we can make noise—not that I plan on doing much of that—or whether we'll need scheduled times for doing laundry. I've lived with all kinds of people in my twenty-seven years. Between the characters my mom used to bring home when I was a kid, the revolving door of roommates in college, and a controlling ex-boyfriend, I've seen it all. I doubt this one will surprise me in any way.

As I go through the motions of getting dressed, making my bed, and tidying my things, I spiral into an array of thoughts.

He didn't have to have the bed made up for me. I'll need to thank him for that and get new sheets.

I wonder if I'll be able to make friends at work this time.

Do I even know how to make friends? Last time I tried it didn't go well, but that wasn't exactly my fault. Or was it? How much of the last three years can I blame on Chris, anyway? Some of it had to be my fault, too, right? I mean, I stayed. Even when his claiming to want me all for himself turned into straight-up isolation.

There's no way the people at this farm have any clue about any of the shit I've lived through. Their lives seem so perfect, from what I've seen.

Well, That's not fair. I don't know them.

Yet.

Once my thoughts quiet down, I keep picturing my new roommate as a Sam Elliot look-alike, complete with the scruffy mustache and everything. The whole house gives off older, single man vibes—the tidiness, the quilt on the back of the couch, the notes left on clean pages of a notebook, his perfect printing, and even the dog.

A huff of breath under my door shakes me out of my thoughts, and I'm momentarily grateful for the dog on the other side of it. I place a shaking hand on the door knob, psyching myself up to turn it, heaving in deep breaths. I know he was friendly before, but I didn't like the way he jumped up at me. Not one bit.

A loud whistle breaks the silence, and after a quick shuffle, I hear the tip-tapping of paws against the wood floor running away from my door.

Silence again.

I head to the kitchen, quickly fill up my water bottle, and when I tiptoe to the front door, the house is still quiet. No roommate in sight. No dog, either. I let out a relieved breath and head to the door, where I find another note on the table.

I'll be away with Luther until Wednesday. Sorry we haven't had the chance to meet yet. Please help yourself to whatever you need.
-A.M.

All right. Guess I have this glorious house to myself for a few days. I can't say I'm terribly mad about that.

let me drink this shitty cup of coffee alone, please

Arthur

I've technically had a roommate for several days, and I have yet to meet her. Hell, I don't even know her first name yet because they've already nicknamed her. According to Gear, who instantly developed a massive crush on the new occupational therapist they've been calling Whinny, she is the prettiest woman she's ever seen. As Mouse so aptly put it, "That says a lot, considering we work for Maeve freaking Howard-James, a whole-ass movie star!"

I wouldn't know, since I haven't seen the new-hire, and while Maeve is objectively beautiful, she has nothing on the woman I met a week ago at Beau's Bar.

Alice shouldn't still be in my head, and I definitely shouldn't be wondering if I'll see her again, given the way I left her last time, too drunk to even stand. I can't get involved with people like that. Not again.

So as I open the heavy door for my scheduled Wednesday night cup of coffee after my weekly NA meeting, I vow not to think about her anymore. Out of sight, out of mind. I have way too much other shit to worry about. A woman is nowhere even close to making it onto the list of priorities I need to focus on.

Turns out I've never broken a vow so fast, because before the door even shuts behind me, I'm taking in the soft, straight hair cascading down her back as she laughs at something Beau said.

Fuck.

I contemplate turning around and leaving. I don't need to come here every Wednesday, after all. It's fine if I do something else. Something outside of my schedule. But that's a fucking lie. I thrive on this routine. On this predictability I've created for myself.

Yet, I can't force myself to walk away from the certain pit of disappointment I'm about to fall into as I walk toward the woman I haven't stopped thinking about. It's been a week of remembering her golden eyes, that unfamiliar lightness filling my chest, and scolding myself for thinking about someone clearly so wrong for me.

I'm an addict.

While alcohol was never how I chose to escape reality, I can't be with someone who lets themselves get so drunk they practically pass out on a bathroom floor.

As I approach the bar, Beau's eyes grow serious as they meet mine. He's a pretty tough nut to crack until he likes you, and judging by the laughter, it seems Alice has won him over.

"Be right back with your coffee, Art." My friend turns his back to us, and the gilded gaze I may never forget burns into me as Alice's hair whips around her shoulder.

I should tell Beau not to bother. I shouldn't stay, and that's made clear when I take in her slightly hazy eyes and the half-empty cocktail glass her fingers are wrapped around. I don't bother sitting, opting instead to rest a hand on the bar.

"I didn't think I'd see you back here, considering a week ago I had to carry you out." I keep my voice low, but I may as well have yelled at her with how quickly her head rears back and the smile on her face falls.

Straightening her smile, she clears her throat. "Yeah, I came back here to thank you for helping me. That was really kind of you, and I'm sorry for what happened. I had no idea—"

"Right. Okay. Well, you've apologized, so…" My eyes flick to the door, and her eyes fill with tears. I should feel bad, but self-preservation has kicked in, and I know it'd be too easy to fall back into conversation with her if I chose to ignore the blatant red flag waving in front of me. So I won't.

"Right. Well, thank you again, Arthur." She stands, gingerly taking her purse in both of her shaking hands. "Have a nice life."

With her head held high, she walks out of the bar and out of my life.

When Beau returns, I'm still standing there, my insides fuming with anger, betrayal and regret, which makes no sense because I know I did the right thing. I can't befriend someone like that.

A cup of coffee appears in my peripheral. "Where did Alice go?" Beau asks, looking around.

"Why did you let her back in, Beau? Aren't people like that exactly what you avoid here?" I brace both arms on the bar as Beau crosses his.

"Arthur, it wasn't like that, she—"

"I don't care, man. I don't *want* to know. The less I know about her, the better. You and I both know it's a terrible idea for me to get involved with someone who can't handle their shit. They certainly won't want to handle mine, too." My own words land like a boulder in my gut, heavy and unwelcome. It's a truth I don't want to admit, but I have to.

"If you would listen to me for a second—"

"Not interested," I interrupt again. "Seriously, Beau, let me drink this shitty cup of coffee alone, please."

He huffs out a frustrated breath, mumbling something as he walks away to leave me alone for the evening. Just the way I like it, right?

going to go live with the creepy dolls

Alice

I guess this is what I get for having high hopes for today.

Instead of sitting alone to wallow after one of my toughest visits with Gran yet, I went to the place that brought me a bit of comfort one week ago. It was a long shot, but I figured the day definitely couldn't get worse.

I was wrong.

I ordered a soda water and chatted easily with Beau, hoping the dim lights would make my bloodshot eyes less obvious. These headaches act a lot like migraines sometimes, making my vision blurry and my stomach upset.

Despite the pleasant conversation, I kept waiting for Arthur to show up.

And show up he did.

He looked disgusted, standing there staring down at me.

Reining in all of the emotions warring inside me, I wished him a nice life with shaky hands, then I walked out.

When I got into my Jeep, I took a naproxen to help with the now-throbbing pain in my head, though I have a feeling it'll do no good given the tightness running from my nape all the way down to my shoulders.

When I get to the farmhouse, there's a light on inside but no car in the driveway. The rambunctious dog is back in his room, and I don't dare let him out.

I manage to hold back the tears until the blissfully hot water of the shower hits my skin, carefully avoiding my hair, which is wrapped in a shower cap. Then I let it all out while I massage my neck and shoulders. My head was already pounding, so it's not like crying will make it any worse.

The visit with Gran replays in my mind as I let the hot water soothe my muscles.

"HELLO," she says timidly. It makes me want to cry, because timid is not a word I'd ever have used to describe my grandmother. Fierce, harsh, brutally honest, yes. Not timid.

"Hi," I say back, though I have already spoken to her three times in the hour I've been here. "Lovely day, isn't it?"

"I'm not sure," she responds. "I don't think I've been out today."

"Oh, well, would you like to go? I can go for a walk with you. The heat from earlier has died down a bit." I'm hopeful a change of scenery will jog her memory, and maybe she'll remember me today. Though I'm never sure if that will be a good thing or a bad thing. Sometimes it's easier when she doesn't know who I am. She's this docile, sweet lady when she thinks I'm a stranger, but downright cruel when she recognizes me.

She doesn't say anything.

"Margaret?" I try again, and again, no response.

After a few minutes of silence, I stand, moving into her line of sight. Her focus has been on whatever is happening outside the window: nothing, because all she can see is a patch of grass.

"Would you like to go for a walk, Gran?" I hold my breath, wondering if using the name will jog her memory or upset her. I even straightened my hair, hoping she would either recognize me or think I was Mom, but neither of those things has happened.

"Dear, you seem like a nice girl and all," she starts in a gentle voice I rarely heard from her when she was my guardian, "but I don't feel much like making small talk with a stranger today, so if you could leave now, that would be best."

With my head low, I do as she asks, saying goodbye to the lovely nurses on my way out.

NOW, in an attempt not to fall asleep before I can take my muscle relaxer, I'm sitting on the couch as quietly as possible with the lights dimmed so the dog doesn't start barking again. It's worked for about forty-five minutes, but then the front door opens, and chaos ensues. The barking startles me, and as my neck tenses, pain shoots up my skull so sharply, I run to the bathroom, not even bothering to shut the door before my head is in the toilet and I'm heaving into it.

Crap. This isn't the way to make a good first impression on my new boss and landlord/roommate. There's shuffling in the hallway, and as I'm collecting myself and drying my hands, there's a soft knock at the door. "You all right?" a deep voice asks.

I clear my throat and prepare myself for the full explanation of my condition. "Yeah. Sorry about that, I—" When I step out into the hallway, I look up to find gentle brown eyes, but they immediately harden once recognition sets in. "Arthur. How—"

He cuts me off, "What the hell are you doing here? Don't tell me you're the new OT." He steps closer and I instinctively step back, nodding at his statement. Once I'm under the bright lights of the bathroom, I wince, and his eyes narrow as he examines my face. "Jesus, what are you on? What the fuck was Owen thinking, bringing someone like you here?"

"I'm not—What? Someone like me?" I'm genuinely confused by his reaction. He's still so mad, and seems like an entirely different person from the one I met.

"What are you on, Alice?" My name on his lips is pure anger and disdain. "There better not be any drugs in my house right now, I swear—"

"No! What? No, there are no drugs here. Who do you think I am?" Crossing my arms defensively, I can almost ignore the throbbing in my head and neck, thanks to the utter shock I'm experiencing.

"Don't lie to me. You were looking dazed as hell at the bar. I saw your drink. Then I come home and you're throwing up again with bloodshot eyes. I won't ask you again. What did you take?" His eyes close when he exhales, like he's trying to calm himself.

"If you must know, I took a naproxen in the car after I left the bar." It's my turn to narrow my eyes.

"An over-the-counter painkiller? You're telling me that's all you've taken?" With furrowed brows, he continues to study me.

"Yes. I don't do drugs. I never have, and I never will. Now, if you'll excuse me, I need to go pack my things." I brush past him and start to head for the stairs. There's no way I'm staying here or working with him.

I need to leave.

"So it's just alcohol then?" His words hit me like a ton of bricks, and I halt.

"Excuse me?" I turn around to face him, my hands fisting at my sides.

"You don't do drugs, but you drink until you puke your guts out?" He scoffs.

"No," I grit out. "I don't."

The lift of his eyebrow is a challenge. He thinks I drank too much last week. And he must think I was drinking tonight, too. "Not that I owe you an explanation, because you're nothing and no one to me, but I was drinking soda water tonight. Last Wednesday was the first time I've ever tasted alcohol. It was also how I found out I have an alcohol intolerance, which means within minutes of ingesting it, I get sick and, as you so eloquently put it, puke my guts out. I have chronic headaches brought on by an old injury, and stress or physical exertion can make them worse. They also make me nauseous, hence the puking today. Is there anything else about my life I need to explain to you before I leave, or can I go now?" I don't wait for his answer before I turn around and storm up the stairs.

I'm halfway there when he speaks up. "Wait." I take another step. "Alice. I'm sorry. Please, wait." The soft voice I remember from the night we met stops me in my tracks, and I turn around, arms crossed, firmly determined not to be swayed about what I thought I knew about this man. "You weren't drunk last week?"

"I've never been drunk," I answer honestly.

"Ne—"

"Never," I interrupt. "And I don't give a crap whether you believe me or not because it's the truth. Whatever idea you have of me in is wrong, but frankly, it doesn't matter, since I was obviously wrong about you, too. Now, if you'll excuse me, I need to pack my things."

Something like disappointment stirs in my gut when I make it to the door of my bedroom in silence, but before I can scold myself for even thinking about anything in this place as mine, there's a gentle touch on my shoulder.

"Don't go." His words are a whisper, but they stop me so abruptly that I nearly fall over. "I'm sorry. You're right. I'm an asshole, and of course I completely understand that you don't want to stay here anymore, but please don't quit your job. I misjudged you based on my own experiences with people who deal with addiction." Once I'm fully facing him, his eyes are on the floor, but given how short his hair is, I get a full view of his furrowed brow. "If you go, Owen and Maeve will be so disappointed, and I can't be the reason for that. And you don't owe me anything, but they seem to think you're perfect for this position. I trust Owen with my life, so I'm sure he's not wrong about you… like I was." He pauses, pinching the bridge of his nose. "Also, Rosemary will bury me six feet under if I'm the reason you quit. Keep your job. Please."

I don't know this man, and right now I don't particularly like him, but I feel his sincerity in a visceral way. The silence between us is charged and tense, and I do nothing to ease it because I don't know *how* to.

"You're not going to go live with the creepy dolls, are you?" Under different circumstances, the question would make me smile. Until he walked into the bar tonight, my memories of our time together last week would make me borderline giddy.

I clear my throat and the emotion in it. "I don't have any other options, so…"

He looks up at me then, brows furrowing impossibly tighter as his head shakes the tiniest amount.

"No," he starts, and I nod sheepishly in return, already mentally preparing myself for the awkward conversation I'm about to have with my ex-roommate and her strange boyfriend. "Stay here. I swear it can't get any worse than this, and this is pretty fucking terrible, I know. But I promise I'm not an entirely horrible person. I'll leave you alone, give you space, cook you breakfast every morning, I don't know. You don't want to seriously live somewhere with haunted dolls and—" His face flushes as he cuts himself off, and I bite the insides of my cheeks to keep from smiling because this rambling, blushing version of Arthur is almost likable.

"Porn noises?" I ask without smiling, which feels like a major feat. He was right about one thing the night we met —my face always gives my emotions away.

Huffing out the tiniest breath of a laugh, he runs a hand down his face. "Yeah. That. You don't want to live somewhere like that."

He's right. I don't. "I also don't want to live with a person who judges me before knowing me. Who makes assumptions about my character and my intentions. Especially when that person is going to be my boss *and* landlord." I puff my cheeks out on an exhale, hoping the frustration with this entire day somehow exits my body with my breath.

"I get that. I fucked up and I'm so, so sorry about that. You have no idea. I might be an asshole sometimes, but I know how to own up to my mistakes, and I'm owning this. But I'm not your boss, and I don't love the idea of being a landlord either, so how about you stay here for however long you need. No need to pay rent. What if we're just roommates and coworkers without any fancy titles or positions that put anyone above the other? We can start over. As equals."

Roommates. Coworkers.

What alternate reality have I entered where the man I

met at a bar, of all places, ends up also being both of those things?

Arthur leans against the wall, hands going to his pockets, and I mimic his stance solely because my ability to hold myself up has suddenly vanished.

This day is giving me whiplash.

now i know why he called me a stubborn idiot

Arthur

The shock on her face perfectly matches how I feel. I offered to let a stranger live here for free after accusing her of being drunk and/or on drugs. But that accusation never felt quite right. I can tell when someone is using something. It's a skill I honed after years of hiding my own addiction from those closest to me.

Maybe a part of me chose to believe she was under the influence of something because I needed a reason not to want her, to not want to be near her. I never would have guessed she had an alcohol intolerance, but I'm sure I would have known if I had bothered to listen to Beau earlier. He tried to tell me something, and I shut him down. Now I know why he called me a stubborn idiot before walking away and leaving me alone like I asked.

"I can pay you." She raises her chin, but I don't miss the slight wobble in it. "I'm no freeloader, and I don't like owing people anything, so as much as you've offended me today." She pauses, swallowing and narrowing her eyes at me. I deserve it. "Staying here temporarily is still somehow better than dealing with the alternative. I'll pay you rent until I find another place to live." She rubs at the back of her neck and winces. The movement reminds me that she mentioned having a headache. If hers are anything like my brother Raf's, she must be in a world of pain right now.

"I understand not wanting to owe people anything. Believe me. But you said you're not feeling well, so why don't you go get some rest, and we can figure this all out later?" Her only response is a relieved sigh and a nod. "Can I get you some tea? Do you need anything?"

At that, her gaze meets mine, and all the warmth in the amber eyes I was so entranced by is gone. "No, other than needing to share a house for a short time, I don't need anything from you, Arthur." After stepping back, she closes the door more softly than I deserve, and I mentally punch myself in the face for so royally fucking this up.

She's my roommate. My coworker. The woman I haven't been able to stop thinking about since our eyes locked for the first time.

How is this mess my life?

THERE HAS BEEN no sign of Alice for the last two days. The woman is like a ghost. I know she's been to the main barn because everyone else has seen her. I've asked Gear and Mouse about her, and they both gave me pointed looks, because apparently it's unusual for me to ask about anyone multiple times a day. Sue me. I'd like to know if my roommate is going to ignore me forever.

When she's home, she moves silently through the house and seems to have perfected the art of avoiding me and Luther. My dog is desperate to be around her, but if she gets home before me, she doesn't let him out. He has a tracker on his collar, since he's a bit of an escape artist and too damn curious for his own good, so I know he hasn't left the house.

I can relate to his curiosity, though, because with every passing hour, I want to know more about Alice, and it has nothing to do with the fact she's living in my house. It has everything to do with the way I felt when I saw her smile for the first time, when we danced like we'd done it a million times before. I want to know her.

NOW IT'S THE WEEKEND, and I figure since we're both off today, there's no way she'll be able to avoid me. But by the time I get out of bed at six, she's already gone. She didn't come home until after eleven last night, but she's gotta be back at some point, so I'm gonna wait her out. I have nothing better to do, anyway.

As I finish cleaning the house and settle onto the front porch swing with a coffee and a book, the telltale sound of tires on the gravel driveway has Luther running at full speed, barking with excitement. He's not dumb enough to get too close to cars when they're moving, but as soon as Alice's Jeep comes to a full stop, he's at her door, tail wagging so hard it makes his entire body shake. He lets out a bark and sits, waiting for her to come out. But she doesn't. Not after she turns the car off, and not after her seatbelt is no longer on. She stares at him, then at me, wide-eyed and looking... scared? No. She couldn't be scared of Luther, could she? I mean, we never talked about it since we haven't talked about much of anything, but I was sure it was fine. Huh. This would explain him not being let out, I guess.

Finally, she mouths the word *help*, and I have to pretend to cough as I cover up my laughter. Not at her, but at the fact she's scared of the world's friendliest dog. I stand, calling Luther over to me. It takes three tries before he makes it halfway to the porch, but once he hears the car door open, he's back, pouncing to get to Alice, whose foot doesn't even touch the ground before she shuts herself in again.

As I walk over to her, I take note of how tightly she's gripping the steering wheel. She really is scared. Shit. I grab Luther gently by the collar and walk several feet away from the Jeep, nodding to her that she can come out.

"S-sorry, I—I don't—Dogs scare me, a-and I know he's friendly, but—"

"Luther, get in the house." The dog knows what's good for him, so while I don't use this harsh tone often, when I do, he knows better than not to listen. He immediately takes off, heading inside through the dog door. Certain he won't move, I lock eyes with Alice, who is visibly shaking. "I'm sorry. I didn't know."

"That's okay." Her arms are wrapped tightly around her middle as her eyes lower to the ground. "I'll get over it."

That's it. I gotta do something.

I can't watch her like this. I place my hands on her shoulders and squeeze lightly, though I inexplicably want to hug her instead. "Luther comes on a little strong. I'm sorry. I should have asked you how you felt about dogs."

"It's fine. It's not your job to—"

"I'm your roommate, and I want to be a good one. I should have asked." As I rub circles on her shoulder with my thumbs, she relaxes. "Can I ask what happened to make you scared?" Her body tenses again. "I want to understand and do what I can to help and keep Luther from triggering you."

I get a small nod, but her eyes remain focused on her shoes. "I was chased by a dog once. I was nine, and I didn't know there was a dog in my house. I stepped on his tail by accident when I walked into the kitchen, and I screamed because he scared me. I guess I scared him, too, because he started barking and chasing me. I ran out into the street, and I fell and hit my head on the curb when he jumped on me. When I woke up, I was in the hospital and—" She stops herself with a shake of her head. "Well, I've avoided dogs ever since. It makes no sense, I know. I work with twelve-hundred-pound animals, but I was lucky because the barn dog at my previous place was so old he would stay in the tack room or the boss' office all day. I know this fear is stupid—"

"No, it's not." Not taking my hands off her, I take a step closer. She doesn't recoil or step back, so I take it as a good sign that she's okay with this. "I'm sorry, Alice. I'll keep Luther with me or in his room when you're around. We can text each other, and I'll make sure he's not going to greet you with barking and jumping, okay?"

"He's your dog. You shouldn't have to do that."

"He's my dog, and it's my responsibility to make sure he behaves. Luther's a rescue, and I haven't had him long, so there are a lot of behaviors we still need to work on. He's a good dog, but he has some trauma, so we're taking it slow." With a final squeeze, I let her shoulders go, immediately wishing I hadn't. I fucking hate the way I'm drawn to her, but since the day we met, it's like I'm incapable of not responding to her vulnerability.

"That makes sense. These things take time." With a step back, she looks up at me. "Thanks. For, um, sending him inside and being so nice about this." She attempts a smile, but it's tight. I wish she didn't feel like she needs to smile to appease me—or anyone, for that matter.

"Of course. Do you maybe want to chat a bit about any other roommate stuff? You haven't been around much, and I was hoping to go over a few things with you." Like knowing literally anything other than your first name and profession…

"Oh. Yeah. Sure." Looking toward the front door, she inhales a deep breath.

"Luther will stay inside. We can sit on the porch. I won't take up too much of your time." I motion for her to walk ahead of me, which is a mistake, because it dawns on me she's wearing bike shorts that hug every single curve of her legs and hips perfectly. I wasn't even aware shorts could hug a person's ass that way.

Fuck. Look away, Arthur. Her ass is not up for grabs.

Literally.

Shit.

I am in way over my head here.

i'll show you how capable i am

Alice

Arthur closes the front door behind him and takes a seat on the chair next to me, setting two glasses of water on the table between us. I considered sitting on the other side—on the swing I've wanted to relax on every day, but haven't had a chance to yet—but ultimately decided it'd be weird to be side-by-side if we're supposed to be talking.

"He's got a treat, so he'll be quiet for a bit." He rubs his hands up and down his jean-clad thighs, and I quickly avert my focus to his shoes, because that is a much safer place to look. The man has thick legs that are incredibly difficult to look away from. Everything about him is hard to look away from. "So," he breaks the silence. "Alice. Alice what?"

"Huh?" I look up, utterly confused.

"Sorry, that was weird. My last name is Machado." He rests a hand over his chest before gesturing toward me. The AM signature on his notes now makes sense. "What's yours?"

"Oh. It's Preece," I respond, waiting for it…

"Priest? Like the guy in a black robe at mass?"

"No, not like that. Preece," I annunciate as if that'll clear up his confusion. It doesn't. "P-R-E-E-C-E. Preece," I say, like I'm in a freaking spelling bee. But it's nothing new. No one ever gets my last name right. Pearce. Priest. Price. Anything but my actual last name.

Arthur's deep chuckle pulls me out of my thoughts. "You obviously get this a lot." I look up, confused by what he means. "That little eye-roll you did when you spelled it said it all, Alice Preece."

I rolled my eyes?

Shoot. I really need to get better at controlling my face. "Sorry," I mutter, feeling my cheeks heat.

"No need. I like that your thoughts are written on your face." He studies me, and my cheeks grow impossibly hotter. This feels like the Arthur and Alice from that first night at the bar, making easy conversation and flirting. Except we're not two strangers getting to know one another. We work together. We live together. And though I hope this living arrangement doesn't have to last long, I'm here now and entirely unwilling to get swept away in his deep brown eyes and kind words.

"Do you have a middle name?" He's completely at ease, taking a quick sip of water. "Mine's Ivan."

"Margaret."

"Hmm. Okay. And how did you get into occupational therapy?" This time he doesn't answer the question before me. He… waits.

"I was originally going into physical therapy. But when I told my PT I wanted to be like her, she took me around the facility and introduced me to the other kinds of thera- pies and the different ways they help people. Everyone there sort of took me under their wing, showing me what they did and the tools they used."

I leave out the part where they probably felt bad for me because they knew I'd come from a home where mom, who was almost never around, had a revolving door of men who looked at me like I was either their next meal or their biggest nuisance. They knew I'd gone to live with my grandmother, who didn't only look at me like I was gum on the bottom of her shoe, but also treated me like it. I skip all of those details, though.

"Occupational therapy felt like this bridge between the physical and emotional rehabilitation, and I really liked it." I stop myself there, where it feels safe.

"And hippotherapy specifically?" He's got one ankle resting on his knee, his gaze intently studying me still, like he's actually listening.

"Oh. Well, I really like horses, and when I found out this was an option, I went for it." I shrug because it really was that simple for me.

"I get that. I'm not sure I could ever not be around horses." Arthur's smile is small, but I can see in it how much he means what he said.

"Was working with horses always part of your goal? Did you always know you'd end up here?" My question instantly feels too intimate, but before I can think to take it back, Arthur scoffs.

"Not even a little bit." He scratches his chin in thought, and the sound brings my attention to the scruff there. My fingertips tingle as I imagine what it would feel like to touch his face. "Not even a little bit," he repeats. "I'm so glad this is where I am, though, you know?"

No. I don't know. Not even a little bit, because being back in Ojai isn't where I pictured myself. I can't wait until I can leave this place and never come back. I won't tell him any of this, though, so I simply hum a response and change the topic. "So what are your house rules?"

"House rules? How do you mean?" He tips his head to the side. It's cute.

No, Alice, it's not. Your landlord is not cute.

"You know, like, should we have sides in the fridge? Would you prefer I keep my food in a separate fridge in my room? Should I make sure not to do laundry at certain hours? Stuff like that." All things I've had to consider when living with other people, even though I couldn't care less myself.

He breathes out a laugh, and when I don't join him, he stops. "Oh, you're serious? Uh, no. Do what you want. Eat whatever you want. Except whatever is in the container with a green lid," he adds quickly. I knew there had to be something. "Yeah, don't touch anything in there." The moment my face changes, he takes notice. "Because that's where I put Luther's treats, and trust me, they might look good, but they taste like shit." The face he makes is one-hundred-percent revulsion.

"How would you know that?" I ask, trying not to laugh. I should still be mad at him. I should be doing everything I can to keep my distance from me. But he's left me fresh coffee and breakfast the past two mornings, and while I know he's doing it out of pity or guilt or whatever, it's still confusing. I know people can be nice, but this nice? Nice like Beau and Josie? I haven't experienced much of that in life.

"I think you know exactly how I'd know that." His smile widens as he stares at a spot on my face where I know I have a deep dimple. "And it's why one shouldn't blindly reach for what one believes to be leftovers, and precisely why one"—he clears his throat dramatically—"*I* —now use the green lid for anything I make him."

"You make him food?" I sound as incredulous as I feel, and Arthur's ears go bright red as he shrugs.

"Well, not all his food. Just a few treats with extra oil for his coat." When I nearly spit out my water, he fidgets with the string of his hoodie. "He has sensitive skin, and he gets dandruff sometimes. Plus, he's extra prone to ear infections because of the floppy ears, and trust me, it's way easier to prevent those things from happening than to deal with them once they do."

So. Stinking. Cute.

I don't even try to stop the thought this time because it's a straight fact. This big, burly man is obsessed with his dog.

"You don't have to explain yourself to me. It's adorable that you make treats for Luther. But my real question is, are you capable of making treats for humans, too?" Oh, no. I said adorable. And now I'm getting into flirting territory again.

Crap, crap, crap.

"Adorable, huh?" Arthur spares me further embarrassment and moves on quickly. "I'll have you know I'm amazing at making all kinds of treats. Stick around, Alice Preece. I'll show you how capable I am." His smile grows, but it quickly diminishes again when I clear my throat and stand.

"Right. Well, it's been nice chatting. I should get inside. I have a few things to prep for next week. Let me know how you want to split chores, or whatever. I'm happy to do my part." I pick up my glass of water, prepared to run into the house and to my room, but then I remember the dog waiting inside and freeze.

"Nah. Cleaning is my therapy, so don't worry about that. Plus, you don't seem to be around often, and Luther is definitely the messiest of us." It dawns on him then.

"Oh, right. Luther. I'll get him so you can go inside. He might sniff around your door, though, so I'd keep it closed if you don't want him in there. He's incredibly nosy." As he rises, I smile at how he talks about this dog like he's a person.

"I noticed," I say, and his brows lift in question. "I did pet him once, but when I stopped, he tried to jump on me and follow me to my room."

"Oh, shit. Sorry. You'd think I never give him attention with how starved he always is for it." He rolls his eyes, but it's beyond obvious that Arthur doesn't mind Luther's behavior one bit. "Anyway, I'll get him out of your way." He moves past me, his arm brushing mine, and his spicy scent sending a shiver down my spine. I almost tell him I'd like to try petting Luther again. It would be an excuse to stay near him longer, even though I'm the one who shut down our conversation. In the end, I stop myself. I'm not sure I'm ready for that, and why bother with spending time with him or his dog if I won't be here that long?

His words replay in my mind then.

Stick around, Alice Preece. I'll show you how capable I am.

Nope. Not a chance.

I MAKE it a point to leave the house early in the morning and not return until the evening on Sunday. It's easier to busy myself with clearing out Gran's house and looking for a rental than to be around Arthur and his inquisitive eyes, and the way his voice tends to soothe something in me. I don't want that.

On Monday morning, there's fresh coffee and a break-fast sandwich waiting for me on the counter with a note:

> *I've never had a roommate before, but I think we're supposed to see one another occasionally? Anyway, Ro mentioned you like almond vanilla creamer in your coffee. There's some in the fridge.*
> *See you at work.*
> *-A.M.*

Ugh. He bought me my favorite coffee creamer? Son of a biscuit. It's going to be really hard not to like this guy.

stay with me, stay at this job, stay in ojai

Arthur

There was no sign of her for the rest of the weekend. I don't know what she does or where she goes, and I'm sure as hell not about to pry and ask her, but damn, I'm curious.

It's Monday, though, and there's no way she can avoid me today since we're supposed to meet to talk about the horses being used for hippotherapy. She's already at the stable when I walk in, laughing at something Paige said.

"Morning, Gear." I tip my baseball cap to the two women. "Alice."

"Hey boss. It's Whinny, remember?" Paige cocks a hip, her hand resting on it. "How was your weekend? Luther get into any other garbage cans? Where is he, anyway?" She looks behind me, no doubt expecting to see the excitable pup. He almost always comes to the stable with me.

"Right. Um, no Luther today." I send Paige a pleading

look, silently begging her not to push the issue. She either can't see my desperation or she ignores me. Hard to tell with her.

"But he's always here, and he was already gone most of last week, so what the hell do you mean no Luther today?" Paige is oblivious to the way Alice stiffens as she talks, but I'm not.

"Sorry, Paige." As I take in Alice's face, it's filled with guilt. "Alice, can I talk to you for a second?" I motion to the tack room, the closest place we may get an ounce of privacy from Paige "Gear" Martinez. That girl hears and repeats everything like a goddamn toddler. Thankfully, she doesn't question my lack of response to her many questions, just goes back to mucking out the stall she'd been working on.

Alice follows me silently, and once we're away from prying ears, she speaks first. "You should have brought him. I know you didn't because I'm here, but that's not fair. I don't want to take you away from your routine. I don't want to take him away from his either." She's pacing, clearly distraught over something I didn't think twice about this morning. "I'm so sorry. I spent most of the weekend looking for a place to live, but anything affordable is nearly an hour outside of Ojai. I swear, everything in this town costs like a million dollars. Who the hell can afford to live here anymore? It's ridiculous. But I'm trying, I swear, Arthur, I'm trying. With it being the end of the month and everything, I thought my chances would be better."

I can't listen to this anymore.

"Alice," I try, but she continues on, telling me she'll be out of my way soon. "Alice," I repeat a little louder, and she looks up, stopping where she's about to wear out the floor. "Is that where you were all weekend? Looking for a place to rent?" She swallows, biting the corner of her lip. "And it's where you've been after work, too." I don't bother asking this time.

"Mostly, yeah."

I don't love that answer. But more than that, I don't like how she's actively trying to move out of my house. I don't think I've given her any reason to, other than the dickhead way I behaved on Wednesday. Obviously, that's why she wants to leave. She must hate that she has to put up with me. "Listen, Alice, I'm sorry, okay? I'm sorry I acted like an asshole to you and made assumptions I should never have made. I'm sorry I've made you so uncomfortable you can't stand the thought of living in the same house as me, if you can even call our current arrangement that, since you're never around and you avoid me better than I avoid my entire family." *Well, that wasn't supposed to come out.* "I panicked when I thought you had a drinking or a drug problem. I've seen what addiction does to people's lives, and I didn't want that for you. I don't want that for anyone. What do I need to do to help you believe I'm not that guy? Do you want character references? A contract of some sort? What can I do?" I didn't expect to be this desperate to convince someone I'm not who they think I am, and yet here I stand. Fucking desperate.

"You don't need to do anything. I'm not uncomfortable around you, Arthur. I've had roommates do far worse things than assume I'm something I'm not. I'm trying to leave because I'm clearly a nuisance, and I'm okay with being a lot of things, but that's not one of them." She shuts her eyes tightly for a moment, rubbing her forehead. "I can't stay. I'll leave tonight. I'll stay at a hotel until I find something, but I can't do this. I can't live in your house and work here and force you to change things you literally do every single day. I won't."

You'd think she was asking me to move out of the country and take on a whole new identity, not adjust how often she's around my dog, an animal who has his own space inside and outside of my house. He's happy, regardless of whether he's here or there.

"This is the second time you've tried to quit this job. Do you not want to work here?" That gets her to look at me, and her eyes turn glassy before I see the fire in them. This woman is a ball of emotions, and they all live right at the surface at all times. And somehow, she's still a mystery to me.

"Are you kidding me? This job is all I've ever wanted. I get to consult on how to start this therapy program and be the sole therapist until more people are brought on. I'm working with Rosemary, a gosh darn legend. Maeve and Owen are giving me freedom to basically do whatever I want, which makes no sense because they don't even know me. The only thing wrong with this job is that it's here, in this godforsaken town I spent too many years of my life in. But this job? This is the job I studied my butt off in school for. This is the job I put myself into debt for. This is the job I *always* wanted and didn't know if I'd ever get. But I'm not going to do it at the expense of someone having to give anything up, so I'm not staying." By the end of her spiel, she's breathing heavily. She obviously cares about this a whole lot. Good.

"I didn't take you for a martyr, Alice." I know I'm taunting her, but sometimes people need a little tough love, and I remember she liked it when I didn't sugarcoat my reaction to her living arrangements at the bar when we met.

"Excuse me?" she asks through gritted teeth.

"You want this job so badly, but not badly enough to take something away from a dog? A dog, who, by the way, will be perfectly fine not coming here every day. He has a great life, I can assure you. But you believe so strongly in not inconveniencing anyone that you're willing to give up your dream job? Come on. Make that make sense." I cross my arms while she seethes.

"You don't know me," she spits out, anger practically bursting out with every word.

"Okay." I remain expressionless, waiting for her to work through this.

"So why do you care what I do? Whether or not I leave?" She licks her bottom lip, clearly pissed off.

"Why do *you* care if my dog gets to hang out here all day instead of in his bed or in his dog run?" I shrug, trying to look unbothered by the fact that she has such few expectations of people. "I wouldn't be the only one to care, by the way. Maeve, Rosemary, Paige, everyone here will care. They like you. They've already nicknamed you. If you leave, how will it force them to change their plans? How much longer will it take to get this program up and running? How many people will have to wait longer to get the care they need? But you know what? You're right. Consider my dog. Please."

Her eyes dart around the room as my words sink in and take root. I can practically see the moment the lightbulb turns on and she realizes I'm right, that her leaving would do much more damage than good. I don't want to guilt her into staying, but she has to see how silly her argument is.

"You're right," she whispers. As her eyes meet mine, they're filled with tears, but she blinks them away. "You're right," she repeats with a nod to the floor.

"So stay, Alice. Stay with me, stay at this job, stay in Ojai. Stay here." Her eyes widen, and for a moment I think she looks scared.

"I can't leave Ojai at the moment, anyway. And I don't want to leave anyone high and dry. I also don't want Luther to be banished from coming here when I'm here, so maybe…" She tucks a strand of hair behind her ear, and I note for the first time that though her hair is hanging straight down her back in a ponytail, this piece is curly. "Maybe we can work on how I handle being around him. I'm obviously not going to stay at your house for long, but we can at least work on being able to be in the same place when we're here."

"No." My immediate response surprises even me, but then my brain catches up with my mouth. "We work on you being able to be around Luther here *and* at home. You stop spending all your free time looking for a rental and stay with me. It's a nightmare finding a place to live around here, and you're going to wear yourself out trying to do that when you should be focusing on the therapy program. I think you'd agree that's much more important." If she hates ultimatums even a tiny bit as much as I do, she's going to say no. But I'm hoping she's not quite as stubborn and hard-headed as I am.

"All right." She puts her hands into her pockets, shocking the shit out of me by agreeing so easily. There's still hesitation in her body language and tone, but she's given me a verbal yes, nonetheless.

"All right?" It's impossible to keep the surprise out of my voice, and I try to recover by clearing my throat. "So we have a deal? No more trying to leave unless it's for a good reason?" I stretch my hand out to her, and she looks at it for a beat before placing hers in mine. Her grip is strong, but her skin is so soft. I don't want to let go, so I don't pull my hand back, but she slips hers away. "We'll take it slow with Luther. He'll be fine."

"Yeah. Okay." She clears her throat when I flip the baseball cap on my head so it's on backward. "I'm gonna get back to work, then, boss." She turns away from me quickly, and it takes me a few seconds to recover.

"Not your boss," I shout at the door, hoping she heard me.

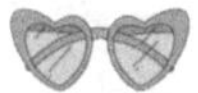

the big ones are just plain awkward to eat with

Alice

"Not your boss."

His words ring loud and clear as I walk toward the building that houses my office and workspace. I smile to myself, remembering the way his ears were already turning red by the time I turned away from him. I bite my lip thinking of the way he adjusted that baseball cap he loves to wear backward when he's working and forward when he's riding. My satisfaction doesn't go unnoticed. Paige, Sam, and Corey are all watching with brows raised and knowing looks.

Son of a biscuit.

BY THE TIME five o'clock rolls around, I haven't seen Arthur because I've hidden in my office all day. I know we were supposed to meet today, but after he so accurately called me out earlier, I couldn't face him, so I pretended to have some calls to make and needed to reschedule.

I knew I'd made the right decision when Paige came to have lunch with me and asked about the "sexual tension that was most definitely tensioning" between Arthur and me. Shutting it down as quickly as possible, and hiding the way my face heated at her comment, I let her words fuel my determination not to let myself get too close to him.

Now, rather than going back to the farmhouse, I opt for a grocery run. I can't keep living off snacks and Gran's leftovers at the care facility. Plus, I'm not going over there today. The nurses asked me to take a break since she's been so upset lately, but they promised to call if she happens to be having a better-than-usual evening.

I don't know how to feel about it. Relieved? Guilty? Numb? I think I'm all of them. It's exhausting.

The people looking after her are so lovely, but they don't know what kind of caregiver my grandmother was. They don't know that resentment was so thick in the air of her house, it was suffocating. Or how she blamed me for my mother's death.

No one does. Because what kind of person would I be if I seemed ungrateful for my grandmother taking me in when I was left with no parents at the age of twelve? No better than her, that's for sure.

So I walk around the grocery store like I have nowhere else to be, because tonight, I don't. I keep my budget tight, opting for bananas, peanut butter, potatoes, chicken, bread, butter, an onion, and some garlic. At the last minute, I splurge on eggs. Despite knowing exactly how much is in my bank account, I breathe a sigh of relief when the cashier hands me a receipt and sends me on my way. Gran's care facility drained me of nearly every dollar

I had to my name. And the moment my paycheck lands in my account, it's essentially spoken for, between the facility, student loan payments, rent that I will insist on giving to Arthur, and all the other bills regular people have. It's all meticulously listed on a spreadsheet I look at no less than twice a week as if it's my lifeline, which sometimes it sort of is.

I text Arthur to let him know I'll be arriving at the house shortly. Owen had already given me his phone number, so I decide to finally use it.

> Hi. I'll be there shortly. Giving you a heads up in case you're outside with Luther again.

ARTHUR:
Who is this?

Kidding.

No worries. Lu's in the dog run, so he might hear you coming, but he can't get to you. Is that okay?

His attempt at a joke has me rolling my eyes with a silly smile, and the *kidding* has me picturing him scrambling to send that in case I did think I had the wrong number. Even the fact that he shortened the dog's name makes me smile.

> Of course. See you soon.

My fingers move of their own accord, asking if he needs anything, but that feels too… friendly, or something. We're not friends. We're colleagues and roommates, and I know better than anyone that those are not guarantees for friendship. I opt not to send it and put the Jeep in drive, following the familiar roads back to the farmhouse.

As I unload the back seat with my bag of measly groceries, Luther's barks greet me from somewhere in the backyard. For a moment, my heart rate picks up and I pause to listen for his proximity, looking around at both sides of the house. Nothing. The barking stops, and if I hadn't been listening so intently, I would have missed Arthur's gentle scolding.

Once I'm in the front door, I'm greeted with the smell of something delicious, and my stomach rumbles. I was planning on a peanut butter and banana sandwich for dinner, which I'm certain will taste like cardboard after smelling whatever Arthur is making for himself.

When I step into the kitchen, he's got a pair of basketball shorts and a cut-off shirt on, his hair is damp, and there's a tea towel draped over his left shoulder. Great. He looks like that while I'm still in work clothes and my hair piled in a messy bun on top of my head with stray curls that refuse to stay straight after a day in the heat of Ojai's late summer weather.

He turns to greet me with a smile, and the bag I'm holding nearly slips out of my hand. He's so unfairly good-looking. Beautiful people have always intimidated me a little. I don't think anyone is truly ugly until their actions make them so. I mean, if you're the kind of person who doesn't give up their seat for someone who clearly needs it more than you, or you scowl at babies, I don't care how objectively beautiful you might be. In my eyes, immediately ugly.

But Arthur? He's… I don't know, this weird mix between pretty, with his sparkly brown eyes and those thick, insanely long eyelashes, and ruggedly hot, with the big muscles, forearm tattoos, permanent scruff on his jaw and a mostly serious expression at all times. And it's not that he doesn't smile, but they're these tiny, crooked ones that pull at one of his cheeks, and if you blink, you'll miss them because they never last long. I may have done a good job of avoiding him, but I have a surprisingly good view of the barn doors from my office, and I may have become a little too acquainted with every detail of Arthur from afar. He's a little rough around the edges, and yet there's a softness to him. I saw it when we met. It was in the way he watched me as I spoke, how he held me when we danced, in the tenderness of his voice when he talked about reading books with Luther, in how he interacted with Josie, looking both annoyed and entertained by her antics. Never mind how concerned he was when he found me in the bathroom.

"Alice?" He wipes his hands on the towel draped on his shoulder and turns away from the stove, directing all of his attention to me. "Did you hear me?"

Crap on a cracker. I didn't.

I got so caught up in my little Arthur daydream, I didn't hear a word he said. Not having enough snacks today wasn't a good idea. I'm so hungry I've lost the ability to act like a regular human being.

"I said, Luther is outside with a slow feeder that will keep him busy for a little bit." He takes pity on me and repeats himself. Given how hot my cheeks are, I have a feeling my blush has become visible even through my tan skin.

I nod dumbly, and that little crooked smile pulls at his cheek, but he licks his bottom lip, erasing it as quickly as he did all my working brain cells with the swipe of his tongue.

"Need any help with that?" He motions to the bag I'm now holding on to for dear life with both hands. Looking away from him momentarily, I loosen my grip, hoping I didn't squish all of my bananas. Or the eggs.

"I'm okay. Sorry, my brain stops working when I'm

hungry." As I set my things on the kitchen island, Arthur gets back to whatever smells so ridiculously good on the stove, and while I quietly put my things away, my stomach rumbles in an obnoxiously loud way. I try to cover it up with a cough, but Arthur's chuckle is confirmation enough that it didn't work.

"It's almost ready, don't worry." He sets a hand on his hip as he continues to work. "I hope you like stew. I know it's not quite fall yet, and it's not like it ever gets all that cold here, but I thought some comfort food might be nice."

"Oh. No, that's okay." As soon as my words are out, his shoulders slump. "Shoot. That was rude, sorry. I do like stew. Who doesn't like meat and potatoes, right? But that's the dinner you made for yourself, so it's all right. I'll come back and make myself something when you're done." And that's code for, I don't want to salivate or have my stomach embarrass me any further, nor do I want you to know I was going to eat a lame sandwich for dinner, so I'll be going now.

"How do you know there's meat in this stew?" He doesn't look away from his task of... Oh my heavens, that's garlic bread he's taking out of the oven and setting down on the trivet. Tossing the towel he used back over his shoulder, he eyes me curiously.

I swallow down the lust I'm currently experiencing over this bread, butter, and garlic. "Um, it smells like it?" That shouldn't be a question, and yet...

"Your nose is right." He casually serves out the stew into two bowls that had already been sitting next to the stove. "Table or island?" With his focus on sprinkling chopped parsley over the food, I stand motionless, mouth agape, taking in the scene in front of me and trying to make sense of what he's saying. I guess we're having dinner together. "If you don't mind grabbing us some spoons, I'm happy to eat wherever."

For some reason, that gets my feet moving, though my mouth is still proving to be quite useless. I grab a soup spoon for him and a dessert spoon for myself. Big spoons are so awkward to eat with.

Something about that thought makes me clear my throat. "Table, if that's okay?" I look over to the kitchen table, noting a pile of napkins already on it. I place two underneath our spoons so we end up sitting across from one another. "Can I get you a drink?" Might as well make myself useful. I hate watching other people work.

"Ice water would be amazing, please." His eyes meet mine briefly before I walk to the open shelves where he has matching sets of minimalist glasses next to the plates and bowls. I let the falling ice and dispenser drown out my thoughts as I pour us both full glasses.

He's already at the table, the garlic bread cut and displayed on the wooden cutting board, and the smell of stew making my stomach rumble again.

"You really didn't have to do this, Arthur." I sit, reluctantly, and he stands, jogging to the silverware drawer.

As soon as he sits back down, he holds his new spoon up. "I like the little spoons, too. Honestly, the big ones are just plain awkward to eat with." He sighs, like this is a serious concern for him, like he didn't reveal we share a quirk I don't think I've ever shared with anyone. "All right, let's dig in!" With a bright smile, my roommate renders me speechless yet again.

we're not going to get married
because of stew

Arthur

Alice is looking at me like I sprouted a second head. I purposely ignored her attempts to make this a big deal. It isn't. So I take a bite and let her sit with her thoughts for another minute before I address her discomfort with something as simple as making her a meal.

"It's not a big deal. We're roommates, I was already making stew, and I always make too much. I'm the oldest of six kids. I've been cooking full meals since I was like ten. I promise you, this is nothing." And I might have been looking for an excuse to get her to sit with me since she avoided me all day and didn't show for the meeting we were supposed to have. She emailed me to say she had to make some calls and couldn't make it.

"It's something to me," she responds quietly, a wince following her words. "I haven't ever had a roommate willingly share, well, anything, really." Her shrug is quick and dismissive, and her reaction to something as small as wanting to share a meal with her stirs something in my chest.

"You haven't had very good roommates then." Shit. I meant for that to come out as a question, not a statement. I must sound like the judgmental asshole she already thinks I am.

But then her lips purse, like she's trying not to smile, and that little dimple pops. "No, I guess I haven't." We stare at one another for a beat. "But I take it you're going to change that." She doesn't ask me, but I answer anyway.

"Yep." I point to her with my spoon before saying, "Now eat the delicious dinner I made us, Alice." As she brings her spoon to her mouth, I smile with the knowledge that she seems more at ease now. I'm hoping it's because I didn't make a fuss about this. Nothing to fuss about.

"You got it, boss." She takes her first bite while I pretend not to be entirely affected by her calling me boss again. Closing her eyes, she slaps a hand on the top of the table. "Ermagherd," she mumbles, going for another bite, even though I'm not sure she's swallowed the first yet. Her palm hits the table again, three times in quick succession. "Arthur, will you marry me?" She continues to eat, clearly not shy about how much she's enjoying this stew. It's not one of my favorites for nothing.

What hits me harder than the fact she seems so relaxed, like she's back to the version of her I met at the bar, is her question. I know she wasn't serious, obviously. We're not going to get married because of stew. It's not *that* good. But for some reason, that's the thing warming my insides.

"I saw you took Scout out today. How did she do?" My question forces her to slow down her eating.

"She was great. I know she's used to a saddle, but for a

lot of people, it's beneficial to ride the horse without one. They get to really feel the animal's movements that way, and it can be great for sensory processing." She pauses, setting her spoon down. "Sorry I missed our meeting today, by the way. I did have a busy day, but I was also feeling weird about this morning. I'm not used to the kindness everyone around here seems to throw around so freely."

I know she means the apology, and I'm glad she's being honest with me. I had a feeling it was more than a busy day. "All good. We can chat another time. And we have that meeting with everyone tomorrow anyway, so we can go over a few things for the new horses then. I'm glad Scout is doing so well, though." This time, when I smile at her, she smirks, like she's got an inside joke I'm not in on. I narrow my eyes at her, but she shakes her head and moves on to asking me about training with Rosemary, and we ease into conversation about the day.

When we finish, Alice insists on washing the dishes. I settle for letting her help me, since she doesn't seem to do well with sitting still. She doesn't stop at making sure the dishes are washed, though; she wants to dry and put them away, too. I've noticed she never leaves dishes on the drying rack. The house always looks untouched, even though I know she has coffee in the mornings, and she's eaten the breakfasts I've left her.

I'm not sure whether she's naturally neat and tidy or if this is something she does because she thinks she has to.

The bowls we used go on a high shelf, and when she struggles to reach, I take them from her and place them back myself. With my chest flush against her back, it's impossible to miss the hitch in her breath. Her flowery coconut scent floats up, and I linger for a moment, inhaling deeply.

I step back and clear my throat. "I can store those on a

lower shelf." Except I won't, because I want to do that again.

We work quietly to get everything put away, and by the time we're done, Luther is scratching at the door to come inside, whining like he's been ignored all day. He hasn't. Paige, Corey, and Sam all took turns coming over here to play with him during the day, and I came at lunch, too.

"Sorry. I'll go out there with him so he doesn't bother you." At least he didn't bark this time.

"Actually…" She places a hand on my forearm, then drops it all too quickly. "Would it be okay if I tried, I don't know, petting him again… or something?" It's obvious she's scared, but she's asking to do this anyway.

"Are you sure?" Her face screams no, but she nods furiously. "Gonna need a verbal here, Alice." Because even though I plan on holding on to Luther's collar tightly if she decides to do this, I need her to be certain, and her wide eyes do not communicate that right now.

"Yeah. Yep. Yes. I'm sure. I did it before, and he was okay until he jumped, but you'll be there this time, and he listens to you, so it's okay." She licks her lips, still nodding like it's going to help to convince herself this isn't terrifying.

"I'll be there the whole time, holding on to him. He won't get his paws on you. I promise." I lower my head, meeting her gaze. Her eyes have taken on a copper tinge in the fading sunlight, and up close, I have a front-row view of the faint freckles on her nose.

"Okay," she whispers. "Let's do this."

I grab his leash and a few treats out of the container by the back door and go out first, giving Luther some scratches and sitting on the ground with my legs outstretched in front of me so I can grab his collar. "I've got him," I shout to Alice. I expect it to take a minute or two for her to work up the courage to come out here, but seconds later, she's standing a few feet away and Luther is whipping me with his tail, hoping to finally get her attention.

"Hey, Luther," she says softly. "You're a good boy, aren't you?" Stepping closer, she rubs her hands together then extends one toward him, which he happily sniffs and licks. That gets a small chuckle out of her, until he tries to pounce. I hold on tightly, but she startles and jumps back. "Okay. That's okay. You're excited." She's talking to him like he'll respond, but I think she needs to process what's happening verbally. "Let's try this again, okay?" She steps forward once more, bending to pet the top of Luther's head. He behaves this time, and with my free hand, I show her the small treat, offering to let her give it to him. She shakes her head, so I go ahead and let Luther know he's doing what we need him to.

"You're doing great." I keep my voice calm and gentle.

"Yeah, he is." Alice's eyes are glued to Luther, watching for any change in his demeanor. Her hands move to his ears, and he sits, panting in delight.

"No, Alice. *You're* doing great." With my hold on Luther steady, she relaxes and lets her gaze meet mine for a second. When Luther goes limp and flops down on the ground with his head landing on my leg, she giggles. It's such a good sound. Like birds chirping on a clear morning. Like rainfall on a tin roof. It's joy and comfort.

She crouches down to keep petting him, and his eyes practically roll to the back of his head, and then so do mine when her hand grazes the bare skin on the inside of my knee. If she's uncomfortable in any way, she doesn't show it. She sits cross-legged and moves to rub his chest and belly, and my dog, who is an absolute ho for any attention, grunts and rolls back and forth, asking for more. It earns us another sweet little laugh.

"I think we can be friends someday, Luther." There's not a ton of conviction in her voice, but I'll take it. She's doing something that scares her, and sometimes we need to talk ourselves into believing something we aren't entirely confident in. I know all about that.

As Luther looks up at me, I give him another treat, and he must think this is the best day of his life. It probably is. He's getting treats and attention from the person he's been trying to bug for two weeks.

"Maybe we should leave on a high note?" Alice's eyes flit to mine. "I don't want to overdo it, you know?"

"Yeah. Yeah, of course."

As her hand moves off Luther, I replace it with mine. He tries to move, but I keep him down as Alice stands and steps back.

"Thank you for today, Arthur. For dinner, for this." Her smile is small, but it's content.

"Anytime," I say honestly.

"Goodnight." She gives me a little wave before turning around to walk inside, and Luther loses his shit. Attempting to get up, he barks, and the way Alice jumps and tenses at the sound has me mumbling a few swear words at my dog.

She looks back, putting on a brave face. But as she walks away, her arms wrap around her middle like the other day when she stepped out of her Jeep, and I decide right then and there I'm gonna make this better for her. Because after sharing one dinner with Alice, I don't like the idea of her having a roommate who isn't me.

i can't wait for my lesson

Alice

One dinner. We had one dinner together, and it feels like we went back to the two people who met at the bar. Before I barfed up everything in my stomach, that is.

I wanted to dislike him after the way he accused me of being drunk or on drugs. I wanted to never look at his judgy face again when I walked away with every intention of leaving. But there was something so honest and earnest about his apology. And I saw that again last night when he explained he's been cooking since he was a kid. I made such a big deal out of something that's so simple to him, but the thing is, he doesn't understand how something insignificant to him can be monumental to me.

It's clear Arthur is a man of actions, but not necessarily words. Though I'm sure he could be good with those, too, if he wanted to. I'm sure he's good with a lot of things, if the way my body reacted to his closeness while putting dishes away is anything to go by. Geez, I need to put some distance between us. I need boundaries here, because we work together, and I'm not staying in Ojai, and it's… a bad idea.

I go to bed with every intention of not thinking about Arthur, but as I fall asleep, he's the only thing on my mind.

OWEN AND MAEVE are joining our meeting today, so I know I can't cancel again, even if the urge is strong, because the thought of being in such proximity to Arthur in any setting has my stomach in knots. Delicious, warm, and fuzzy knots I don't exactly hate.

Despite my feelings, logically I know I need to keep my distance, especially when we're at work. And I've been good at that.

I see him for the first time all day at two o'clock when he walks into my office, taking off that damn baseball hat and running his fingers through his hair. I wonder what that feels like.

Hard no, Alice.

I clear my throat, determined to stay as far away from him as possible and to separate our responsibilities with the horses in every way I can think of.

"Hey there, roomie," he says in that casual way of his.

"Hi, Arthur." Pulling my notebook closer to me, I fidget with my pen, waiting for him to sit down. He opens his mouth to say something else when Owen and Maeve walk in, whispering something to one another. Rosemary is a few steps behind them.

"Hello, lovelies," Maeve says brightly. "So nice for us all to be together, finally." They take their seats at the table, and Owen, ever the efficient one, opens his laptop. "Arthur,

I take it you've been a wonderful roommate to our delightful Alice?" The way she calls me 'our Alice' makes me feel warm inside. I've spoken with Maeve several times since I arrived, and she's always been kind.

"I'm doing my best. She's easy to be around," Arthur answers easily. Well, crap, this is awkward. I don't handle compliments well, and surely it's written all over my face because Owen quickly pulls us back to our reason for being here.

"Glad it's going well. Maevey and I want to discuss the new horses we'll need for the therapy program." He clicks on something, squinting at his screen. "Alice, I know you agree Scout will be a good fit, but we'd like at least a couple more. Rosemary and Arthur have been working on a shortlist, but ultimately, we feel like it's something you should all agree on."

"Oh, well, I'd be happy to give my input, sure." I've never been asked to do this before, but I've worked with horses in a therapeutic setting long enough to know pretty quickly when they have the right temperament.

"Great. Art, can you set up a trip for you three to go back and see some of the horses you liked? You're the experts, so I'm confident you'll bring back the perfect additions to the roster." Owen types something, likely notes he'll add to the software we use to keep meetings and tasks organized. He's insanely techy. It's awesome. But I'm stuck on what he said.

"A trip?" I keep my features as schooled as I can, but darn it, it's hard.

"Yes. We think you should spend some time with these horses to make sure you're comfortable with them." Rosemary nods, unfazed by my surprise.

"Plus, it'll be fun! You're going to be cooped up here, setting things up a little while longer, so this ought to be a nice little break. And a chance for the two of you to bond, too." Maeve swings a finger between me and Arthur and smiles innocently, but Owen sighs, throwing her a sideways glance.

"Um. Okay." I think about what this means professionally rather than personally because personal feelings have no place here. "Thank you for asking me to be a part of this. It means a lot that you trust me to be the one starting this program alongside you, you both know that." I've told them before, but it bears repeating.

"Thank you, Alice. We couldn't do this without you." Maeve reaches out and squeezes my forearm.

"Kid, I don't know how many ways I can tell you that you were by far the best candidate for this job, and we had been looking for *months*." Rosemary stresses the last word, reminding me what she's told me every single day since I started here, which is that *they* feel so lucky *I* accepted this job. Every time she says it, I think someone is going to come around the corner with a camera and say, "Gotcha! Just kidding!" because it honestly doesn't seem plausible they would be the lucky ones.

Owen nods in agreement before adding, "Other than this, I think everything else is running smoothly, but are there any questions or concerns either of you has so far?"

"Actually," Arthur says, "I'm curious as to whether we're using English or Western tack." It's probably something we would have talked about if I hadn't so actively avoided him.

Everyone looks to me. "I see you're set up for both here, and though it's much more likely that people with little-to-no riding experience will use Western, I'd like the option for English, too, if that's all right." Again, not something I've ever had any say in before, but gosh, this feels nice.

"Of course," Arthur responds. "We're always ready with both since Maeve only rides English, anyway." Arthur rolls his eyes at her playfully, and she laughs.

"Oh, you're mad because you can't handle it, Arty." Pointing to me, she says, "Perhaps Alice can teach you, since you won't even get on one when I ask."

"Perhaps she can," he shoots back with a mocking British accent, making everyone chuckle—even Owen. But my laughter is all nerves as I imagine the potential of riding with Arthur and exploring the ranch. I've gone out on Scout with Paige and Sam, but I know it would feel different with Arthur. Everything else seems to.

"Anything else?" Arthur and I answer Owen with headshakes, and he closes his laptop. Rosemary gives us a salute and makes her way out the door.

Before they stand, Maeve reaches over and touches my arm. "Alice, we're having a girls' night this Friday. It'll be me, my twin sister Charlie, and our bestie Elaina. We'd love for you to come, if you can." Again, she is the nicest human, but I'm not used to having friends, and I worry I'll be the awkward person out among such a tight-knit group. My hesitation either speaks volumes, or she's always got a lot to say. "It's super low-key. We'll be in our jammies, eating junk, and talking about boys. Charlie and Lainey are the loveliest girls, and they've asked to meet the newest addition to our team since we won't shut up about you. Will you pleeeeeeease come?"

"Maevey," Owen warns with zero heat as Arthur watches.

"If you're sure I won't be imposing, I—"

"Oh, wonderful! And imposing? Never! I'm so excited!" She claps her hands, bouncing in her seat.

"All right, blondie, let's go before you make any other plans." Owen stands and pulls Maeve's chair out for her as she smiles sweetly at him. They are too cute together. "See you both soon." They wave goodbye at us, and I stand, unsure of where to go, but needing to not be left alone with Arthur.

When he walks past me, he leans in close, putting that damn cap on backward. "Didn't know you rode English, tesouro. I can't wait for my lesson." That lightning-quick smirk comes and goes, and then he goes, too, leaving me to unravel in the middle of my office on my own.

his trip back from lustytown takes a little longer than mine

Alice

Arthur texted to let me know he wouldn't be home until later since he's got his Wednesday visit to Beau's Bar tonight, so I had the rest of the leftover stew for dinner. Now I'm scouring the shelves in the den for a book to read since I couldn't shut my brain off. I'm restless. My mind and body are tired, but both are also completely wired, and I'm not sure I'm capable of actual sleep at the moment.

I catch a glimpse of the book Arthur had recommended to me the night we met, but it's on a high shelf I can't quite reach. After looking around for something I can use as a step stool, I settle on the small ottoman in front of a chair and drag it over. I'm on the tips of my toes, fingertips nearly touching the book, wondering why the heck these shelves are so high, when a deep voice has me tumbling backward.

"Need some help?" Arthur catches me around the waist when I ungracefully make my landing. "Shit. Sorry. I thought you heard me come in."

With his chest against my back warming every part of me and rearranging my brain cells until they're mush, I don't feel any pain. I rush to step out of his hold, sitting on the ottoman I fell from as we lose our connection, and the ache from my awkward landing finally registers in my ankle.

"I didn't hear anything. Luther didn't even bark." I brush the hair from my face and look up at him, finding his gaze raking over my mostly bare legs, up to my chest and shoulders. I run hot, so a tank top and sleep shorts are my go-to. He wasn't supposed to be home so early, or I definitely wouldn't be out here like this, even if the way he's looking at me is making my entire body buzz.

"Yeah, I took him for a run earlier. He's tired." Pushing up the sleeves of his shirt puts the tattoos on his tanned forearm right at my eye level, and while I could happily sit here and stare at them, I need distance, so I stand. The moment I attempt to step around him, my stupid ankle gives out and forces him to catch me again.

"Son of a biscuit," I whisper. We're chest-to-chest now, his arm firmly wrapped around my body. The tremors of his chuckle vibrate right through me, and I force my eyes to remain open, though all I want is to melt into this feeling.

"You all right?" He studies my face, lingering on my nose where I know there are freckles. Freckles I've always loved, but my mom and grandma always hated. Freckles I surely got from whoever my biological father was, because neither of my so-called caregivers had them.

"Yes," I respond, my voice coming out softer than I'd like.

"Are you hurt?" The intensity in his brown eyes is enough to send a shiver running down my entire body.

"Yes," I breathe out unthinkingly. I don't remember

what the question was, but apparently I'm prepared to answer yes to anything this man asks me.

"Where, tesouro? Where are you hurt?" Not loosening his grip on me, he scans my body from top to bottom. With how close we are, and the thinness of my top, never mind the fact my nipples hardened the moment he touched me, my lack of bra is undoubtedly obvious. "Alice." My name is a whisper I'll never be able to unhear. It's a sound I'll think about for days, weeks, months to come. It's a plea and a promise, and when his eyes lock on my lips, every cell in my body comes alive at his attention.

When his shallow breath lands on my lips, and I'm certain we're about to cross a line I'm not sure I'd ever want to uncross again, Luther's deep bark comes from the room he's been in all evening. It jolts me back to reality, where kissing my roommate and coworker is a badder-than-bad idea.

I blink out of my daze and clear my throat. "You can let me go now."

"Can I?" His trip back from Lustytown takes a little longer than mine, but then he loosens his hold when he asks, "Will you fall again if I let you go?" There's a playfulness to his tone that cuts the tension ever so slightly, and I'm incredibly appreciative of the way he can do this.

I narrow my eyes, playing into it. "Believe it or not, I've made it twenty-seven years without having anyone to catch me when I fall. I don't need anyone to start now." After swatting at his arm, he finally releases me, and I limp away. "I'm fine," I say, swiping a hand to keep him from touching me again because I truly don't believe I could take it. "I landed funny. I've handled way worse."

He huffs out a frustrated breath, then his steps fade as he walks into the kitchen, and I hobble up the stairs. When

I get to the door of my room, Arthur is suddenly there, placing something cold in my hand.

"Put this on it, at least?" With his warm fingers wrapped around mine, the cold from the ice pack hardly even registers. I whisper a thanks and limp inside, shutting the door as my heart threatens to leap out of my throat.

I'VE TOSSED and turned for the last two nights. Not because of my ankle, though that hasn't help, but because every moment Arthur and I have had together kept replaying in my head, like a movie on a loop I couldn't end.

Yesterday, when he handed me the book I'd been trying to get, he tried to say something about the other night, but I shut it down fast, thanking him for helping me then handing him a loaf of banana bread I'd baked. Avoidance seems to be my strategy, and so far it's working beautifully.

It's almost time for me to head to Maeve's, and dinner is nearly ready, so I decide to do a few stretches on the back deck while Luther is in his dog run. I haven't had a ton of time with him, but he was at the stable yesterday, on a long leash that made it so he couldn't reach me whenever I walked from my office to see the horses. And he's happy enough to be around people, playing with his toys and napping in the sun.

I've just gotten into rabbit pose when the back door opens and Arthur steps out. He doesn't say anything, and I don't flinch when Luther makes an excited noise. I give myself ten seconds in the stretch before I slowly unfold and sit back on my feet.

"Hey." I look up to find his eyes already on me. "Was everything okay with Jasper? I was out with Scout today, and I swear she knew something was up with him. She didn't seem herself, and as soon as we got back, she kept pulling me toward Jasper to check on him."

Surprising the crap out of me, he lowers in front of me on the deck, crossing his legs. "Yeah, he's colicky. Doc came quickly, and thankfully, it seems to be pretty mild. He's on painkillers now, and Corey is taking the first shift walking him and making sure the rest of the horses stay calm. Thanks for the heads-up on that today. Jasper is always up to something, so no one thought much of it, but you did." His serious gaze is equal parts intense and gentle.

I shake my head, brushing off his words. "It was Scout. She knew."

"And you followed her lead. You're really intuitive, Alice, and Scout knows that. She trusts you already." Like every other time Arthur speaks, his compliment is sincere, and impossible to ignore this time.

"Thanks," I mumble, mostly because I don't want to be rude.

"What were you doing out here before I interrupted you?" He cocks his head to the yoga mat I'm on.

"A few stretches for my neck and shoulders. If I don't keep up with them, I end up with a headache and many trips to the bathroom where my face becomes intimately acquainted with the toilet." I wince at the thought. This man has now witnessed me being sick twice, and now I'm talking about it. How unsexy. Come to think of it, that's probably what I should be doing—reminding him how I'm the pukey girl.

Distance. Create more distance.

"So your headaches are brought on by shoulder and neck pain?" He doesn't seem fazed by the barf talk. Crap.

"Yeah. It's from an old injury when I was a kid." That's always the vague response I give when people ask about my chronic cervicogenic headaches.

"The same one that happened thanks to the dog?"

Damn, this man remembers everything.

"The very one," I answer quickly, moving to stand. He does the same, and before I can begin rolling up my mat, he's already starting to. "Oh, you don't have to—"

His look stops me from continuing. It reminds me of the way Owen looked at Maeve when he feigned frustration with her. It's a loaded look, but there's no menace in it.

"Okay. Thank you. Anyway, dinner's nearly ready for you. It's not much, just chicken and potatoes." I take the perfectly rolled mat from him, careful not to let our hands touch.

"For me? Are you not eating?"

"Girls' night, remember? Plus, you cooked for me the other day, so it was my turn to pay the kindness back." I give him a small smile, but before I can head back inside the house, he arrests my movements with his words.

"That's not how this works, Alice." My mind swirls with confusion and worry. "There's no paying anything back. You didn't have to make me dinner, like you didn't have to thank me for giving you ice for your ankle with baked goods." He steps into my space, and I'm grateful for the mat in my arms that forces our bodies not to get too close. "I appreciate that you cooked, but I'd much rather have dinner with you. The banana bread you made was delicious, but it would have been better if we'd shared it with a cup of coffee. If I help you with something, it's not because I want or expect anything in return. I really need you to understand that, okay?"

I gnaw on the corner of my lip, unsure how to respond because I'm not sure if I know how to do what he's asking. Kindness has always been transactional, especially with the people closest to me. "I'll try," I answer honestly.

"Good." He reaches up and tucks a stray strand of hair behind my ear. "I have the next shift with Jasper, so I might not be home when you get back."

"Oh. Okay."

"Thanks for dinner, goldie. Have fun tonight." That's the second nickname he's given me that I don't understand. His tiny smile lingers a little longer than usual before he hooks a thumb over his shoulder. "I'm gonna give Luther some attention before I eat that delicious-smelling dinner you made me."

"Okay," says the broken record, also known as Alice. "I-I'll see you." And with that, I leave.

In the car, I do a few more neck rolls for good measure and head to Maeve and Owen's house. Whatever nerves were lingering about meeting new people tonight have been replaced by the little knot of tension pulling at my ribcage, also known as Arthur Machado.

the kind where you have a box she can check off. yes. no. maybe

Arthur

Jasper seems to be feeling better, and when I tag Sam in for their shift, I'm certain it'll be an uneventful few hours. I'm so tired, though, I can feel it in my bones, but all of that dissipates when I walk into my house and find Luther lying in his bed, not in his room. Alice must have let him out, and my face pulls into a smile, knowing what it took for her to feel safe enough to do that.

"Hi, buddy," I greet Luther quietly, knowing Alice must be asleep in her bedroom. But as I walk deeper into the house, I catch a glimpse of white socks hanging off the couch. As I round the space, I take a moment to take her in. She's fresh-faced, and while her body seems relaxed, there are two little creases between her eyebrows, and her lips are pursed.

There must be some sort of magnetic force at work here, because even though I know it's a bad idea, I walk closer, crouch down next to her, and bring my finger to her forehead, smoothing gently. She lets out a low hum, and my fingers trail along her hairline, my palm cupping her cheek. I practically preen when she nuzzles into my touch, taking a deep breath in as a smile has her lips tipping up.

"Arthur," she whispers as my heart squeezes. When her eyes open, I don't move my hand, letting my fingers play with her hair. "You're home?" Her question is mumbled, but that word, home, sounds so fucking good coming out of her. It's always "the house" or some version of that, but she called this place home.

"I'm home, tesouro." The nickname slips out more easily with each day that passes by. When she wiggles and moves to sit up, I let my hand fall. "Sorry, I'm sure I stink."

"I'm used to it," she responds, and I chuckle. "Oh geez. I mean, I'm used to the smell in general, not that you stink. You never stink." She catches herself and slaps a hand against her face. "Ugh. I'm going to shut up and go to bed." Her eyes are hazy with sleep, and I'm not sure I've ever seen her look more beautiful.

"Good girls' night?" I know she's tired, but I'm not ready to let her walk away yet.

"Yeah. It was really nice. They're all so…likable and funny." She smiles, and I know my face matches hers. I'm happy she's making connections here. "How's Jasper?"

I let out a sigh, still relieved the night's going so well. "He's good. Much calmer, and doesn't seem to be in any pain."

Her smile widens, and she closes her eyes. "Good. I'm happy to hear that." She sways on the couch and snaps her eyes open. "Now I need to go to bed before I fall asleep sitting up. You get some rest, too." She taps my shoulder, using me to brace herself as she stands, then drags her feet all the way to the stairs.

"Hey, Alice?" I call as I rise to my full height, and she turns her head. "Thanks for waiting for me and taking care of Luther." She lifts her gaze to mine, but it's too brief. She licks her lips, cheeks turning pink, and nods, not saying anything as she takes the steps up to her room slowly.

IN A MATTER OF DAYS, Jasper had made a full recovery, and in the last couple of weeks, things between me and Alice have started to become less tense, in a way. If I grab her favorite coffee creamer when I go to the store after noticing she's run out, she doesn't immediately insist on paying me back. And when I made dinner two nights in a row, she didn't say anything about it being her turn the next night. Sure, she bought more treats for Luther since he's been going through them faster now that I'm trying to teach him to stop being so reactive, but it didn't come with a reason or as payback for anything. She thought of him —*of us*—and got them.

She has no idea how deeply I understand that feeling like a burden to someone can tear you down in a way that's difficult to recover from. With each passing day, though, I like to think she's starting to realize that she's not a burden here.

The problem is, as we become more friendly toward one another, and I see the way she cares about the horses, interacts with the staff, and laughs so easily in their company, the more difficult it is to remember why I shouldn't want her the way I most definitely do. It's *all* I think about sometimes.

Like right now.

I've been distracted while working with Rosemary today, and she knows it.

"Are you gonna tell me what's going on, or are you gonna keep staring off into space until you trip over something and give me a good laugh?" She's not one to beat around the bush, that's for fucking sure.

"It's nothing. Just got a lot on my mind." It's not a lie.

"I can tell. What's weighing you down more? That your brother and his daughter will be here in a few days, or that, at some point, you're gonna have to get over yourself and tell Alice you like her? You could do one of those little note things. You know, the kind with a box she can check off. Yes. No. Maybe. Or you could ask one of her friends to ask her out for you, so you don't have to talk to her." Rosemary is one of the toughest people to read. She can be completely serious when she's joking, or sound like she's kidding and be serious. I don't know how to take her.

"I'm not thirteen, Ro," I say, focusing on the movement of my hand as I brush Jasper.

"Then stop acting like it." Ah, there it is. She was kidding. I scoff and shake my head. "You liked her when you met. You decided you couldn't like her when you thought she was abusing alcohol or drugs. And you stuck with that decision, what? Because you're living and working together? I get it. It's a little complicated, but so is life, kid. Don't be an asshole about it and you'll be fine. She's not one of your ride-'em-and-ditch-'em girls."

"Jesus, Ro. I know that." I gotta stop talking about my love life with my seventy-year-old coworker. She knows too fucking much.

"And that's what's got you scared?" She continues inspecting the horse in front of her, murmuring to him softly in between scolding me. I swallow hard, because that's not it at all. Rosemary lets the silence linger before she says, "Your past doesn't define you, Arthur. Look at you now. You've come a long way. Sure, you still have more to go, but every day you take steps in the right direction. I know because I'm watching you take them." She pauses dramatically. "And I know what I'm talking about, remember?" She chuckles at her own comment.

I told her one time she always seems to know what she's talking about, no matter the topic. She's one of those people who knows something about everything. And I've never lived down my comment.

"Wow. Give a person a compliment one time…" I mumble and she laughs.

"One time is all it takes, kid. I never forget." She winks at me when our eyes meet, and I chuckle.

he wants to eat you for breakfast, lunch, and dinner. and then go back for seconds

Alice

This is my second time at Maeve's in the month since I got back to Ojai, and I'm not sure the shock of feeling at ease here has worn off yet. Elaina and Charlie are easy to talk to and more down-to-earth than I had expected at our first girls' night. After last week, they decided we'd do this as often as possible. It so happened we were all free again tonight—because, well, I'm always free—and now here we are.

So far, we've eaten our body weight in cheese, crackers, and various meats, had three different kinds of ice cream, and Charlie and I are currently witnessing Maeve and Elaina having a dance party in the kitchen.

"Some things never change," Charlie says as the two women walk back to where we're gathered on pillows around the coffee table.

Panting, Elaina, who is Owen's sister and also married to a movie star, flops down next to me. "I don't have the stamina for these like I used to, so I'm officially not leaving this spot for the rest of the night."

"Is that it, then? We enter our thirties and can't even handle a little dancing?" Maeve, who is also panting, throws herself dramatically onto Charlie's lap.

"I don't know about you, sister, but my stamina is fine, thank you. Ask Raf." The innuendo isn't missed by anyone, and Elaina perks up at the comment.

"Oh, have we reached the portion of the evening where we talk about all the crazy sex we're having? Except you, Maeve. You keep your fucking mouth shut about my brother." She points a finger at her best friend, who rolls her eyes as we all laugh.

"Well, I'm not having any sex, so I guess I'm out of this conversation." I pop a grape into my mouth, and Charlie openly gapes at me.

"How on Earth are you living with a Machado and not having sex? Have you seen those men? They are literally all attractive as hell. Even Ivan, but you never heard that from me. Rafael would have a conniption if he knew I thought his dad was fit." Charlie's British accent is stronger than Maeve's, and it's incredibly endearing, but her comment makes my cheeks burn.

"We're just roommates. And coworkers. And once he takes over for Rosemary, he'll be my boss." I chance a look at Maeve, and find her looking at me with a sly smile and brows raised.

"As our resident romance author knows," Elaina starts, "those are some great tropes. I mean, my husband was once *just* my roommate."

"I bet Arthur totally knows what he's doing, too. He'd probably handle you like he handles the horses, you know? All commanding and strong, but still sweet." Maeve sits up a little taller. "You'll have to tell us if it ever happens, Ali."

Her words have my eyes practically jumping out of their sockets, but the way she so casually gives me a nickname makes me want to share parts of my life with them.

But she's my actual boss. My boss' boss.

And I'm eventually going to leave this place and never come back.

"You'll have to excuse Maeve. She's never taken an HR course in her life." Elaina giggles, shaking her head.

"Listen, if you and Arthur can keep it profesh at work, it's totally fine. You're looking at me like I've lost my marbles, but I'd hate for you two not to give it a try because you sometimes see each other at work. The chemistry between you is hot. We've all seen it at the ranch. And I have never seen Arthur this way about a woman." My eyes must only be getting wider, because she keeps going, "But if you don't like him, then you do you. If the chemistry is strictly platonic, that's all right. No pressure."

She pauses, and I finally swallow and take a full breath. "But, Alice?" I meet her eyes. "That man looks at you like he wants to do *very* naughty things to you. Like he wants to eat you for breakfast, lunch, and dinner. And then go back for seconds!" Her brows dance on her forehead, and a shocked laugh escapes me.

"Ohhhhh, girl. You're in trouble. What a Machado wants, a Machado gets." Elaina's green eyes sparkle as she speaks. "I've known Raffy and his siblings for a long time. I mean, Raf played the long game to land Charlie, for fuck's sake. If Art's already looking at you like that, you better gird your loins. He's coming for you!" My loins choose that moment to react to her comment, because my gracious, I've thought about Arthur coming for me. In more ways than one.

"I—He doesn't—It's not—" I can't form a thought, let alone a sentence.

"Take your time processing it. There's no rush, anyway, right? You're getting to know one another, and this part should be fun, whether it's platonic or romantic. So let it be fun." Maeve reaches over and takes my hand, giving it a reassuring squeeze before letting go.

"Anyway, what are you all reading these days? I've found myself in a slump of sorts, and I need something new." Charlie, bless her heart, changes the topic and I couldn't be more thankful, though it doesn't help to take my mind off Arthur.

"I'm reading a sci-fi, horror, thriller romance. I know that's a lot of words, but this book is difficult to describe," I say as I pick up my sparkling water. When Charlie's brows raise in curiosity, I continue. "It's called Grave Matter. I've been devouring it, though I'm a big baby and can't read it at night because it's so atmospheric and creepy, so if you're into that…"

"And it has romance?" Elaina asks curiously.

"Sure does." My cheeks heat as I think about the scenes in the book. I definitely didn't expect Arthur to read romance books of any kind. "The sex scenes are… hot."

"Fucking right! I am so in! Text us the book details later?" Elaina—who swears more than anyone I've ever met, yet is a literal angel of a human—always gets me to laugh. I nod my response, and when I look at Maeve, she shakes her head.

"No books for me, thanks. I leave the smut reading to these two. I read enough scripts as it is. Though it's remarkably unsexy reading a sex scene when there are instructions between the dialogue." She shrugs, and the rest of the night goes by in a blur of cheese, chocolate, and laughter.

THIS MORNING I'm in the clinic barn, setting a few things up for our first trial patient tomorrow. Arthur's brother has a daughter with autism who has been having a harder time than usual with transitions, and he wants to try hippotherapy for her. I'm equal parts excited and nervous.

"Hey, Whinny." Sam waves at me as they walk into the barn, and I mentally remind myself to use the nickname instead of their name. It's not something we did at any of my previous jobs, but I like it.

"Hi, Mouse. Catch any more friends trying to break into the barns today?" I swear there is always a critter trying to bust in, and Sam is the one to catch—and release—them.

"Just the usual culprits." The wide smile on their face lights up the space, and Paige walks in with a handful of hooks we need to hang in the tack room today.

"Hey, beautiful people. Ready to pretty up this barn?" She lifts her other hand and revs the power tool she's wielding, making us laugh. Paige got the nickname Gear for being the one always fixing things, with a love of tools and a constant need to know how things work.

We all head into the tack room, and while Paige gets the hooks up, I continue organizing, and Sam works on unpacking a few things.

"All right, Whinny. Be honest. How are you liking working here so far?" The question comes from Paige, who is hardly ever silent.

"Oh, I love working here. You know that." She knows because I told her nearly every day the first week I got here.

"Yeah, but that was only a few days in. You've had some time to adjust now, so I wanted to make sure your answer is still the same." She smirks, quickly turning back to her task. "And how are things going with your grandmother? You mentioned going to visit her. Is she okay?"

I forgot I'd let that slip. I didn't give any details, so I'm not surprised she's asking.

"Yeah. I mean, sort of. She has Alzheimer's, and because she lived alone, no one really caught it. She lives at an assisted-living facility in town now." I keep it vague on purpose. It's hard to talk about this when people expect me to be sad about it all the time.

"Are you two close?" Paige mumbles with a screw between her lips.

"Not at all," I answer honestly. "She raised me after my mom passed, but we've… never gotten along." Understatement of my life, right there.

Even Sam, who mostly keeps to themselves, quirks an eyebrow at that, but I don't elaborate.

"I hope you know I'm not asking to be nosy, but you leave here after a full day of work and get in your car to go somewhere. Sometimes you're not back until late. And I swear I'm not stalking you, but I mean, I can see your driveway from my place. There isn't exactly a whole lot of traffic around here, and I see your headlights heading toward the farmhouse really late some nights. Is everything okay?" I know she means well, and I hate that I'm causing any worry.

"Um, yeah. I usually go to Gran's house before or after I visit her to pack up her things and get the place cleaned up. She has a lot of stuff, so it's taking some time." I shrug, knowing damn well that's not the entire story.

"Wait, so your grandmother still has a house close by? How come you're not living there?" She turns to me, but

Sam shooting her a look makes her wince. "Sorry, that didn't come out right."

Wanting to put Paige out of her misery, I divulge more details. "Yes. My grandmother was born and raised in Ojai. So was I. Her house is only ten minutes from here, but I can't live there because she nearly burned it down. It needs extensive work now, so I need to figure out what to do with it. I'll probably sell it to help pay for her care facility bills, but I need to clean it up before I can do that, so that's where I am when I'm not here." There. Secret's out.

"Next time you go, let me know. I'll come help you," Paige says easily as she moves on to her next task.

"Yeah, same," Sam adds.

Tears pool instantly, and I hold my breath in an attempt to keep the sob building in my throat at bay. I swallow hard, looking down at the floor and attempting to gather myself. That wasn't the response I was expecting. I guess I thought there'd be more questions, or we'd move on to something else.

"Thanks, but you don't have to do that. The house reeks of smoke, and Gran has newspapers from 1975 stashed in the linen closet. I'd hate to put anyone through having to clean that stuff up."

I'd also hate to put anyone through having to witness me crying when I see that the only things she's ever gotten rid of are my things. She's always had a hard time parting with stuff, unless it was something of mine. She even turned my old bedroom into a plant room, which makes no sense because it's only got a small window and hardly gets any light. It's shelves and shelves of random dying plants everywhere. She'd rather that than to have any proof I even exist.

"We know we don't have to," Paige says, pausing to

screw another hook into the wall. "But it's what friends do. And if you'd hate to put us through dealing with old newspapers, you must have forgotten we clean up literal horse shit every single day."

Sam chuckles at that. "True. And, Whinny?" I lift my chin to look at them. "You moved here to take care of a grandmother you say you're not close to, and you spend all your free time visiting her or cleaning up her house. If we didn't already know you're a good person, that confirmed it."

Paige points at me then, nodding. "Yep. And so you know, I won't ask anything else. I know too well that family stuff can be complicated. It's why we gotta lean on our chosen family, you know?"

I don't, but I nod anyway. The rest of the time we spend chatting and working side-by-side, I keep replaying those words in my mind.

Chosen family.

It hadn't ever really occurred to me before that I could choose one, or that one could choose me.

i need to know where you got that pickle

Alice

Scout's been prepped, and I went over the plan with Rosemary and Arthur yesterday afternoon, but I'm still a nervous mess as I pace inside my office. I know this is a trial run, and nothing is official, but it still feels like a big freaking deal. I'm so caught up in my own thoughts, I don't hear the door opening. When I turn around to pace in the other direction, Arthur is there.

A sharp breath hits my lungs, and he gives me an apologetic look.

"You always sneak up on me," I say, forcing a smile.

"No, you're really good at getting in your head and focusing on whatever's going on there." He taps his temple, and I know he's not wrong. I can easily get lost in my thoughts. "I knocked and everything, but still, I'm sorry I startled you."

"It's okay. I'm a little nervous about today." The honest words slip out, and he nods, walking further into the room as the door remains open.

"I see that. I'm nervous, too." My brows furrow because it's nearly impossible to imagine Arthur ever being nervous about anything. He's confident and calm at all times. "Cece is my niece. Gabriel is my brother." I already know this, so I nod as if I understand why that should be the reason he's worried, but my face must still communicate otherwise. "I don't see them much. There was some family drama, mostly between me and my dad, and it's sort of bled into my relationship with the rest of the family. So I'm a little anxious because I'm not sure how Cece is going to do, if she's going to want me there, or if it'll be weird talking to my brother." He swallows hard after the last word, looking down at his boots. We talk for a few minutes almost every day, but it's usually about work, or Luther, or what we're eating. We don't really do… this. And yet, I'm so thankful he's opened up because it's like he knows that sharing his nervousness with me must help. I'm not alone in my feelings now, and neither is he.

"How can I support you?" I can't fix this for him, but maybe I can make things a little easier. I expect him to say that it's okay, that he'll handle it, or that he doesn't know.

"Um, maybe you could talk to my brother first? I might need a minute. We text every now and then, but it's always a little harder when it's in person, you know?" He keeps his eyes low, a quiet sniffle breaking through the air.

I don't know. I don't know because I don't have siblings and my family drama is… different, but I know this is hard for Arthur. I can understand that much. "I bet it is. I'll do that. I'll introduce myself first and go through the plans for today with him and Cecilia to give you some time."

His pretty eyes lift to meet mine then, those dark lashes looking impossibly darker and thicker with the wetness between them. "Anything I can do for you?"

"You just did." My smile is genuine, and when the

timer on my phone beeps, indicating it's time to go, we walk out of my office together. When we part ways, I walk toward where Gabriel will park and Arthur heads toward the barn. We exchange a quick look, an even quicker smile, and my nerves settle.

"Feeling good?" Rosemary asks, meeting me outside.

"I think I am, actually. We have a good plan in place." When I turn to face her, she's smiling and a small chuckle leaves her.

"Atta girl." She doesn't remind me she'll be there to support me, to support Arthur, or that she agrees that the plan is good. She doesn't have to. Those two little words give me all the confidence I need.

A few minutes later, a blue SUV pulls up, and it's obvious that the tall, dark, and handsome man who steps out of it is related to Arthur. They share the same dark hair, tanned skin, and kind eyes, but Gabriel is clean shaven, with his hair lightly styled and no baseball cap in sight. As he helps his daughter out, he lowers his forehead to hers and whispers something only for the two of them, and only when she nods, does he step back, take her hand, and start walking toward us.

I take a few steps forward as Rosemary stays behind. It's part of our plan, not to overwhelm Cecilia, who stands behind her father when we're close enough to shake hands.

"You must be Alice," he says to me with a bright smile that I return.

"I am. It's nice to meet you, Gabriel." We shake hands, and I take the lead. "We're really excited you could both be here today. I think it'll be fun. And I bet I'll even learn a thing or two myself," I say, peeking over Gabriel's side to look at the little girl holding a stuffed pickle. "For starters, I need to know where you got that pickle." That gets her attention, though she doesn't meet my eyes. I crouch down to her level as she fidgets with her toy.

"Daddy got him for me. His name is Pickle, and he's my best friend," she says, not taking her eyes off the toy.

"It's really nice to meet you, Pickle. And it's really nice to meet you, too, Cecilia. My name is Alice, and I'm going to do some activities with you, if that's okay?" Technically, there are more people involved, but if that's overwhelming, it could just be me.

"Yeah. That's okay. But Tio Arthur will be there too, right?" The way she says Tio is so sweet. It sounds like chee-oh.

"When we're with the horses, he will be, yes. And Rosemary, the person behind me, will be there, too. She's very nice, and she's been riding horses longer than I've been alive." I state it like the fact it is, not animating my voice any more than necessary.

"And how long have you been alive?" Her father clears his throat, then, giving her hand a squeeze, but I look up at him and smile to let him know it's okay.

"Twenty-seven years. How about you?"

"Five years and eleven months. I'm almost six. Can we go now? I want to meet the horse." She's so straight to the point. I love it.

"We can. Would it be okay with you if Rosemary and your uncle help you pick out a helmet and some other gear? You probably won't need them today, but it's good for us to be prepared and for you to know what they feel like. Pickle can come, too. I have to do some boring paperwork with your dad before I join you."

"Yep. That would be okay because Tio Arthur will be there." Looking up at her dad, she lets his hand go. "Come on, Pickle. We're going to meet a horse today," she whispers as she hugs her stuffed friend.

With all the confidence in the world, she walks over to Rosemary, introduces herself, and asks if they can go get her horse helmet.

"I like your style, Cecilia. You don't waste any time," Ro says to her as they walk away.

"Nope," the little girl replies with a pop, and they walk in silence toward the barn.

"Wow. She just did that," I say with a laugh. "That's incredible."

Gabriel watches his kid with what can only be described as pride in his eyes. "That's Cece." His eyes meet mine as we both laugh, in awe of this little girl. "I thought we had all the paperwork done. Is there more?"

"No, but I wanted to give you a chance to ask any questions or tell me anything about how she's doing today before we get started."

"You were thorough. It's why I was able to prepare her so well for today, so I think we're good." It's a nice compliment, but I feel like I'm failing Arthur if I don't give him a little more time. "And she's had a good day. Usually, it's hard to tell when she's excited about something, but not today."

"Oh, I could definitely tell. The way she whispered to Pickle? So freaking cute." I clutch my chest, and Gabriel lets out an easy laugh. He's certainly different from Arthur, who makes me feel like I deserve a gold medal anytime I manage to get more than the lopsided smirk out of him.

The realization that I want to earn those smiles, though, that's what sits with me as Gabriel and I walk to the barn.

kinda gross, but I also kinda like it

Arthur

I watched their entire interaction from the barn. I saw the way Alice carefully let them approach, that Gabriel smiled at her, and she smiled back, how she won over my niece easily, which didn't surprise me one bit.

And when Cecilia started walking toward the barn with Ro, I saw how my brother laughed easily with the woman who's occupied most of my thoughts over the last few weeks. The kick to the gut, though? How she smiled and laughed back. How she clutched her chest watching Cece. I saw it then, a perfect little family forming right before my eyes. It's what my niece and brother deserve, and if it's what Alice wants, it's what she deserves, too.

As Cece gets closer, with Rosemary quietly walking alongside her, my nerves amp up. I try to still see her every few weeks when Gabe and I can make it work, but I'm always worried she'll stop asking to see me. As I step toward the door and she spots me, she takes off in a full sprint.

"Tio!" There's the smallest smile on her face, and I wonder if it's being related to me that she gets that from. You gotta work for a smile from Cece, and I'm always willing to. She doesn't have to work for one of mine, though. Seeing her face is enough to have me grinning from ear to ear.

"Hey, if it isn't my favorite niece." She barely comes to a stop before barreling into me, her little arm wrapping around mine in a makeshift Cece hug. When she looks up at me, she rolls her eyes. "Funny seeing you here. I had no idea you were coming."

"Tio, your dad jokes are even worse than Daddy's." She tugs on my hand. "Where's my horse?" I laugh, leading her into the barn, but not quite to Scout's stall yet. I know Alice has a plan for introducing her to Scout.

"Cece, you know she's not *your* horse, right?" I drop onto one knee to get a better look at her. She's growing so fast.

"I know, I know. But for today, this is my horse to spend time with, right?" This kid is too smart for a five-year-old.

"That's right. But before you meet Scout, we're going to get your helmet fitted and show you a few important things. Then you can take a carrot over to Scout, and she'll probably wanna be your bestie." I boop her on the nose, and she scrunches it up.

"But Pickle is my bestest bestie." She hugs the stuffy closer, rocking back and forth a few times.

"That's right," I agree. We all know how much she loves this thing. Pretty sure Gabriel has like six or seven as backup in case anything ever happens to it.

"But I guess if Scout is nice, she could be one of my besties, too. Like Daddy, and all the tios, and tias, and Vó and Vô and Bisa." She seems satisfied after she's named all of her favorite people, but it makes my chest ache that she didn't mention her mom. "So, Miss Alice mentioned a helmet. What else do I need to protect myself with before going near a one-thousand pound animal? Daddy said I don't need gloves to touch horses, and I've got my boots on, see?" She stops and kicks out a leg in front of her, showing me her shiny black boots, I'm sure Gabriel had a hell of a time picking out with her.

"Those are perfect boots," Ro says from next to us. Cece nods, and that tiny smile appears again. As we get her helmet sized and show her the different belts used during therapy sessions, she asks questions about saddles and a few other things. We remind her that, for today, she won't need them, but I know for her it's important to understand things and have set expectations.

Alice and Gabriel walk into the barn, talking quietly, and all of Alice's attention is on Cece. Like she did before, she crouches next to my niece, but doesn't force eye contact.

"What do you think about the barn so far? Does it smell different in here?" Alice scrunches her nose, and Cece takes a deep breath.

"Yeah, it smells like what I thought a barn would smell like. Kinda gross, but I also kinda like it." We all hold in a laugh at her answer, because she's absolutely right. You either love this smell or you hate it.

"That's a fantastic way to describe it, actually." Alice chuckles as she moves on to the next thing. "And is there anything you're curious about in here? There are a lot of new things to see and touch."

"The helmet was cool. I learned horses need their hair brushed, and I see brushes around. Can I touch them?" The kid's a natural. It's like she was meant for this.

"Cecilia, you're making my job too easy," Alice jokes. "Can I ask you one more question before we go explore the grooming tools?" Cece nods, looking at Alice's face for the first time. I can tell she's studying her freckles, because it's exactly what I do when I look at her. "Do you prefer to be called Cecilia or Cece?" I'm not sure if my brother is getting all warm and tingly, too, but watching Alice with my niece is making me feel things. I'm pretty sure this is what swooning is.

Do guys swoon?

Whatever. I just did.

"Whichever seems appropriate in the moment," the five-year-old responds casually.

Alice looks up at Gabriel first, as if to ask, 'is she serious?' And then finally, fucking finally, her gaze lands on me. I give her a quick nod and a wink, and she blushes so beautifully.

"Uh, great. Okay, let's go explore." As she stands, she clears her throat, gesturing to the bench with tools left out for today. "Your unc—tio," she corrects herself, and my heart fucking gallops faster than Jasper when he hears the whistle indicating it's time for dinner. Alice looks at me briefly again before continuing, "is going to show you what we use to groom the horses. He's the expert."

"I thought Rosemary was the expert since she's been riding horses for longer than twenty-seven years." Again, Cece is stating facts. Though I don't know where that number came from.

"You're right." Alice chuckles. "But Arthur is learning from Rosemary, so you get two experts today."

"Everything on this bench is safe for you to touch, Cece," Rosemary explains.

"And we'll tell you how we use them and what they're for, if you want to know," I add. Cece nods again and reaches for a brush, not letting go of Pickle. When Scout shuffles, a few stalls away, she looks up, searching for the source of the sound. "Scout is right in there, but she can't come out. She doesn't know how to open the door. We can stay here as long as you want, all right?"

"All right, Tio." She keeps touching things, exploring with one hand. "Did you know a horse's heart is as big as a basketball?" she asks no one in particular.

"I don't think I did," Alice says. "Maybe that's why they're so good at making people feel better." It's a nice sentiment, but I can see what's coming next from a mile away. My brother, who I've yet to talk to, looks at me with that same friendly smile he gave Alice and raises his eyebrows knowingly, waiting for Cece to be Cece.

"Actually," Cece starts, "it's because they have to run really fast, and they need big hearts to pump blood through their bodies."

Alice pulls her lips between her teeth to keep from smiling or laughing. She's as enamored with this little kid as we all have been since the day she was born, and I'm so glad I'm here to witness it.

After another thirty minutes of fielding questions, Cece decides she's ready to get closer to Scout. Rosemary and I take turns showing her from afar how we approach the horse, and how calm she is. We explain what she can expect things like Scout's mane to feel like, or what sounds she might hear.

When Cece starts to fidget with Pickle, Alice asks her if she'd like to go outside, and I stay back, giving them space. Gabriel stays, too, while Rosemary takes a few things back to the tack room.

Neither of us moves, but he's the first to speak. "That was really amazing, Art. You're really good at this." His words hit their target like an arrow straight to my heart. It should feel good to have my brother compliment me, but in my mind, all it does is highlight all the ways I've failed. "And Alice managed to win her over quickly. She prepped us for nearly every possible outcome. She's pretty incredible."

I remain quiet, but clench my jaw so tightly that my molars are about to crack. I sniff, crossing my arms to keep from responding to my brother's clear admiration for the woman I already know is, as he says, incredible.

"She's a little young for you, though, no? Twenty-seven… That's eight years younger than you, old man." Annnnd there it is. He's trying to rile me up, and it's fucking working.

"Guess that means she's too young for you, too, then, since you're all of a year younger than me." I hardly even finish my sentence before he's laughing.

"Who said anything about me? She's going to be my daughter's therapist. I'm not doing anything to get in the way of that." He turns to me, slapping a hand on my shoulder. "Besides, it was obvious from the moment we walked in that you were jealous as hell. All we talked about was Cece and Alice had a few questions about her grand-mother's house."

Her what?

"I was giving her some advice, and she didn't show any signs of being interested in me like that. Not like how she nearly melted into a puddle on the ground when she looked at you earlier." He gives my shoulder a squeeze, not moving his hand. "I miss you, bro. It's been really good to see you like this today."

I lower my chin to my chest, trying not to let my emotions get the best of me. Trying not to dwell on what he said about how Alice reacted when she looked at me. Trying not to think about why she told my brother, a near stranger, about her grandmother, whom I've hardly heard anything about. "I miss you, too," I manage to get out.

The rest of the afternoon is a blur. I somehow focus on my tasks, but barely, and for the first time, maybe ever, I'm thankful Rosemary went home early so she can't call me out on my bullshit.

i told her to respectfully fuck off

Alice

The energy in the house has shifted since Cece and Gabriel came a few days ago, and I wish I knew why. I mean, I can easily explain why things have shifted for me. It doesn't take a genius to see I'm increasingly attracted to Arthur. And if my face is doing its thing, I wouldn't be surprised if there's not actual drool on my chin when I do see him.

Though he doesn't have to see proof of it since he leaves for work before six o'clock almost every morning, and still there's always coffee and breakfast made for me. Sometimes it's a bagel with cream cheese and honey—Josie's honey is the best I've ever tasted. Sometimes it's overnight oats and fruit, or chia pudding, or fresh bread I still don't comprehend the existence of because there's no way he has time to make that if he sleeps at night.

Add to all of this that he shared something personal with me when he saw I was having a hard time, and the man is a whole swoony package. Don't get me started on the baseball caps he likes to flip backward when he's grooming the horses. It's truly unfair to be living with a man like this. Hence the drool.

Now I get what Charlie was saying. It's impossible to live with a Machado and not at least think about sex constantly. I've never thought about it this much. I've never *wanted* it this much. And though it's not something I should have time for when I'm either making morning or afternoon visits to see Gran, on top of trying to figure out how to fix up her house to sell, my brain finds any available sliver of opportunity to dwell on Arthur.

I've just finished my avocado toast when Luther's whimper pulls me out of my thoughts. I've been trying to spend more time around him. Now that Scout is staying in the therapy barn more often, I'm not always in the main barn where Luther likes to stay. Since the first girls' night, I let him out of his room for a bit if he's not being too rambunctious. He's only gotten calmer, though. I don't know what's changed, but he hardly ever barks, and there's no more jumping up at me, either.

Opening the door slowly, I lower my other hand for him to sniff, which he happily does before licking it. When I kneel down, he approaches me carefully and sits in front of me, waiting for ear scratches. "Such a good boy, Luther." He licks at my face, making me giggle, and the force of his kisses throws me off balance enough that I topple over. He keeps licking me, eventually throwing himself on top of me for belly rubs while he kisses my face off. My laughter erupts out of me, and I wonder how I ever felt afraid of this dog. He is nothing but pure joy and love.

Someone else's laughter registers, and I look up to find Arthur taking in the scene in front of him.

"I get it now," he says with his hands in his pockets and

a smile that reaches all the way up to his brown eyes. "I get the nickname now. Whinny."

I gasp in mock shock because I know why Sam picked the name and everyone agreed. My laughter is loud, like a horse's whinny, and though it doesn't always come out, when it does, you know. And now Arthur knows.

"No, it's good. You have a great laugh." He watches me for a beat, eyes studying every part of me. "The best," he whispers so low I'd have missed it if I hadn't been watching his lips move. He makes a tsk sound that he usually uses to call Luther to him, and he obediently goes to his owner, sitting and patiently waiting for a reward. "Stay, Luther." Again, the dog does as he's told, and Arthur walks to me, extending both of his hands to help me up. I take them, and when I'm on my feet again, we're so close I have to strain my neck to look up at him.

"Thanks," I mumble, taking a step back. "Did you come back to get him?"

"Yeah, he's gonna be at the main barn today, then go home with Paige." Something about the tightness of his expression doesn't sit right with me.

"Is there anything else you need to do to prep for leaving? Anything I can help with?" As I ask, he takes a step away from me.

I'm hit with a wave of doubt, wondering if I shouldn't go on this trip after all. But it's part of my job, so personal feelings need to be set aside.

We're only going to be gone for a couple of nights, and Rosemary is coming, too, so this will be fine. If anything, it'll be nice to have a little separation between Arthur and me now that we won't be sharing a living space.

With his stony expression firmly in place, he answers me, "I'm good. How about you? Need help with anything?"

"Nope. I'm all set." When I smile, he doesn't return it, he studies me in that way of his that makes me feel like he sees right through me.

"All right, then. I'll see ya." With a nod, he turns, patting his leg for Luther to join him and finally rewarding the dog with a treat.

TWO HOURS LATER, I'm about to load my bags into Rosemary's trunk when a large hand covers mine, taking the probably too-heavy duffel with more ease than I ever could. "You're with me, goldie." Arthur places my bag gently in the backseat of his truck while I stare in horror. Or shock. Or both?

"Yeah, I'm gonna drive on my own. You two kids go together so I can enjoy my peace and quiet, and you can listen to whatever singsongy shit you like. In case anything happens here and one of us needs to come back, we have two vehicles." My current boss smiles proudly at me before getting into her car. I watch her drive away, still not sure I understand what's happening.

"It was her idea," Arthur says from behind me. Well of course it was. It couldn't possibly be Arthur's idea to want to spend more time with the person who's already infiltrated nearly every area of his life.

I turn on my heel, and awkwardly hold up the purse in my hand. "It's fine." Feeling like an idiot, I get into his truck, trying not to breathe in his spicy scent that's mixed with leather. Turns out trying not to breathe is a really good way to get lightheaded, and when I take a deep inhale, I catch him watching me in my peripheral.

"You good?" he asks, turning the ignition as the truck rumbles to life.

"Mmhm." I keep my eyes locked on the view in front

of me as it changes from the long driveway out of the ranch and onto the quiet street. As we drive through town, I keep my head down, unwilling to look at the park I always wanted to play at as a kid but couldn't because my mom never took me. I keep my eyes on my lap when we pass the elementary school where I was endlessly teased for having a mom who was responsible for at least two divorces in my fifth-grade class.

"Do you mind if we make a quick pit stop here? Figured we can get snacks. It's about a four-hour drive." He waits for my quiet yes before turning into the parking lot of the convenience store. Normally, I avoid places close to where I used to live, but I haven't had any run-ins with anyone since I got here, so I walk into the store next to Arthur, hoping today will be no different.

He's picking out chips while I grab a couple of candy bars and a Diet Coke. As I set my things on the counter to pay for them, the woman behind me puts a hand on my shoulder and says, "I was so sorry to hear about your grandmother." I face her, not wanting to be impolite as she continues talking. "After what happened with your mom, too. She probably couldn't handle it all, you know? Losing a daughter like that and then having to raise her kid? It's a lot for anyone…" She keeps talking, unaware or maybe uncaring of the wounds she's opening up. I can't hear her anymore because all I'm able to focus on is Arthur's face as he walks up behind her, so I do the only thing I can. I leave my things on the counter and rush out the door.

It's not until I'm back in the truck, hugging my knees, that the tears register, and before I can wipe them away, Arthur is inside, heaving like he ran over here with his arms full of snacks. He tosses everything into the back seat before facing me.

"Alice," he says, so softly it has a sob bursting out of

me. I can't look at him. It'll make me cry harder. "I don't know who that was, but seeing that this is your reaction, I'm really glad I told her to respectfully fuck off."

That gets a watery laugh out of me, because it's exactly what she deserves. Minus the respectfully. The laugh becomes more sobbing, though, because now there's no controlling it. In a flash, Arthur moves across the bench seat and pulls me into him. "It's all right, tesouro, I've got you."

I don't like to let myself dwell on sadness. Normally, I find something to pull me out of it, like thinking of something I'm grateful for. This time, having his arms wrapped around me is what makes it easier to let go of the hurt that person unwittingly caused. Or maybe it's that I believe him when he says he's got me, and right now, he's what I'm grateful for.

Once I wipe the last of my tears away, he takes a deep breath. I know he wants to ask me, but I don't need him to. "That was an old neighbor. Jan or Jane, I don't remember. She was talking about the fact my mom died when I was a kid, and since no one even knew who my biological father was, my grandmother took me in. Gran had also been a single mom, so raising another girl on her own wasn't exactly something she was excited about. In fact, she never let me forget how I had put a wrench in her plans of retiring early and traveling. Now she's sick. She has Alzheimer's, and I had no idea because I left Ojai when I graduated from high school. I never came back, but then she nearly set her house on fire, and her doctor determined she'd either need me to care for her full-time or put her in a facility. That's why I'm here. The fact that my job became available exactly when I needed it to felt like an absolute miracle."

"Maybe it was," he responds quietly. "Thank you for

telling me. For being honest with me." As his words land, I shut my eyes tightly to keep any more tears from escaping.

"I can't stay. I'm leaving," I whisper, almost hoping he doesn't hear me.

"Leaving where?" His calmness never falters.

"Ojai. I can't be here. Eventually, I'll have to figure out how to sell Gran's house, and I don't know how much longer she has, but I can't live in this town. Not when all my demons live here, too." The swell of his throat bumps against my forehead when he swallows and nods. There's nothing left to say.

not because I'm a sexist asshole, but because i value my life

Arthur

She let me hold her for a few more minutes, but the bomb she dropped was still detonating in my chest by the time we parted and I started driving again. The further we got from Ojai, the more Alice seemed to relax, and eventually she fell asleep. I've got some music on low enough not to disturb her, but then she lets out a snore and wakes herself up, making me chuckle.

"Are you laughing at me?" She turns to me with sleepy eyes and a wide grin, and this is the most beautiful she's ever looked. The most at peace. And fuck, I love that it's happening here. With me.

"I would never," I answer, my voice serious while a smirk tugs at my lips.

"Yes, you would. As you should. I woke myself up with a snore, and I was probably drooling, too." A small laugh quickly rolls through her before she shimmies a little, sitting up taller.

"I hope you don't mind the music. Feel free to change

it, if you want." I point to my phone, which doesn't have a password on it—much to Owen and Raf's dismay, since they work in security—but she shakes her head.

"No, this is great." Her knee bounces along to the Post Malone song playing. "I don't trust anyone who doesn't like Posty. If you have Kendrick Lamar on this playlist, too, we're officially allowed to be friends." She smiles to herself again, looking out the window and mouthing the words to the song, and I hope and pray the next song is one of the several by Kendrick on this list.

ROSEMARY BEATS us to the hotel we're staying at in Paso Robles because she's a speed demon. The woman is seventy and her right foot has only gotten heavier with every year I've known her.

I take my bag and Alice's while she grabs what's left of our snacks, and we walk in to pick up our keys. We're on different floors, which I hate.

"You sure you're okay to head to the first place in an hour?" I glance at my watch, making sure that's all the time we have.

"Of course. You and Ro did all the work today. I was just your passenger princess." Tilting her head to the side, she smiles, batting her eyelashes as she takes her bag from my hand. Playful Alice is truly something to behold. She's light and sweet, funny and silly—and she's these things despite clearly having a tortured past.

"You were a great passenger princess and snack buddy." We get to her floor, but I place my hand on the elevator door to make sure it doesn't close before I get my next words out. "But, Alice?" She turns halfway, meeting my eyes. "Don't downplay what you already did today, okay? Driving was nothing. Get a little rest, and I'll see you soon?" She nods, and I let the door shut, counting down the minutes until I'm next to her again.

WHEN WE ALL meet an hour later in the lobby, Alice has changed out of her jeans and into the breeches I have a love/hate relationship with. She wore them the day we worked with Cece, and apparently, it'll be what she wears during sessions with clients, along with the branded polo. Her hair is up in a ponytail, and she has her backpack on. It's adorable, seeing her so prepared and eager. But also hot as hell. Because this woman takes her job damn seriously, and she's really fucking good at it.

"Stop staring," Ro whispers to me with a light smack on the back of my head. "All right," she says loud enough for Alice to hear, adding a clap. "I'm drivin'."

"The hell you are, Ro," I cut in as Alice watches with raised brows. "*I'll* drive, thank you very much. And not because I'm a sexist asshole, but because I value my life. And Alice's. You're too heavy-footed for these roads." That gets Rosemary laughing.

"Fine," she says, "but only if we can all sit on the bench seat in the front of your truck. We can make an Alice sandwich." She starts laughing at her own silliness, and Alice joins her.

"Rosemary, I really like you, but I'm sitting in the back." Alice opens the back door as we approach my already unlocked truck, and as she slides off her backpack, Ro takes it from her and places it on the back seat.

"Nah, you go up front. Sitting in the back seat makes me feel like a kid." She shuts the door, deciding for us what the seating arrangements will be.

Nine minutes later, we arrive at the farm where there are two horses that are no longer needed since they're transitioning their operations to mechanization. Alice seemed excited about these two because they're draft horses—a Percheron and a Belgian—and naturally patient and calm animals.

Once introductions are made, one of the owners gives Rosemary and me space to evaluate the horses. He eyes Alice a little too closely, especially when she's not looking, and I must make some kind of sound, because Rosemary tsks before saying, "Down, boy." I blow out a breath and focus on the task at hand.

I haven't met these horses before, so we take our time to see how they interact with each other, check them for scars or other physical issues. Alice is watching and taking notes on how they respond to us before coming to meet them.

So far, Moose, the Percheron, is doing great, but Buttercup has a diagonal corneal scar, so we need to make sure there isn't any major vision loss there.

"What do you say we get to know each other a little bit, Mister Moose?" Alice approaches the gentle giant slowly, her voice soft. "Oh, I see those ears paying attention to my voice. That's nice. Thank you." She places a steady hand on his neck, and the damn horse leans right into it. "What if I try to lead you over here? Will you come with me?" Of course, he does, and she rewards him with more gentle touches. "That was so good, Moose. Can we try using a brush?" She moves slowly, picking up a brush where he can see it, and he remains calm. When she picks up each hoof, he remains watchful, but at ease, and when she gives him a squeeze to the fetlock, it's clear her encouragement works. They're both doing great, and my God, I like watching her. I don't think she knows, *truly* knows, how good she is at putting people—and horses—at ease.

I wasn't there when she got to know Scout and the other horses, but the team were so impressed with how calm she was with them, how she never pushed them too far, too fast. I see it now.

Moose doesn't seem to mind the brushing, and when Alice moves quicker than before, he perks up, but doesn't startle. She's not showing any exterior excitement, but she must be pretty damn happy right about now because this horse is being an angel. Or maybe she's the angel and Moose knows it.

I continue to watch from afar, not interrupting or making any noise. Rosemary isn't far away, and I know she's going to have something to say about the hearts in my eyes as I watch Alice work, but fuck, how can I not?

"How did he seem to you?" When she turns to face me, her eyes are like champagne bubbles, pale gold with an inner shimmer when they meet mine. She looks back at the horse, who's nudging her for attention, and she giggles. "Oh, I see. You want all my attention, huh?" Smart animal. He lowers his head, and she embraces him. "Oh my gosh, I think I love him," she whispers as I walk closer to them.

"He's great. Seems super healthy, though a more thorough physical by a vet will give us a better picture." As I approach, Moose sighs, lips smacking when he sniffs Alice, and I'm jealous of a damn horse.

"Do you mind helping me for a minute? Maybe give

him a few unexpected touches to see how he reacts while I'm standing at his head?"

"Whatever you need," I answer.

She continues to stroke his neck gently, and I move to his side. "Okay, Moose, we're going to try a few things now." Alice nods, giving me the signal to touch him, and when I do, his ears perk, but stay soft. Damn, this horse might be perfect for the clinic.

"Such a sweet boy," she praises. "Now we're going to move a little faster. I'm going to lead you, and Arthur is going to stomp his feet for us." I follow her instruction, and again, Moose reacts to the noise, but never in a bad way. After a few more minutes, Alice stops, praises him some more, and says goodbye to the horse I'm pretty sure just fell in love with her.

We walk out of the barn, and once we're out of sight of the horses, she does a giggly little run on the spot, fists pumping into the air. "Oh my gosh, Arthur, did you see him?" She lunges into me, arms wrapped around my neck as I catch her waist. "He was perfect," she mumbles into my neck.

When she pulls back, hands still on my shoulders, I have to swallow before coming up with actual words or thoughts, or anything that isn't blurting out, *Can I please kiss you now, even though we're both working and people can probably see us?*

I settle for, "Yeah, goldie. He was awesome."

Awesome? God, I'm a chump.

Alice smacks my shoulders a few times, then lets me go. "He was, wasn't he? I'm not sure how any other horse is going to top Moose. I mean, Buttercup was great, too. So gentle, but I think she'd need a little more training, which is okay, I mean, that's to be expected, you know? Oh my gosh, I feel like I could run five miles with all this adrenaline coursing through me. Sorry, it was hard to keep this contained in front of the horses, so it's all coming out right now. I promise I'll calm down soon." She runs a hand over her forehead, catching a few stray hairs and tucking them back. There are a couple of curly pieces again, and I wonder if she straightens her natural curls.

"You don't have to calm down. I'm glad you're excited." In fact, I'd like to see her this happy every day. Alice opens her mouth to say something, but stops short as she looks at something over my shoulder.

"Hey, kids," Rosemary says brightly. "How did it go with Moose?"

Alice's giant grin gives her the answer I suspect she was expecting. "So good. He's incredible, and responded really well to different stimuli. He's an amazing animal," she says, looking over at the owner, a man likely in his early forties who is officially looking at Alice with a little too much appreciation in his gaze.

"Yeah, he's always been great. I'm not surprised he took to you so easily. Probably decided he liked you the moment he saw you." The way his eyes linger on her chest and his cheeky grin has me grinding my molars, but it's Rosemary who clears her throat loudly.

"Well, thank you very much for letting us come today. We'll be in touch in the next few days, if that's all right." She extends a hand to the man, shaking it quickly and with what I know is a death grip, and then she nods to the two of us. Alice waves and says a quick goodbye, but I walk away with zero pleasantries.

Rosemary, being the badass she is, doesn't let the awkwardness of the moment linger and quickly moves us on to talking about more pleasant things, like how she's picking the music for the drive back and that we're having an early dinner because she said so.

tell me if it's too much. or not enough

Alice

We got on the road early this morning to drive a couple of hours to another farm. After yesterday, I'm a little more apprehensive about how today's going to go. Not because of what the owner said to me, which was awkward and unnecessary, but because I'm pretty confident we have already found two horses we can use for the program, and I'm not sure we'll be as lucky today.

There are quite a few more to see at this place since these are retired racehorses, along with some broodmares that have aged out for breeding.

By lunch, though, we haven't had much luck, so we head to a food truck nearby. Even Rosemary is quiet as we eat at a worn picnic table. I'm starting to feel the strain of the morning on my upper body, so when I finish, I move down to the grass to do a few stretches.

"Neck or shoulders bothering you?" Rosemary asks.

"Little of both," I answer truthfully, closing my eyes against the sunshine beaming down on us. "I'm okay, though. I came prepared." She knows all about my condition, so she understands what I mean when I say that.

"Sorry, my old arthritic hands are no good to you," she says, flexing her wrinkled fingers.

"What does being prepared look like?" The question comes from Arthur, who hasn't asked me any questions since I told him I had chronic pain.

"Oh, well, I usually have muscle cream, naproxen, ginger candies, and muscle relaxants, though those are a last resort for me if the pain and nausea can't be managed with everything else, plus ice and yoga or stretching." My eyes remain closed as I answer him, and a battle wages inside my brain, trying to decide whether I want to open my eyes and see the usual disinterest that glazes over people's eyes when I tell them about an invisible condition that doesn't sound all that bad. Part of me wants to witness it from him to prove to myself he's like everyone else, while the other part is already disappointed by that being true.

"What condition do you have?" That's definitely not a lack of interest in his tone.

I reach for my shoulder and start massaging it before giving him the mouthful. "Chronic cervicogenic headaches. When I fell as a kid, one of the bones in my neck got knocked out of place and never went back quite the same way. Now the muscles at the base of my skull are always trying to compensate for my wonky bone, which means they're almost always a little tight. That and I get the occasional migraine, which isn't fun either, as you've already witnessed." The table creaks as he gets up, and my stomach sinks, knowing he's likely about to clean up our plates and move on.

I swallow down the disappointment and gasp when a strong hand moves mine off my shoulder and takes over gently massaging where I'm sore. The heat of his body on my back is impossible to ignore, and as I look down, I note that his legs are stretched around mine. Like on the bathroom floor at the bar.

"Here?" Arthur asks gently. I nod, unable to form words. "Tell me if it's too much. Or not enough." I bite the insides of my cheeks so hard I'm sure I'm about to start bleeding, but I refuse to moan while he touches me. Especially while Rosemary is sitting right next to us. So I remain silent as he helps soothe an ache so much greater than the one that came with my injury. The loneliness caused by a lifetime of feeling ignored and unimportant lessens significantly when people acknowledge what they can't see.

Minutes, or maybe hours, later, Rosemary shifts. "Dang it. I lost again," she mumbles. Must've been playing Solitaire. She's obsessed. "All right kids, I'm gonna hit the loo and then we should head back. Alice, I don't want you to go as hard this afternoon. It's not worth the damage you could be doing to yourself, all right?"

Sensing her eyes on me, I open them and give her a tight smile. I know she's right, but I want to see as many horses as possible. "You got it, Ro." She walks away, taking our trash with her. "Thank you," I say loud enough for her to hear, though she doesn't reply. I touch the top of Arthur's hand gently and turn until I can see his face. "Thank you," I repeat, this time just for him.

With a sigh, he removes his hands from my shoulders. "Please take it easy this afternoon, okay? Let me help with anything that might make this worse?" I adore the way he asks me without telling me.

I'm about to protest, say I'm fine, promise to go easy, but I don't get to because he erases all of my thoughts with what he says next. "Rosemary's gonna eat and be passed out before seven o'clock tonight. If you're not too tired, I'd really like to take you out to dinner. We gotta do something other than look at horses while we're here, right? I won't keep you out late, I promise." He tilts his head, the silent question hanging between us.

"Oh, um, yeah."

Geez, Alice, got any words with more than one syllable?

"That sounds good."

That's better. Wait, those are all still one-syllable words.

The knowing smile he steals my breath away with does nothing to help with the heat rising from my neck to my cheeks.

"All right. Shall we, then?" He stands, offering me a hand. I don't need the help, and we both know it, and yet…

TWO HOURS LATER, a smaller dapple gray horse with kind eyes watches me approach. His silver coat is speckled with charcoal rings that speak of good breeding and gentle years. The gelding caught my eye earlier as he grazed next to a brown goat. As I read more about him, I find out he's a retired steeplechaser, moved here from Virginia for retirement, and is extremely calm. He could be the perfect temperament for therapy work, and Ro's already given me the green light to see how we work together.

Like with Moose, I connect with Winston almost immediately, and after thirty minutes, I'm feeling great about his potential.

"Sorry to interrupt," a gentle voice comes from behind me, and Winston remains perfectly calm. Another great sign.

"Hi, there," I greet the young woman, wiping my hand

on my breeches to shake hers. "I'm Alice. I'm with Agape Stables."

"I'm Amy, one of the volunteers. I happened to see you spending extra time with Winston here, so I wanted to give you a little heads-up." Her wince does nothing for the confidence I had in this gorgeous boy. "He's lovely, but he's bonded to his companion goat, Goaton Ramsey—named for his, uh, strong opinions about feeding time." Her low chuckle has me clasping a hand over my mouth to hold in my laughter. "I know, right?"

"Oh, that is too good," I say, running a hand down Winston's neck.

"What's too good?" Arthur asks as he and Rosemary come around the corner, and I watch the horse closely for any indication of nervousness or discomfort. He's curious, but not reactive, which makes me smile.

"This lovely boy has a BFF—Goaton Ramsey!" My eyes go wide, and I can't help the huge grin splitting my face as I tell them.

Rosemary immediately laughs, but Arthur is very much giving a *you've got to be kidding me* look. "Sounds like a winner," Ro says. "Let's walk out and chat a little more."

We leave Winston with Amy and step out of the barn, but before we can talk about the goat, Rosemary takes a phone call. It's Arthur and me again. And sure, there are plenty of people around, but even a farm like this feels small when I'm standing in front of him, the object of all of his attention.

"A goat? Really?" He doesn't seem upset, more… incredulous.

"Oh, Arthur, pleeeeeeeease?" I beg. "Winston was wonderful with me. And he's on the smaller side, so he won't be as intimidating for people who aren't used to horses. And kids will love a goat, so I could use him as part of the therapy program. And, I mean, Goaton Ramsey? It's hilarious!" He's watching me with those magical brown eyes, and I tuck my hands into my back pockets to keep myself from any more hand gestures or fidgeting as he considers taking on a farm animal.

"All right, goldie. I guess we have a goat now." He smiles when I gasp in shock, and that smile turns into a full belly laugh when I break into a happy dance, right there, in the middle of the farm. I think it might be even more rewarding to make him laugh than it is to find a horse we can bring to the ranch. What a good, good sound it is.

have we died and gone to food truck heaven?

Arthur

Fuck, I'm nervous.

I guess some part of me thought she'd laugh at me for asking her to dinner, or maybe think nothing of it because we're roommates and therefore eat together all the time, but she was nervous, too, when I asked her. Like she knew this was different.

I didn't plan on doing this here, but after today, I'm not sure how much longer I can keep my feelings to myself.

Since we got back to the hotel, I've been overthinking every single thing. What I'm wearing, which is only slightly nicer than my everyday uniform of jeans, a T-shirt with a flannel for the early mornings, and a baseball cap. At least I had enough sense to bring a buttoned shirt that isn't plaid and a clean pair of boots.

Every time the elevator opens, I stand. I got down here ten minutes earlier than the time I gave Alice, so I've stood and sat enough times for the guy at the front desk to be watching me pretty closely.

I run my hands through my hair and opt to try to chill the fuck out. It's still three minutes to seven. Resting my elbows on my knees, I look at the floor and mentally laugh at myself for acting like a teenager going on his first date. When I look up, though, I know I have every reason to feel like this because there she is, in creamy white pants, heeled brown sandals, and a denim jacket. I can only see a sliver of the shirt underneath, which matches the pants. But none of that is important, because the thing that takes all the breath out of my lungs is her hair. It's full, and curly, and goddamn it, she's the most beautiful thing with that smile on her face as she walks toward me.

Me. A man so broken and with more faults than she might ever know about. She's looking at me, and she's happy.

By the time my brain catches up enough to tell my legs to move, she's nearly reached me.

"You are so damn beautiful." The words fly out of my mouth before I can catch them, and her smile grows as that adorable blush of hers covers her cheeks.

"You look pretty nice yourself." She playfully tugs on the collar of my shirt, and I instinctively step into her.

"No, tesouro. You *are* beautiful. Always." Her amber eyes meet mine, and like the first time, every part of me feels a little more alive, a little more alert with her attention on me. "And your hair," I say, looking at the curls framing her face.

"Oh, I forgot my straightener, and one of the horses tried to eat my hair today, so it was sticky and I had to wash it." She touches a strand self-consciously.

"I think you should always forget your straightener." As I run my mouth, her eyes go wide. "I mean, or, you know, wear your hair however you want. I'm not trying to tell you what to do. It always looks amazing, anyway, but damn,

Alice, these curls…" I puff out my cheeks and blow out a breath in lieu of finishing my sentence. "Not that I don't like your hair straight, though—"

"Arthur?" She tucks her lower lip between her teeth in an attempt not to laugh. "Thank you. Can we go get dinner now?"

"Yep. Yeah. Good idea." I pinch the bridge of my nose, so annoyed with myself for acting like this, and Alice giggles. I will gladly make a fool of myself all day, every day to hear that.

We chat about the day, since we spent so much of it apart, and she lights up talking about Winston. I might not be super excited about bringing a goat into the mix, but I can't bring myself to care when she's this happy.

The restaurant is nice, but doesn't seem too fancy. At least not until I notice what's on the menu. It's all locally grown food, and everything can be made either gluten-free or dairy-free. The names are completely pretentious, and save for the low jazz music playing, the place is quiet. It's weird.

Our server approaches, introducing himself as Jarod. "Can I get either of you a drink? Our signature is the Gin Crush, which is made with locally grown oranges and passionfruit."

"That's okay, I think—"

Cutting me off, he continues, "We also have some great wines. I'd be happy to recommend a bottle."

"I'm happy with a soda water, if that's okay," Alice politely responds.

"Same. Thanks." I smile tightly at him and continue to look at the menu, struggling to find something that sounds appealing.

"Maybe a beer or a cider is more your speed? We have some great local selections as well." This guy is pushy, and when we both look up at him, shaking our heads, his smile falls, and he walks away.

"Hey, Arthur?" Alice asks as she closes her menu. "How set were you on having dinner here?"

"Uh, well, I don't know what else is around, to be honest. I know that guy was a bit annoying—"

"That guy sucked, Arthur. I'm sure the food here is amazing, but is it going to taste as good if we have to put up with that?" She doesn't seem upset, yet I feel like an idiot for already messing this up so badly. I should have waited. I should have planned better. "One of the volunteers at the farm told me there was a food truck event starting tonight. She said she never misses it because there's always so much to choose from, and there are always new vendors from all over. What do you say?" I drop a twenty on the table. Her genuine excitement over food trucks has me pushing back my chair and reaching for her hand. She takes it, and we scurry out of the restaurant like we're dining and dashing, which we're obviously not.

When I open the passenger door for her, we're both laughing, and I'm wondering how I got so lucky that she walked into Beau's Bar on a random Wednesday.

After a quick search, we find that the festival is close by, and damn, she wasn't joking when she said there was a lot to choose from. It's in a huge field, and after I get our entry tickets, the lanky teenager helping us hands us a map, explaining that there are areas for different food types. Drinks in the middle, desserts on the north side, and so on.

"Have we died and gone to food truck heaven?" The kid laughs at Alice's question and tells us to enjoy. I have no doubts we will.

. . .

FOUR KINDS OF TACOS, a chicken korma that changed my life, and cannoli that were probably a mistake later, we're both stuffed. "That was likely the best meal of my life," Alice sighs, chin resting on her palm as she dreamily looks around at the sea of food trucks in front of us. We opted to sit on a bench and try everything together with all the containers between us. As I return from tossing them all away, I make sure to sit closer to her. Leaning into me, she whispers a thank you, then pulls away again.

"This was your idea, so thank *you*," I say, leaning into her the same way.

"Can I ask you something?" Her gaze lowers to her lap, her voice tentative.

"Of course you can."

"When you thought I was drinking too much, you were really intense about it. Tonight at the restaurant, you ordered water, and there's plenty of alcohol here, but you're not drinking any, and while it might be because you know I can't drink, I feel like there's more to it. Am I right?" In anticipation of my answer, she looks up at me, hands clutching the bench on either side of her.

"You are. I've seen what addiction can do to people, and I thought… well, I was worried about you." It's not the whole truth, I know it and I hate it, but this isn't the right time or place for whole truths.

"You were worried? You weren't judging me?" Her eyes search mine, and I'm so thankful I can answer these questions completely honestly.

"I was never judging you. I was scared *for* you." I place a tentative hand over hers, much like that first night. She doesn't move away.

"Oh," she says quietly. "I think maybe I misread the situation, then."

"I think we both did." I squeeze her hand and give her

a smile I hope communicates that we can move past it. That I already have.

"I'm overheating from all that food." After sliding her hand from beneath mine, Alice slips her jacket off, and my mouth goes completely dry. Her top hugs across her chest and arms, leaving her shoulders completely exposed. "Should we walk off these food babies and see what's going on at the market?" Nodding my response, we both stand. Alice hangs her jacket over her purse, and we walk side-by-side in comfortable silence.

The sun has set over the hills, and our path is lit by hundreds of strung lights between the tents of local makers and vendors. Alice insists on getting Luther a leather toy he will destroy in less than six seconds and some handmade treats, saying she can even put them in the container with the green lid to make sure I don't eat them. I love that she remembers that and calls me out on having eaten dog food. More than that, though, I love how carefree she seems tonight.

She takes off ahead of me, and when I reach her, she dramatically turns around with a pair of pink heart-shaped glasses on. "What do you think?" she asks, wiggling her eyebrows and flipping her curls behind her, that toothy grin hitting me straight in the heart.

"Gorgeous," I answer honestly, but she rolls her eyes and sticks her tongue out at me, reaching up to remove the glasses. I catch her wrist, lowering our hands and linking our fingers. With my free hand, I reach into my back pocket, pull out a bill, and hand it to the woman watching us with a knowing smile that reminds me of Rosemary.

We continue exploring, and as it gets darker, she flips the glasses to rest on top of her head, but doesn't let go of my hand. When we reach the end of the market, she keeps walking toward a quiet spot lit by a firepit that no one seems interested in since it's warmer than usual.

"Arthur, is this a date?"

Her question takes me by surprise, but I don't hesitate to answer, "I hope so."

Turning to face me, her eyes reflect the fire, and she's entirely golden. "You do?" She licks her lower lip, and I track the movement, moving closer to her because I can't help myself.

"Yeah, tesouro. I hope the fact that I haven't been able to take my eyes off you all night, and that I really don't want to let go of your hand, and that I wish this night could last forever means this is a date for you, too. I'm tired of pretending you're not on my mind every second of the day, that I haven't wondered what your lips taste like since the night we met." We're so close I can feel her breath on my lips. "I don't know how much longer I can go without begging you to let me kiss you."

you don't have to beg

Alice

"You don't have to beg," I start, as my hand finds purchase on his torso, fisting his shirt. "You don't even have to ask," I confess in a whisper. And that's all it takes. His lips touch mine in a kiss so reverent, so hungry and explorative, I'm not sure I'll ever experience anything like it again in my life. I don't think I want to either.

The way his fingers tangle in my curls has me floating into the night like the embers of the fire beside us, but his other hand clutching mine tethers me to the ground, reminding me this is real. That his lips are, indeed, touching mine in a kiss that's so much better than I've imagined these last few weeks.

He pulls back, resting his forehead on mine, but I can't bring myself to let this moment end.

"Not enough," I whisper before reaching for him, bringing his lips back to mine, begging with a whimper to never let this end. His response is his tongue tasting mine languidly as a deep groan builds in his chest. No other sound has ever made me feel so alive, so needed, so wanted.

When we finally break away from one another, the sky has darkened completely, and we're both out of breath. The sounds of the fire crackling, the people chattering in the distance, the nighttime insects buzzing nearby, all fade back in slowly. I stare into his eyes, as dark as the night itself, and he stares back, his fingers still in my hair, but gentler now.

I shiver as the breeze hits my skin, and Arthur pulls my jacket from where it hangs over my bag, gliding it up my arms and tugging it closed over my chest. "Let's go home?"

The word home has never sounded so sweet. And I let myself play into this little fantasy where his home is my home, where we come back to each other, day in and day out, because we want to, not because we have to.

We walk hand-in-hand to his truck, then drive back to a hotel that is certainly not home, but that makes this date feel much more like one.

As he walks me to my room, the heat of his touch on my back burns through my clothes, even as we come to a stop and I turn into him.

My stomach flips as a nervous energy rolls through me, and he must feel it as his grip on me tightens, his thumb drawing circles on my spine.

"I hate to be this person, but… what now?" And I do hate it. I hate that I'm asking this moments after the best kiss of my life. I hate that I suddenly feel the eight years between us because he is a man. A real man. And I feel like a silly girl. But I shouldn't, because Arthur's gentle smile immediately tells me he's not worried.

"Now I need you to be sure that you want this. That you want me." He kisses the corner of my lips, my chin, my jaw. He leaves tiny kisses all over my skin until I'm ready to melt and mold into him so we can never be separated again. "Because if you do, we're not just roommates anymore. Not just coworkers. Now we're more. So much more." But when his lips land on my neck and goosebumps rise over every inch of my exposed skin, making me stiffen, he stops and waits for me to process his words. "You can tell me."

"I—" Oh gosh, how do I say this? How do I *do* this? "I got out of a toxic situation last year, and I haven't dated since. We'd been together for years, so I don't really know how to do… this." The heat from his kisses is replaced with the heat of embarrassment, but it's temporary.

With a deep inhale, he runs his hand soothingly up and down my back, straightening to meet my eyes. "If this is all I ever get of you, Alice, to know what your hair feels like in my hands, to taste your tongue, and know how your body feels against mine, then it's enough. It's more than enough."

"I want more." I swallow quickly, so annoyed with myself for saying that without thinking. "I—I mean, I will want more. But not right now. Not tonight." His patient eyes and his gentle touch coax me to continue. "I'm tired of being scared of anything good."

"Okay. Keep telling me when it's not enough and when it's too much. Do you think you can do that?" As he traces my jaw with his fingertips and our bodies become flush with one another, I'm once again drawn into his warmth.

"I will," I promise.

"Can I kiss you again, Alice?" His question, the way he says my name, it might all be my undoing because even though I told him not tonight, I'm tempted to drag him into my room and throw even more caution to the wind.

The only answer I can give is to pull him down to me and kiss him until we both run out of breath again. And when that happens, he wraps me in a hug, burying his face in my neck and holding me tightly for a few seconds.

"Goodnight, tesouro," he whispers into my skin, stepping back with a sigh and a smile I've never seen on his gorgeous face before. A smile I know is all mine, only for me, and because of me. I want to see that smile every day and be the reason for it always.

I want the impossible.

THE FOLLOWING morning is a little bit rushed as we make a stop at a hobby farm to see a sweet old mare who can no longer keep up with her young owner, and I walk away thrilled with the prospect of another therapy horse being added to the roster.

Before heading back to Ojai, we confirm Winston and Goaton Ramsay will be going to the ranch, and then it's Arthur and me alone in his truck.

"You feeling good about the last few days?" He seems to catch himself and the double meaning of the question, and adds, "In regard to the horses, I mean." His lopsided smirk makes me smile.

"I think the horses are going to be amazing." Chancing a look at him, I note the tension in his jaw and reach for his hand resting on his lap. "And I feel really good about everything else, too." I might not understand why Arthur second-guesses himself so much yet, but I hope he can open up to me about it one day. I hope I can open up about things I haven't told him, too.

. . .

WHEN WE GET BACK to the farmhouse, Paige is waiting with an excited Luther on the front porch. She holds on to his leash, knowing about my hesitance with dogs, but Luther hardly even pulls at it. He doesn't bark, either. It's incredible.

As we approach, Arthur gives him a quiet command along with a hand signal, which he follows. Once they're done with their hellos, Luther sits again, facing me this time. And he waits with ears perked up and hopeful eyes.

"Hi, buddy," I say to him quietly. Arthur's grip tightens on the leash, and I'm thankful for the precaution, but I want him to know I'm okay, so I get on my knees in front of Luther and scratch his ears. He leans into me, and if Paige's gasp is any indication, what I do next is surprising to more than just myself. I hug him. And the sweet dog rests his head on my shoulder, sniffing loudly before turning his face to lick mine. I giggle, letting him kiss my cheek.

"All right, Luther, that's enough," Arthur calls out gently.

"Jealous, boss? Your dog gets more action than you do." Paige cackles at her own joke, and I laugh with her, watching Arthur's cheeks blush as his heated eyes meet mine. "I guess that trainer is really paying off." I don't understand what she means but there's no time to think about what she's saying because in typical Paige style, she continues on. "Anyway, I'll let you three be a happy family. Thanks for letting Lu stay with me." She gives us a salute and takes off to her car, peeling away down the driveway as Arthur shakes his head.

"That girl is a firecracker," I say, getting to my feet. "And you, boss, are you jealous of your dog?"

He turns slowly, that gaze still burning through me. "No." When he steps into my space, he drops the leash and wraps both hands around my waist, pulling me flush against him right before his lips crash into mine. My arms instantly wrap around his neck as I stand on my tiptoes, a low moan slipping out of me as he deepens our kiss.

"See, when Luther kisses you, you giggle and push him away when he doesn't stop." He kisses me again, his tongue instantly finding mine, coaxing another needy sound out of me. "And when I kiss you, you make these sweet little sounds and press your body closer to mine." His lips lower to my neck, and I lean back to give him more access. "You push your fingers into my hair and hold me to you like you want more."

"I do." I moan again when his tongue swirls on my skin.

"So, no, tesouro, I'm not jealous. Not unless you plan on letting anyone else kiss you like this." He kisses my lips once more, so softly, it's barely there, but with vulnerability embedded in it.

"I don't. No one's ever kissed me like you do," I admit truthfully. I've been kissed before, but it's never felt like this. Like the other person couldn't bear to be without me. Like I couldn't bear to be without them. Never. "And what are your plans, Arthur?" I hope he understands my need to know he won't be letting anyone else kiss him either.

With his eyes locked on mine, he gives me the answer I crave. "Yours are the only lips I want, goldie." And I know it's the truth, because I know liars, and Arthur has never lied to me. He might not trust me with everything yet, but he doesn't lie.

I reach up to kiss him again, but before I can, Luther shoves his face between our legs and whines, clearly not enjoying the lack of attention, and perhaps picking up on the new dynamic we're about to test out.

And while we laugh at this sweet dog wedging himself between us, all I can do is hope I don't mess it all up.

AFTER UNPACKING my things and a quick shower, I left to go see Gran. One of the nurses said she was having a good day when I checked in earlier, so despite being tired, I decided to attempt a visit.

I knock on the door gently. "Gran?"

At the sound of my voice, she turns away from where she has a puzzle laid out on the table. "Alice," she sneers, and a chill runs down my spine at the familiar tone. "What are you doing here? Isn't the point of putting me in this place so you never have to see me again? I hate it here, you know? I wish you'd left and never come back. I could still be living in my own house, not in this hellhole." She scoffs, turning back to her puzzle.

The place she calls a hellhole is nicer than anywhere I've lived and costs thousands of dollars a month. The reason she can't live at home is that she nearly burned the place down, but she doesn't remember that.

Reminding myself this is her anger talking, and she's dealing with an unimaginably difficult illness, I round the table and take a seat across from her. "I'm glad you're trying the puzzles. Dr. Chen said this would be really good for you."

"Don't act like you care." She tries a piece that doesn't fit and tosses it in frustration, looking up at me with narrowed eyes. "You probably look like him, with that awful curly hair and those freckles on your brown skin. I figured you'd be like him and take off when life is inconvenient for you, like you did when you were eighteen."

Whenever she talks about my father, it's always to point out how I'm like him and not like her or my mother. All my life, I straightened my hair to look more like them, even though I've always liked my curls. I covered up my freckles with makeup, even though I always thought they were cute. I avoided being in the sun because my skin is already so much darker than theirs. Every part of me I love, I tried to hide so I could look more like Gran, more like my mom, more like I belonged in this twisted family.

I remain quiet because I know there's no point in arguing with her. I know I'll never win this battle, or any other. I also know that if I do, she'll only make it worse.

With hard eyes still on me, she raises her voice. "I don't want you here. No one in this town wants you. No one in this town has ever wanted you." I open my mouth to speak, but she keeps going, "I'm going to tell the nurses not to let you back in here. Go, Alice. I'd rather die alone in this place than to have to look at the person who ruined my life for another second."

"Gran, I—"

"Get out!" she yells. "Get out of here. Leave!" Two nurses appear at the door upon hearing the screaming, and I stand, nodding at them to let them know I'm leaving. One of them stays with Gran while the other follows me out.

"I'm sorry. She had been doing great today." Melissa, the nurse I normally speak to, places a gentle hand on my shoulder.

"It's fine. She's never liked me, so this is… normal. Minus the screaming." I push my emotions as far down as I can, taking a deep breath before facing her. "Do you think she meant it about not letting me back here?"

Melissa sighs, shaking her head. "No. You're her only family, so of course you can still come. Honestly, Alice, I've seen family members stop visiting their relatives for far less than what you've endured during your visits."

I know what she's saying, but when I left at eighteen, I was leaving my grandmother to enjoy her life. I was giving her what she wanted. Now, I'm all she has, and she's my only known living relative. It's not as easy to turn my back, even if some days I wish I could.

After getting confirmation that Gran had calmed down and was going to bed early, I walked to my Jeep as pain shot from my neck to my shoulders and back up to my temples.

I've grown so used to the pain that occasionally it takes a minute to even notice it's there.

I wonder, sometimes, if I'll ever have a day where my head doesn't hurt, a day where my heart doesn't hurt this much. I wonder if it's possible to experience joy without also experiencing pain.

now my dick is officially inviting himself to join this conversation

Arthur

After a quick shower, Alice left to see her grandmother. All I wanted to do was go with her, at least for emotional support, but of course, she insisted she'd be okay. I've busied myself with things around the house and prepping meals for the week. I even called Beau to give him a life update because though it feels like Alice and I should have been together from the day we met, this is still a pretty major life event.

As I'm packing up a salad, the front door opens and Alice scurries to the stairs. "Goldie?" I call out to her, but she doesn't answer. She's shuffling something around upstairs, so I drop what I'm doing to check on her. I find her in the bathroom, cleaning the toilet. "Everything okay?" I ask from the doorway as she finishes wiping every-thing down, then heads to the sink to wash her hands.

She sways a little, and when I catch her reflection in the mirror, she's as pale as a sheet. I move quickly, standing behind her as she scrubs her hands.

"I think I'm going to be sick." She barely gets the words out before she's sucking in a deep breath and wiping her wet hands down her face. Her hair is already up in a messy bun.

"So why are you cleaning the toilet? Come here." I pick her up, setting her on the countertop, then look for a towel to soak in some cold water.

She leans back, taking another deep breath. "I can't throw up in a dirty toilet, so whenever I feel like I'm going to be sick, I clean it first." I think back to the bar and the cleaning products next to her. "I'm not a germophobe or anything, but seriously, hugging a toilet that's literally covered in… you know what? This isn't helping." She winces, placing a hand on her stomach.

"It's okay, I get it. Have you taken anything yet?" I place the cool cloth on her forehead, and she sighs, shaking her head. "Need me to get anything for you?" Another small shake. I don't want to jostle her too much, but she can't be comfortable here, so I pick her up again and set her on the floor, getting myself into position behind her and pulling her into me until her head is resting on my shoulder.

We sit like that for a little while, and I move the cloth a few times. When I think she's fallen asleep, her voice breaks through the silence in the bathroom where Luther has been watching us from the bathmat he's curled up on.

"She knew who I was today. She asked me why I bothered coming back when there's no one here who wants me. Then she said she'd tell the nurses not to bother letting me in anymore. Said she'd rather die alone than with the person who ruined her life." Her quiet sniffle nearly breaks me. "I—I don't know what to do anymore. I'm spending nearly every penny I have so she can be taken care of, because, even when she didn't want to, she took me in.

Because like me, she's alone and doesn't have anyone else." With her voice breaking on those last two words, she turns into me, and I wrap her up in my arms. There's nothing I can say to make this better for her, but I can be here. I *will* be here.

I expect sobbing, or at least more tears, but she holds on tightly to me, her breathing even and steady. I massage her shoulder and neck gently, trying to relax her muscles.

Eventually, she sits up a little straighter, her watery eyes sad, but a small smile on her pretty lips. "Thank you," she whispers before attempting to move away. I hold on to her and she doesn't fight me.

"How about I get you into bed with a heating pad and some tea?" I brush a curl from her forehead, and she leans into my touch.

"I can manage on my own, it's okay."

"Yes. You can," I say, cradling her face in my hands. "But you don't *have* to. I'm here." My favorite pair of golden eyes fill with tears, and the lips I'm starting to memorize with my own quiver. When she blinks, twin tears stream down her cheeks, caught by my thumbs, and when she nods, relief floods me.

Once she's settled in bed with the heating pad on her shoulders and a mug of mint tea in her hands, I get to work on some chicken broth. She doesn't want to eat anything, but at least this way, she'll get some sustenance. When I walk in with the bowl and a few crackers on a tray, Luther is lying on the bed with his head on her lap.

"Did you send Luther to training?" Alice asks, her hazy eyes meeting mine as she strokes the top of Luther's head.

I set the tray carefully on her nightstand, knowing all too well that Luther won't be gentle when he gets off the bed. It buys me a few seconds to think about how to answer this.

"Paige already ratted you out, so you might as well tell me." Her smile makes her dimple pop, and I huff out a laugh.

"Yeah, well, he needed it. I didn't send him anywhere, but I did find someone to help me train him, and we have video calls three times a week so she can see him and guide me through the exercises." I shrug it off, patting Luther's leg so he'll get off the bed and let Alice have her soup. He practically rolls his eyes at me, but he jumps off, settling on the rug instead. "How does chicken broth sound? Think you can stomach it?" I hope changing the topic means we don't have to talk about why I've got him in training. It's pretty obvious anyway.

"It smells amazing." That's a good response. When I rest the tray over her lap, she places a hand over mine. "Thank you."

Once she's had about half of the crackers and broth, her eyelids grow heavy, so I tuck her into bed and leave water on the nightstand.

The little crease between her eyebrows softens, but it only disappears after I kiss her there, and a soft sigh leaves her lips.

AFTER A NIGHT of mostly restless sleep, four in the morning seemed like a good time to start the day. Luther disagreed. He stayed in his bed while I brushed my teeth and pulled some sweatpants and a flannel shirt on. The coffee brews quietly, and I sit at the kitchen table, making a mental list of the things we'll need to tackle at the ranch before the horses—and goat—arrive. Thinking about that damn goat makes me think of Alice, which makes me smile like an idiot.

"What are you grinning at this early?" Like I conjured her, she stands at the entrance to the kitchen. With her hair piled high on her head, a white tank top and leggings on her slender body, she's a vision. And she's walking toward me with a sleepy smile I'd sure like to see on the pillow next to mine every morning. "Hi," she whispers, stepping into the space between me and the table. Her eyes soak up every inch of my body, gaze traveling slowly over my torso where my open shirt has left my skin exposed.

"Morning," I respond in my still-raspy voice. She moves to lean back on the table, but before she can, I take her hand and pull her to me. "How are you feeling?" I bend forward and place a kiss on her palm.

"Good as new. Thank you." With her free hand, she reaches for me, running her fingers through my hair.

"I didn't wake you, did I?" I sigh as she continues to comb my hair back with her fingers, a touch so simple, but so intimate, like we've done this a thousand times before. But that's how things tend to be with Alice. Even when something is brand new, it feels like it's always been a part of us, like we're meant to be doing it.

She shakes her head. "I fell asleep too early. I think I was dreaming about you, though."

With that little confession, I pull her closer again, and when she stumbles, she widens her stance so my knee is between her legs. The tiny strap on her tank top falls off her shoulder, and when I track the movement, my eyes catch on her hardening nipples. She's not wearing a fucking bra, and now my dick is officially inviting himself to join this conversation.

"You *think* it was me you were dreaming about?" My brain manages to get me back on track for a moment.

"Yeah. It just…" She pauses, nails raking over my scalp as she leans down, bringing her face closer to mine. She's so short, it doesn't take much. "It felt like you. It felt like this." Her lips touch mine in a kiss that's tentative at first, but when I put my hand on her hip, she lowers herself to straddle my thigh, and our kiss turns hungry. Needy.

Both of her hands slide under my shirt, fingertips exploring the skin on my shoulders and upper back until she's pushing the sleeves down. Once my arms are free again, I wrap them around her waist, pulling her closer. The friction makes her gasp, then moan, and her cheeks are that perfect rosy hue when I push back to look at her.

"And how does this feel?" I ask into her neck, nipping at her, then soothing her skin with my tongue.

"Warm and safe," she whispers, and my heart somersaults. "Hot and hard." My dick jumps for attention this time. Her voice breaks when I lick at her collarbone. "Wet," she gasps, grinding against my thigh and arching until her breast is nearly touching my lips.

"Please, Arthur," she whimpers, and I lick her nipple through the thin cotton of her top until it's nearly see-through, until she's moaning louder, grinding harder.

"You are perfection." I slide my hands up her torso, cupping her breasts. When my fingertips dance along her collar and her hooded eyes meet mine, she gives me a small nod, and I pull her shirt down, mumbling a curse as I get my first look at her.

I lavish her with kisses and licks and sucks while she writhes on my lap, her hands in my hair, pulling and scratching in the most delicious way. "That's it, tesouro. Ride me." My lips travel up her neck until they meet hers again, and she kisses me like she never wants to stop. And I do it back like I hope she doesn't.

Her hand travels to the waistband of my pants until

she's gripping me through the material. I throw my head back, hissing out a breath. "Fuck, baby, that feels—" She grips me tighter, moaning at the same time I do. "So fucking good," I manage to get out. "So good, Alice." Too good, in fact, because damn it, I'm so close to coming in my pants. "Ride my thigh, baby. Ride it so I can feel how wet you are for me." Her hand moves in time with her body, up and down my shaft.

"Oh," she breathes out softly, circling her hips, then letting out a small gasp. "Oh my—" As she throws her head back, she groans, and her body tenses up. Fuck, if she comes, I don't stand a chance of not embarrassing myself. "Arthur, I'm—I think—" I don't want her to think, so I pull her nipple into my mouth and suck until she's gasping for air, until her body is completely flushed and all her muscles tighten—and until mine do, too.

I come with a loud groan, and she does with a quiet whimper, and when her hold on me loosens and her body relaxes, I kiss the soft skin on her chest and neck until she's humming contentedly and her fingers are stroking my hair gently. I've never wished for time to stop quite like I do now.

I breathe her in as her arms wrap around my neck, and when I glance up, there's a look on her face like I've not seen before. She's entirely happy in this moment, in this afterglow, and I can't believe I get to have it with her.

"That smile," she whispers, tracing my lips with her fingertips. "That smile is all mine." If she only knew it's not only the smile that's hers. That every part of me is, too, even the ones I'm sure she doesn't want. Even the ones I know she won't like.

"You know," I say, straightening her tank top. "The night we met, I thought you were the most beautiful person I'd ever seen. I saw your eyes, and I didn't think you could get any more stunning. And then," I pause, cradling her face in my hands, "you smiled. And then," I say, kissing her cheek, "you blushed. And then," I mumble into the skin behind her ear, "you laughed. And then," I suck her pulse point, "you came. Every single day you do something that convinces me you're even more beautiful than the day before." I kiss her lips softly, and she hums again, that sweet, happy sound making my chest impossibly fuller. "I really need to clean myself up, but after, do you wanna come watch the sunrise with me?"

"I'd love that," she answers immediately, sitting up straighter and looking toward the now-silent coffee machine. "I'll make our coffee." With a kiss to the tip of my nose, she stands and heads for the mugs.

I walk away, unsure of how I'll survive when she does the same.

she's a very good girl

Alice

While Arthur got himself cleaned up after what was easily the hottest sexual experience of my entire life, I got our coffees ready and put on his flannel shirt. As I'm washing Luther's water bowl before I refill it, strong arms wrap around my middle, pulling me back.

"You're wearing my shirt," Arthur says, burying his face in my neck. I'm starting to think it's his favorite thing to do. I giggle as his stubble tickles me, leaning into his touch, the forgotten bowl overfilling in the sink.

"Is that okay?" His response to my question is a groan I feel all the way down to my toes. "I'm taking that as a yes."

"Never take it off," he mumbles between kisses. "Well, maybe not never." He pulls his face back, but hugs me up tighter, and the way his voice lowers makes me want to forget the sunrise and climb into bed with him instead. That thought makes me stiffen, and of course, Arthur notices. "You can tell me."

"Um it's—is this okay? I mean, *was* that okay? I said I

wanted slow and then—" Ugh, how do I even say it? And then I walked in here and humped your leg?

Ever the calm one, Arthur turns off the faucet and spins me in his arms, taking my face in his hands. "I told you, I'm happy with whatever parts of you I get to have, at whatever pace you want to give them to me."

I pull him closer, tugging on the material of his shirt and kiss him, hoping he can feel how thankful I am that he's an anchor when I feel myself drifting away.

As is par for the course these days, Luther gets our attention by wedging his body between ours, and once he's got fresh water and food—and decides he doesn't actually want either—we all get into Arthur's truck. He drives us to a spot on the ranch beside a small pond, and the three of us settle on the bed of the truck, watching the sun make its way through the foggy air.

I wonder how much it's going to hurt when I fall.

Probably not as badly as when I leave and have to pick myself back up again.

AS THE WEEK BLURS BY, Arthur and I have found ourselves working together more often as he passes his ranch coordinator duties to Paige and continues his training with Rosemary. Today is no different as we're getting ready to take Cecilia out on Scout for the first time since this is now her fourth session.

Having all this time together has definitely helped ease any concerns I had about us not being able to be profes-sional, because when we go home at the end of the day and he kisses me senseless, telling me he'd been thinking about doing that very thing all day, the giddy feeling that bubbles inside me is almost too much to take.

Almost.

Harder to take is the fact that *all* he does is kiss me. Since that morning in the kitchen, we've made out, and every night he kisses me sweetly in the hallway before saying goodnight and walking to his room. And every night I consider kicking down his door and climbing into his bed.

Naked.

Not that I've ever done that before, or that I would be bold enough to now, but I'm seriously considering a major personality change if it means getting under the covers with Arthur.

Car doors closing pull me out of my lusty thoughts, and I look up to find Gabriel and Cece walking toward where I've been waiting at the clinic's entrance. I like to greet people at the door rather than having them wait for me. "Hi, you two," I say with a wave, which they both return.

"Are we starting in the classroom today?" Cece asks, referring to the therapy room we were in last time.

"Nope. Straight to the barn today, Cece." I look back to see if Arthur is outside, but he must be with Scout. "Your tio is in there, if you want to go see him." Not needing any further convincing, the little girl takes off toward the barn, Gabriel and I laughing as we watch her.

"She's not excited at all," he jokes with an easy chuckle.

"Not even a little bit." Looking up at Gabriel, I get to the reason I wanted Cecilia to go ahead of us. "Hey, thank you for sending me all that information on the fire damage and steering me toward the contractor. It's been really helpful. I think I'm going to end up selling the house as it is, let someone else make the decisions on how they want to fix it up."

"Makes sense. You probably don't need to take on a house renovation right now anyway." There's no pity in his voice, only understanding.

"So do you want to come in or watch from afar today?" I ask as we start our walk to the barn.

"Mmm, maybe somewhere in between today. She told me I was hovering too much last week," he says with another laugh.

"Well, that's good. She's comfortable. But I know she likes having you here. I catch her looking back to make sure you're there every now and then." The love between these two is pretty special.

His smile falters a bit. "Yeah, she's always worried I'll leave and not come back, like her mom. It's all so fresh, and with starting school last month, it's been a lot for her." He swallows, brows furrowing as he shoves his hands into his pockets. "But she's doing okay. This is helping a lot, and there's an artist who's been volunteering at her school who she seems to love, as well."

"I'm glad, Gabriel. I know it's been tough for you both, but you're doing great, and so is she." I give his arm a reassuring squeeze as we walk into the barn.

"Thanks. You're doing great, too, you know. And Art's never seemed happier." He delivers his statement casually, but my entire body goes rigid as I stare at him, unable to move or speak. He chuckles, unfazed. "Don't worry. You two are perfectly professional. I just know my brother well. It was obvious how he felt about you the first time we came here."

I let out a relieved breath, trying my best not to overthink what he might mean by how Arthur feels about me.

Following the chatter, we find Arthur helping Cecilia

get her helmet on, something she's used to by now. Once they're ready, we get started by going through the visual schedule we built for her today so she knows what to expect.

"First we're going to brush Scout. You did that last time, remember?" Cece responds with a quick nod, looking to the bench where the grooming tools are laid out. "Then we'll put on the saddle, and then you get to sit on Scout and ride around in the pen. Sound good?" This smaller indoor arena is the safest place for her and Scout, free from noise and distractions.

"Yep," she replies quickly, picking up a brush.

Scout is calm and ready, having been prepped by Arthur earlier, and as we go through the motions, we both check in with Cece constantly.

"All right, the saddle is on. This is how you're going to get on." I gesture to Arthur, who comes up behind me to help me the same way he's going to help Cece. "Then you'll hold on here," I continue, showing her how to grip the neck strap as Arthur moves to the front of the animal. "And Arthur will hold on to Scout to make sure she doesn't go too fast or in the wrong direction. Sam will be on the other side to help. How does that sound?"

Cecilia's eyes move over me, the horse, her uncle and Sam, who has been quietly observing. We allow her to take her time taking everything in. "Okay. And Scout will listen to you, right, Tío?"

"She sure will. She's a very good girl." The way his voice lowers when he says that as he pats Scout's neck shouldn't make me shiver, but it does.

I play it off as though I'm getting ready to dismount, but Arthur's smirk is far too knowing. He helps me again, so we can demonstrate to Cecilia, who looks focused and ready. I know it's important for her to understand each step, but I can't wait for when she gets to understand Scout's movements and simply let herself enjoy that moment.

Slowly, we get her mounted. "Do you think you're ready to start moving?" I stand next to Cecilia, keeping my hand on the saddle as Sam takes to the other side to ensure safety. Arthur remains ahead, keeping Scout company and ready to lead her.

After a few deep breaths, the brave little girl mumbles a few words to herself before saying, "I'm ready."

The smile shared between Gabriel and Arthur as the brothers simultaneously find one another's eyes is filled with pride and joy, and I'm so lucky to witness it.

"Is it okay for me to put my hand on your leg to help you feel safe?" Cecilia gives me a yes, and with the first few steps, her hands tighten around the strap. "You're doing great, Cece. Try to let your body move with Scout's, sort of like when you're in the ocean and you feel a wave coming."

"Oh," she whispers, and I feel her relax a little more.

"That's it," I encourage her again, and she relaxes a little more.

I keep my eyes on her face as Arthur leads us slowly around the pen, and Cecilia closes her eyes, a smile as bright as the sun lighting up her face. When she opens them, she searches for her dad, who is clearly trying not to cry. Instantly, I look at Arthur, to find him already looking back at me, and whose own teary gaze tells me he didn't miss the special moment.

Cece not only trusted Scout today, she trusted herself, and that's the biggest win. We all remain mostly quiet for the final lap, but with triumphant smiles firmly in place.

hungry for this man standing in front of me

Alice

We're at the end of another session, quietly brushing Scout, Arthur fiddling with something close by, when Cece asks, "Miss Alice, would you like to come to my birthday party?" She doesn't stop what she's doing, nor does she look at me, but I know she wouldn't ask if it hadn't been something she was seriously thinking about.

I don't hesitate with my answer. "If you want me there, Cece, of course. I'd love to."

Her lips turn up slightly. "I do want you there. I'd like Scout there, too, but Daddy says that's a big no." She rolls her eyes, and I pull my lips between my teeth to keep from laughing. "Tio Arthur will come, too. He always comes to my birthday, even though he's not at family dinners anymore." The way she so easily states that fact about her uncle makes my chest pinch. "But I think if you came to family dinners, he would come, too. Maybe you could do that." She doesn't ask, and this time, I find myself pausing. I wouldn't know what to do at a family dinner any more than I'll know what to do at a child's birthday party, but knowing it's for one day and I can leave after an hour or two makes it less overwhelming.

"Oh. Well, I'm not part of your family, Cece, so I'm not sure that would be appropriate." Keeping my voice gentle, I hope she understands, but all I get from her is a little hum, and then she's back to quietly brushing Scout and whispering words of encouragement to her.

When it's time to go, Cece gives Scout a hug, and it feels like another small win for today and for this program. I want to be hopeful that I'll find something like this when I leave, but I know there will be a few key pieces missing wherever I end up. A few key people, specifically.

"Hey kiddo, look who's here!" Gabriel waves over at his daughter, who lights up at the sight of the gray-haired woman with a neat bun low on her head.

Cecilia rushes past me, yelling, "Bisa!"

As I reach them, Gabriel greets me with a warm smile. "Alice, this is my grandmother, Ana Maria." He places a gentle hand on her shoulder. "Vó, this is Alice, the occupational therapist here at the clinic."

"It's lovely to meet you, Ana Maria. I've heard all about your incredible ability to whistle from Cece." As I extend my hand to shake hers, she waves it away, pulling me in for a hug that is quick but tight.

"Call me Vó. And thank you for the work you're doing here. The boys have been raving about you." Her accent is thick, but also lovely. Like every word she says is intentional. My confusion must be written on my face as she explains, "This one and Rafa, they have only good things to say about you."

I met Rafael a couple of weeks ago for a tour with Charlie. They were both so kind. He's Owen's friend and business partner, and another Machado brother. I wonder how many brothers there are. But before my mind can wander too much, a familiar deep voice comes from behind me.

"Bença, Vó," Arthur says before kissing his grandmother's hand, then her cheek. She pulls him in for a hug, then palms his cheek, tapping it three times. Her smile is so big, her eyes nearly close altogether.

"So good to see you, Netinho." Tears well in her eyes, but she quickly looks away, giving her attention to Cecilia, who wants to tell her about what we have done today. We all listen attentively as she recounts how she sat on Scout with no saddle today so she could feel how her body moves, and that she got to give her a carrot, and how you have to flatten your hand to make sure you don't lose any fingers.

"Sounds like it was a good afternoon," Gabriel says as he attempts to tighten the ponytail on his daughter's head, which is currently hanging on by about five hairs.

"Yep. And Tio Arthur and Miss Alice are coming to my birthday party. Can we go home now?" Before she gets an answer, she's already walking toward the spot she knows her dad always parks in.

Gabriel shoots me an apologetic look. "Sorry, Alice. She got this idea in her head, and you know how it is. She's determined."

"I do know. I like that about her." I admire it. She's five, and she goes after what she wants without fear. "And if I won't be in the way, I'd be happy to come."

"It would mean a lot to her, actually. She really likes you." Gabriel's smile is kind, but the throat clearing behind me is not.

"We'll be there," Arthur confirms, and I run my tongue along my front teeth in an attempt to distract myself from the warm, fuzzy feelings that sentence gave me. "We" sure does sound nice coming from his mouth.

Ana Maria and Gabriel exchange a look I can't decipher, then he says, "Great. I'll text you both the details."

We say our goodbyes, and Arthur and I go our separate ways, though I swear I feel him watching me the whole time. This man is trying to make me lose my mind.

BY THE TIME FRIDAY ENDS, I'm beyond spent. I spoke to three real estate agents this week, who all told me I should gut and renovate Gran's house before selling it to make more on the sale. I swear none of them heard me when I said I don't have the money, energy, or desire to tackle a renovation. They also didn't seem to understand that I want to get rid of the house as soon as possible.

Gran is continually getting worse, and my visits now are mostly to speak with the medical staff. Battling with the emotions that come with her illness and our strained relationship is becoming more than a hardship. At times, it's an all-consuming, physical thing that leaves no room for anything else. The tsunami of feelings hits at the most random times.

I'm frustrated and tired.

So when I get back to the farmhouse and Arthur is outside in jeans with no shirt on, I'm not sure whether to feel more frustration or unadulterated joy. Luther rushes to greet me with no barks or jumps, only licks and tail wags.

"Hey, you." Arthur sets down a few tools, and walks up to my Jeep, where I'm still petting Luther. He kisses me quickly on the lips in a completely natural and unforced way, as if we'd been doing this for years, not weeks. "I'm almost done here, then I'll take a quick shower. If you're hungry, you don't have to wait."

Oh, but I'm hungry. Very, very hungry for this man standing in front of me with glistening skin and a spot of dirt on his cheek, wearing a backward hat and jeans that sit low on his hips. I'm starving.

But I don't say any of that.

"I can wait."

For the food, yes, I can wait. For him? I'd rather not.

"'Kay, I'll be there in a few minutes. Need help with anything?" I'm a little obsessed with how at ease he is and how he's always offering to help. I'm a little obsessed with *him*.

I shake my head with a smile, and he winks at me before walking back to whatever he was working on. I sigh at Luther, who cocks his head, not having a clue what I'm swooning over.

"All right, pup. Let's get this pizza out of the car and grab a cold drink. What do you say?" Turning his head the other way, he sticks out his tongue at me. "I'll take that as an affirmative."

True to his word, Arthur comes in a few minutes later, heading straight for the shower. I busy myself with prepping a salad to go with our pizza, then rush upstairs to change out of the dress I wore to see Gran and into something more comfortable.

When I step out of my room, Arthur opens the bathroom door and nearly walks into me.

"Sorry," he mumbles, trying to step around me as he holds his towel. It doesn't go unnoticed that he's in nothing but a sheet of terrycloth, but more obvious than that is how his demeanor has completely shifted. This isn't the carefree man I came home to minutes ago.

I step in front of him, placing a hand over his racing heart. We're both silent, and when he finally heaves out a sigh, his muscles relax.

"Gabriel texted me about the party on Sunday." He swallows, his jaw still tight and his features tense. "It's at my parents' house."

He's alluded to not having a good relationship with them, though he's never told me why, and I haven't pressed. It's obvious this is a surprise to him, and not a happy one.

"Tell me what you're thinking. What you're feeling." I know he doesn't want to. I know I wouldn't. "I want to understand."

"I don't know. I haven't been there in years, but I told Cece I'd be at her party. They've always been at Gabe's house." He rests a hand over mine, still on his chest. "I try not to miss out on my siblings' big moments, you know? As long as it means I'm not going to the house. It's... I don't want to cause a scene or make things weird for anyone." His fingers wrap around mine, and I step closer to him. "I haven't talked to my dad in three years. I don't even know if it's because I'm too stubborn or because he is anymore."

His admission makes my heart hurt for him. "I'm sorry," I whisper, bringing my other hand to cup his cheek. "It won't be easy, but I'll be there with you. To support you. To be whatever you need."

Lowering his forehead to mine, he whispers, "Thank you." We stand together for a moment as he lets me carry some of this burden for him. Arthur is strong and solid, but it's in the moments where he lets me see his softness that I feel the closest to him.

He turns his face to plant a kiss on the palm of my hand, lifting it to kiss my wrist. It's a simple move, but it's a

tectonic shift in our relationship that we'll be feeling indef-
initely.

TWENTY-EIGHT

I've had to do all the touching myself

Arthur

My lips shift to her wrist as her hand lowers from my chest, over my belly button, and finally to where my towel hangs. With a flick of her wrist, it falls to my feet, and her gaze falls to where I am very much naked.

"Alice," I warn, dropping her hand as I look for any ounce of self-control I might have left in me.

"Do you have any condoms?" She peels off the sweats she must have just put on, then lets my flannel shirt she wears almost every night join them in a pile on the floor.

"Yeah." The single word comes out strained, and I bite my fist when she turns and slips her T-shirt off, walking into my room in nothing but a white cotton thong.

Fuck, this woman is my undoing. My end and my beginning. If I wasn't already in love with her, I am now.

My brain finally catches up with what's happening and tells my legs to move. When I stumble into my room, she turns around, but suddenly her eyes widen at something behind me, and she covers her chest. Twisting to see what's shocked her, I find the culprit.

My dog is trying to cock block me right now? I think not. I slam the door shut before he can sneak inside. As I turn back to my girl, she's got one hand covering her mouth to stifle her giggles, so I rush to move her hand away.

"Your laugh is the best sound in the world. Please never hide it from me." Kissing her fingers, I pull her close, and can't help my groan when we're finally chest-to-chest, skin-to-skin.

Fuck, this feels good.

Burying my face in her neck, I run my hand up her spine until my fingers reach the back of her head, tangling in her curls.

"I love it when you do that." She sighs as my tongue meets her skin, and when I pull her head back, she moans, fingers pressing into my back hard enough that I feel her blunt nails dig in. "More," she begs.

In a swift move, I pick her up and lay her on my bed, committing every detail to memory, from how her curls fan out over my pillow to the way her golden eyes shine, even in the dim light. Her bronze skin glows against the white sheets, and as I hover over her, she reaches down to slide her thong off, wiggling until it's lost in the sheets.

She reaches for me at the same time I lean down to kiss her. Instantly our hands are everywhere, touching every inch of skin, and when I reach her hip, she lifts her knee, spreading herself open for me. With feather-light touches, I tease the inside of her thigh as she writhes underneath me.

"I've thought about touching you so many times," I confess.

"Me too," she pants out. "But you've been torturing

me with nothing but kisses for weeks, so I've had to do all the touching myself."

Fuck. She's been touching herself across the hall? All while I've been holding back, taking it slow, trying not to rush anything, trying not to fall even harder for her than I already have.

"Have you touched yourself thinking about me, baby?" Her response is a nod, cheeks turning red at the admission. "Do you use toys on yourself, wishing it was me?" A head-shake this time.

"I don't have any," she says as I inch my hand closer to where she wants me. "Just my fingers, and they're never enou—" She ends on a gasp when my thumb runs from her entrance to her clit. "Oh my—Yes." Her back arches when I spread her wetness around it. I push the tip of my finger into her, and the sound she makes have me hissing in a breath as I thrust my hips against her leg, searching for friction.

"Like this," I mumble. She hums, circling her hips as I push deeper into her. "I want you like this every day." When I add a second finger, she closes her eyes, throwing her head back. I give her a few slow strokes, loving the way she squeezes my fingers.

"How?" she asks, locking eyes with me again.

"In my bed." My mouth finds hers, and I nip at her bottom lip before releasing it.

"Naked."

I lick from her collarbone to her breast, flattening my tongue over her nipple, making her moan.

"Dripping wet for me."

I keep my thrusts shallow, only pushing an inch or two into her. When my thumb meets her clit again, and I suck her nipple into my mouth, she finds her climax, eyes popping open to meet mine as she gasps and moans quietly.

Once her body relaxes, I kiss her neck, her collarbone, her chest, up to her cheeks, and finally her lips. The little minx spreads her legs more and reaches down to grip my cock, pumping it twice, which is enough to make me lose any potential train of thought I might have had. I rest my forehead on her chest, trying not to lose my mind.

"Where are they?" She grips me tighter, and I groan, pulling her nipple back into my mouth.

After a few seconds, I remember her question and reach for the nightstand drawer, pulling out a condom and quickly rolling it on.

As much as I want to sink into her, I force myself to slow down, to drink her in, and feel everything in this moment. I spent so much time trying to numb my feelings, to escape them and reality as often as possible. Then I learned how to handle them without needing to hide behind anything. And now, here with her, I'm not afraid to feel it all.

I want to.

I need to.

Sensing the shift, she glides her fingers over my cheek, up to my forehead, pushing my hair back. She gives me time to process, even if she doesn't understand what it is I'm feeling.

"Sometimes I can't believe you're real and that you're here," I admit.

"I'm right here." She pulls me down for a soft kiss. "I'm right here," she repeats with another kiss. "I'm here and I want you. All of you." This time, she kisses me deeper, shifting until the tip of my cock is gliding to her entrance. All I want is for those words to be true. "I'm here and I'm yours, Arthur."

I push inside her, and we both moan, breathing one another's air.

Has anything ever felt this good?

"No, it hasn't," she murmurs. I push deeper, and her eyes widen, a silent gasp forcing her lips open. "Nothing's ever felt this good."

I can't be bothered to care that I let that thought slip out of my mouth. Not when she agrees with me.

"Tell me if it's too much or not enough." I rest my forehead on hers, giving her shallow thrusts like I did with my fingers.

"It's both," she whines. "It's so much, but I'm not sure I'll ever have enough of you. Go slow, but give me all of you."

I already have.

We're panting, despite how slowly I'm moving. When I'm all the way inside her, I hold myself there, breathing her in as I burrow into her neck again. She shifts beneath me, circling her hips and whimpering when the base of my cock brushes her clit.

"Alice, baby, you're driving me crazy. You feel so fucking good. So perfect for me." I give her a deep thrust, and she moans loudly, nails digging into my shoulders.

"Arthur," she whispers, gasping when I push into her again, then pulling me down for another kiss.

Time slows, and we move at this languid pace, kissing one another as thoroughly as we're fucking. It's all-consuming, the way we move, the way we swallow one another's moans, and our bodies move in sync.

She lifts her knee, and her noises become more desperate. When she comes, our mouths are still fused together, and when I follow her immediately after, we're both slick and spent.

Gasping for air, I slide out of her and quickly tie the

condom, not wanting to miss out on another moment of being this close to her. I pull her body into mine until her head is on my shoulder, and I hold her tightly despite the sweat on our skin.

When her stomach rumbles, I kiss the top of her head and move quickly to get the pizza she brought home.

She doesn't bother putting clothes on, but when I forget to eat because I keep staring at her naked body, she giggles and tucks the sheet around herself. Once we're both satisfied in every possible way, I put the box on my dresser where Luther won't reach it and shuffle back under the covers, pulling her close to me again and listening to her tell stories about past horses she's worked with until eventually we fall into a content, happy silence.

I can't say how long we lie there for, quietly stroking one another's skin, but when she finally shifts, it's late enough that my eyes are growing heavy.

"I should go," she whispers, lifting her head to look at me. Before I can beg her not to, she strokes my cheek. "I need to shower, and I'm not sure it's a great idea for me to, um, sleep here?"

I say nothing, and she must take that to mean I agree with what she's saying. But really, I'm looking for words that aren't *no* or *don't go*.

After peeling her body away from mine, she looks around the room, quickly realizing none of her clothes are in here. "Night, Arthur." Clearing her throat, she stands and walks out of the room, completely naked. I watch her with a pang of regret in my chest, then stare at the ceiling long after she finishes her shower.

It isn't until Luther nudges me with his ice-cold nose, likely needing to go out, that I finally get out of bed. By that point, the lights are off in her room and the door is closed.

BY THE TIME I woke up, the sun was beaming in through the window, which told me it was late morning already, since the fog had cleared up. Made sense, since I didn't fall asleep until early morning.

Between the way Alice left last night and the anxiety about seeing my dad tomorrow, I've been on edge all day. I've read, talked to Beau, gone to check on the horses, and deep-cleaned the fridge, but none of it is helping. Making it all worse is the fact that Alice hasn't been around all day.

After taking Luther for a long walk, we get back home in the dark. His tail wags excitedly when he sees her Jeep in the driveway.

Inside, I listen for any sounds around the house, but when there are none, I head straight upstairs, stopping in front of Alice's door.

Either she's quiet or she's sleeping, and I hope it's the former as I knock three times.

you can't laugh while my dick is still inside you

Alice

The front door closes, and Luther's nails pitter-patter on the stairs as I listen for Arthur. I didn't expect to be gone so long today, but Maeve wanted to have brunch with the girls, and then I spent the rest of the day cleaning out more of Gran's house. Before I knew it, the sky was getting dark. I was surprised to get back to an empty house, but it gave me a chance to eat something and have a long *everything* shower.

Once I finished my curly hair routine, I slipped Arthur's shirt on. I've been sitting on my bed staring out the window since, thinking about how much my life has changed over the past couple of months, and what meeting Arthur's entire family will be like tomorrow. Gabriel and Rafael are lovely, and it helps that Charlie will be another familiar face there, but family events are very far outside of my comfort zone.

Now Luther is sniffing at my door, and the three hard knocks that follow startle me enough to jump off the bed.

I swing the door open and find Arthur, arms spread wide as he holds on to either side of the door frame. His head is lowered, but as the seconds tick by, his chin rises as he takes me in, starting at my toes, over my bare legs, to where his shirt opens wider at the collar. Every inch of my skin warms with the heat from his gaze. I'm practically panting by the time our eyes meet.

Reaching for him first, I wrap my arms around his neck and kiss him. It's fierce and needy, it's wild and entirely uncontrolled. I never want it to end, but he cradles my face in his hands and pulls back.

"Are you okay?" His question unsettles me, because I don't know.

Am I?

I'm on the brink of falling for a man I can't have, in a town I don't want to live in, while I make decisions I never wanted to have to make about someone else's life. But with him, I feel more than okay. It might be the only time I do.

"Yeah. I didn't mean to be gone all day, I'm so—"

He cuts me off with a kiss, shaking his head. "I just wanted to make sure, baby. You don't need to explain or apologize."

Him calling me baby does obscene things to my body, and the way I try to climb him like a tree, wrapping my leg around his hip, does nothing to hide that fact.

"You're wearing my shirt again," he says, gripping my outer thigh, slowly massaging his way higher and higher, where he's about to discover… "And nothing else?"

His groan makes my core throb, and when his other hand slides beneath the hem of the shirt, grazing my inner thigh, I'm mewling, ready to beg him to touch me. "Tell me, what am I going to find when I touch you, Alice? Is your pussy soaked for me?" I nod vigorously, and he tsks. The way he talks to me isn't entirely unexpected. Arthur is a competent, confident man, and while I adore how tender he can be, this side of him makes me absolutely feral. "I said, tell me." He pinches my skin lightly, enough to make me gasp, enough to make me wetter.

"Yes, my pussy is soaked for you, Arthur." I barely know what words are as he inches closer, no doubt already feeling how wet I am.

Instead of touching me like I need him to, he spins us until my back is against the bedroom wall, then he drops to his knees, lifting one of mine until it drapes over his shoulder. The flat of his tongue meets my clit, and I'm certain I levitate. He licks and sucks until I'm riding his face, reaching for the high only he can provide. His response? A desperate-sounding moan followed by his fingers gripping me tighter as he hums, like he's entirely satisfied.

The tip of his tongue circles my clit as his fingers tease my entrance. Just as I consider begging, he slides two fingers into me, curling them into a spot no one has ever touched before. I slap a hand against the wall as my legs tingle and heat rushes over my skin. He doesn't pull them out, just keeps curling and uncurling his fingers until I'm gasping for air, screaming as I come harder than I even knew was possible. When I look down, I find his reverent, hungry eyes already on me, and I'm certain it makes my orgasm last longer.

As I begin to calm down from the high, he stills his fingers and sucks my clit into his mouth. Somehow, I come again, my hands gripping his hair, trying to decide whether to push him away or pull him closer, and settling on holding him exactly where he is.

With me melted into the wall, he leaves a gentle kiss on my oversensitive skin, lifting his head to look at me again. His lower face glistens with my release, and he licks his lips before taking the hem of my borrowed shirt to wipe his chin.

He stands slowly, his hands never leaving my body as they settle on my hips. "You've been so quiet when you come. I was wondering if I'd ever get to hear you scream for me."

His mouth hovers over mine, and I close the distance, tasting myself for the first time. I moan into him, palming his hardness through his jeans, then reaching for the button and lowering the zipper. I shove his pants and boxer briefs down, desperate for him, so, so desperate.

This new energy between us is loaded. We're both processing a lot of feelings individually, I know that. But it feels so good to have this one thing that we can give each other, to know he feels at least some of what I feel, and that we can both find some type of relief together.

I lift my knee again, and he grips the backs of my thighs, lifting me until I feel his hardness between my thighs. I rock against him until his hard cock is slick with my release. When I start to move faster, his groan is almost pained as he throws his head back. "I need to get a condom, baby."

I don't stop moving. I can't.

"I'm on birth control, and I was tested not long ago. You have nothing to worry about. Do I?" Slowing down, I lock eyes with him.

"No. Nothing to worry about. Are you sure?"

How do I tell him I've never been more sure of anything or anyone than I am of him?

"Yes. Now make me scream again." I notch him at my entrance, gasping at the feel of him with no barrier between us. "Fuck me, Arthur."

With one thrust, he pushes inside as a feral groan leaves him, and his fingers grip me hard enough to bruise. I hope they do. I hope he marks my body the same way he's marked my heart. Permanently.

"Yes," I whisper. "More," I beg, and he delivers, relentlessly fucking me hard but slow, lavishing my skin with kisses. "You're perfect." My words come out between pants, but I don't miss the way he moans at my praise.

With one hand, he grips the collar of my shirt and pulls until buttons go flying, then his fingers are deftly pinching and pulling my nipples. He picks up the pace, and the noises I make are savage. Again, liquid heat fills me as I find a climax unlike any other. I wonder if it would always be like this with him. But then there's no time to wonder, as Arthur's face strains as he empties himself inside me.

"Alice, fuck," he whispers before kissing me deeply, shivering with the aftermath of his release, his hold on me softening as his kisses do the same. His lips leave a warm trail across my jaw, down my neck, until his face is burrowed there again, his inhale so deep, it seems never-ending. He stays inside me, and while I know this was us needing a physical connection to make up for the emotional turmoil our families have us in, it feels like more. So much more.

As he lifts his head, he kicks his pants all the way off, and my back comes away from the wall. He carries me to the bathroom, somehow grabbing a towel out of the closet while I'm still wrapped around him. I laugh, imagining what we look like right now.

"Tesouro, you can't laugh while my dick is still inside you," he says, sounding sad, but smiling from ear to ear. He kisses me quickly. "Just kidding. You can laugh whenever you want."

Somehow, he's still semi-hard, and when we shift, I

moan, despite knowing that there's no way I could possibly come again right now. He lifts an eyebrow at me, and I giggle again, shaking my head.

Setting me on the edge of the countertop, he kisses me again, just two soft touches on my lips. "I'm gonna clean us up, then you're coming to my bed. I'd say we could do yours, but mine is bigger, and I'm pretty sure more comfortable. But if you want yours, I'm gonna be there, because there's no way I'm not sleeping next to you tonight."

It would be so inappropriate for me to cry right now, but it's exactly what I feel like doing. He's so hot and so sweet, so serious and so funny, so hard and so tender.

"Yours." It's confirmation of two things: where we're sleeping tonight and what I am.

I quickly latch my mouth to his again, and two tears race down my face. He lets me kiss him without rushing me, even though we really do need to get cleaned up. As I shift closer to him, I moan again because apparently it's not possible for my body not to call attention to how much this man turns me on.

When I do it a third time, he bites down on my lower lip gently.

"Alice," he warns, in that deep voice that makes me clench around him.

"Goldie," he says even more sternly, and when I roll my hips,

"Baby," he gasps. His hips push forward almost involuntarily, making us both groan.

"Tesouro," he calls, gently, pressing his forehead to mine. "As much as I'd love to tell you we can go for round two right this second, I'm a fairly normal thirty-five-year-old man, and there is no way my cock is getting hard again. Not for another hour or two." He sounds disappointed, which makes me want him more. "But I will gladly give you my mouth, my fingers, or my thigh again if you need more."

It's tempting. So very tempting.

"I don't think I could come again anyway. I'm pretty sure you drained my body of all the necessary orgasm hormones or whatever."

What am I even saying?

I don't know anymore. He might have also drained my brain of working cells.

"That sounds like a challenge," he starts, then chuckles when my eyes widen and I shake my head. He slides out of me, wincing. "Just kidding, baby." He uses a towel to catch some of our mess, then reaches around me to turn the faucet on.

I watch as he cleans himself up, and even as he takes care of me, that serious look of concentration I've come to know well firmly on his gorgeous face.

When we finish brushing our teeth, he takes his shirt off. He tosses it into the hamper he leaves in the corner of the room, then he pushes the flannel off my shoulders and does the same with it. We're both naked, but it's not sexual. It's weirdly comfortable.

He picks me up again, spinning us around as I yelp and grab onto his shoulders. With a laugh, I say, "You don't have to carry me."

He's quiet until we get to his room. He sets me on his bed, making sure I'm underneath the covers. "I know. And yet, I'd carry you anywhere," he adds simply, then walks to the other side of the bed. I turn to face him, and he mirrors my position. "Tell me something." He plays with one of my curls, his eyes never leaving me.

"I really like it when you call me baby," I immediately reply, feeling my cheeks heat. He smiles that full, just-for-me smile.

"I really like it when you say *fuck*. Especially followed by the words *me* and *Arthur*." We both chuckle, inching closer to one another. He heaves out a sigh and kisses my forehead. "I'm worried my dad will ask me to leave tomorrow." His confession is followed by silence, but I nod to let him know I heard him.

"I'm worried my Gran will die and I won't feel sad about it." My confession is followed by his gentle touch on my chin, tipping my head up to look at him.

"You can feel however you feel, Alice. There isn't a right or wrong way for you to process her illness or her eventual death, whenever that comes." My eyes well with tears again, but I know I have to get the next words out for him.

"And if your dad chooses to ask you to leave, it will say far more about him than it will about you." His brows furrow, and he scoffs, clearly not believing me. "I'm serious, Arthur. Whatever happened that made him so upset with you, the reason we're all going to be at his house tomorrow is a sweet little girl who wants all the people who love her there on her special day. You're giving Cece that.

"And if your dad can't see it, then I'm sorry, Art, but that's on him. I'm proud of you for choosing to go, and I'm going to support you regardless of the outcome of your decision because I'm seeing firsthand how hard this is for you, and you're doing it anyway. That means something. That means… everything!" Taking a deep breath to calm myself, I find Arthur watching me with soft eyes and a small smile.

"You have no idea, do you?" I honestly don't know

what he's talking about, so I shake my head. "No idea how incredible you are." He pulls me into him, and we settle into a comfortable position of intertwined limbs, his hand in my hair. As my eyes get heavy, I swear I hear him say, "I think you might be my favorite person."

you also found your pickle

Alice

I wake slowly, taking stock of the position I'm in to make sure it's not going to cause my neck or shoulders any pain, but when I try to move, I can't. I'm trapped under a very warm, very naked, and very cuddly Arthur.

"Too early, tesouro. Go back to sleep." Geez, his morning voice might be my new favorite sound.

"That's rich coming from the guy up at four in the morning nearly every day." I snuggle into him, and he hums happily.

"It's Sunday. I wanna stay in bed with my girl and snuggle." My brain snags on those two words.

My girl.

But not for long, because Luther comes in, puts his front paws on the bed, and lays his head on Arthur's pillow, panting into his face. "Buddy, I love ya, but seriously?" Luther answers him with a lick to the face, and I laugh at these two silly boys who feel more like home than any place I've ever been. "Ugh. Fine." He kisses the top of my head and slides away from me.

"I'll get up, too. I can let him out if you make the coffee?" Just when I think I'm about to avoid any awkward, potentially gross morning breath, he leans down and kisses me. And it's not awkward or gross. It's amazing, because it's Arthur.

"Sounds like you know who makes a better cup of coffee in this house." He kisses the tip of my nose and stands in all his naked glory. After pulling on a pair of sweats, he takes a fresh shirt out of his closet and leaves it at the foot of the bed for me. I have the insatiable urge to squeal and kick my legs,.

How is this my real life right now?

THE MORNING WAS QUIET, both of us feeling the pressure building as the minutes ticked by. And now, as we pull into a long driveway, Arthur's grip on the steering wheel tightens to the point that his knuckles turn white. I place a hand on his thigh, and when he puts the truck in park, I unbuckle my seatbelt and slide closer to him. "You can do this." I kiss his cheek and he nods, swallowing hard.

He opens the driver's door, slipping out and then reaching for me to help me out through the same side. We grab Cece's gifts out of the back seat and walk slowly to the front door, which is wide open. As we step inside, there's chatter coming from the back of the house, and as we take our shoes off, a gorgeous woman walks down the stairs. When her eyes land on Arthur, she runs down the final few stairs, practically lunging at him.

"Mano," she yelps. "You came!" She pries herself off him and jumps a few times. "This is the best day ever!" Facing me, she smiles brightly, the same dark eyes as Arthur's shining back at me. "Hi, I'm Dani. Little sister," she says, pointing to Arthur with her thumb.

"I'm Alice. It's so nice to meet you, Dani." I extend a hand, but she wraps her arms around me, pulling me into a hug.

"Thanks for coming with him," she whispers so only I can hear. *Oh boy, I think I like her already.* "All right, come on! Cece's been talking about you coming for days." She takes my hand, pulling me into the house, and Arthur follows closely behind.

"Cece!" Dani calls out. "Ceciliaaaa," she tries again. "Ana Cecilia Machado, get your butt in here!"

The birthday girl emerges from another room, a book in hand, looking like she's about to give her aunt sass, until she sees me and Arthur.

"You're here!" Cece rushes to us, hugging Arthur around the legs, then looking up at me. "Hi, Miss Alice. Thanks for coming to my party. Do you want to come see all the desserts Bisa and Vó made for today?"

"Hey, I helped, too," Dani interjects, making me laugh.

"I'd love to, Cece." I look back at Arthur, who nods, letting me know it's okay to go as he stays back with Dani.

Cece gives me the rundown on the Brazilian goodies laid out on the dining room table that I absolutely cannot wait to try. As she finishes, I notice we have an audience. The couple, who could only be Arthur's parents, smile at us from the doorway.

"Good work, Cecilia. Would you like to introduce us to your friend?" the man with a full head of salt-and-pepper hair asks.

"Vó, Vô, this is Miss Alice, my teacher at the ranch.

I'm gonna go get Pickle." She walks out of the room, leaving me alone with her grandparents.

"Hi, Mr. and Mrs. Machado. It's great to meet you. I'm Alice Preece." I extend a hand to Arthur's mom first, and she takes it, wrapping both of her hands around mine.

"Alice. It's so good to meet you. Gabriel and Cece have said wonderful things about you." Her slight accent is endearing, and I love the way she says Gabriel. "And please, it's Andrea." She pats my hand before letting it go, and I reach for her husband, who gives me a hearty shake.

"Thanks for coming today, Alice. It means a lot to Cece. And please, call me Ivan." His kind smile eases some of the concern I had about him not being open to Arthur coming today. "Can we get you something to eat or drink?" He extends his hand toward the kitchen behind him and Andrea. "Our sons are vultures, so you might as well get to the food before they obliterate it all." He laughs, and the tenderness in his voice when he speaks about his children is apparent, but I wonder if he's including Arthur in that statement.

In the kitchen, Arthur is at the table with his grandmother, laughing at something she said, but when he looks up and sees his parents, his joy immediately falls away. He stands, clearing his throat. "Mãe. Pai." He nods to his parents, and Ivan blows out a heavy breath while Andrea walks across the room to embrace her son.

Every person in here is acutely aware of the weight of the tension around us.

Another man with a boyish face claps his hands. "Bro! I'm so fucking happy you're here." He slaps Arthur's back as he hugs him.

"That's five bucks, Tio Gustavo!" Cece pipes up from her spot at the table.

"Ce, I bought you a really nice present. Can't I skip

paying into the swear fund for one day?" Gustavo pleads with his niece.

"Nope," she answers, popping the "p' and not taking her eyes off her plate of cheese and crackers.

He groans, patting his back pockets. "Put it on my tab, kid." Turning to me, the dangerously adorable smile is back on his face. "You've gotta be Alice. I'm Gustavo, the best-looking Machado brother." He winks at me, and Arthur clears his throat next to him, though it sounds more like a growl. "Oh, my bad, Art." They exchange a look, then Arthur takes a plate and begins quietly putting some food on it. Grapes, cheese, meat, fresh bread, and some little round things I don't recognize, but look delicious.

He walks to me and hands me the plate. "I suggest you grab anything else you might want before the vultures attack. I know Marcelo is around here somewhere waiting to pounce."

"What did I tell you, Alice? Vultures." Ivan chuckles, but the sound dies when his eyes meet Arthur's, realizing they've both said the same thing.

"Do you want anything to drink? I'm gonna get some water," Arthur whispers to me, tucking a strand of hair behind my ear. The motion seems to soothe him as much as it does me.

"Water is great. Thank you." I lean into his touch, making sure to lock eyes with him for a moment. When we do, his face softens, his lopsided smile making an appearance before he steps away to get our drinks.

"It's really wonderful to see Arthur looking so settled. So happy," Andrea says from behind me. I turn to look at her as she watches her eldest son with watery eyes. "He deserves so much happiness, after everything he's gone through. And I can tell he's very happy being near you." She reaches out to squeeze my elbow. "I know we've only just met, and I'm sure you probably have an idea about the difficult relationship Arthur has with his father right now, but as his mother, I can see he's different. And before I miss the chance to say it, I want to do it now. Thank you." She pulls me into a hug then. It's quick, but tight, complete with a little extra squeeze at the end. Just like her mother's. I focus on keeping my plate upright rather than the chaos of emotions warring inside my head. I expected this to be awkward, hard, uncomfortable, not quite so natural, easy, and comforting.

AS WE SIT around the chairs outside, there is no shortage of embarrassing stories being shared between siblings. Charlie fills me in on a few family details as they all talk over each other, and she eventually asks me if I want to take a break from the chaos. It's an easy yes.

We walk to a nearby pond in silence, and when we reach a bench, she sits first, leaving more than enough room for me to join her.

"They are the best people, and I love them all dearly, but they are so bloody loud." Charlie looks out at the water as she speaks. "I hope you know you've been welcomed into the fold, Alice. Dani won't shut up about you, and the boys think you're pretty damn cool."

"Oh." It's the only response I can come up with.

"I know. It's a lot. They love hard and fast, those Machados." There's a wistful smile on her face as she's undoubtedly talking about Rafael, too.

There's some rustling behind us, and Cece approaches with her stuffed pickle. "Hi. Miss Alice, do you like our quiet spot?"

"It's gorgeous, Cece."

"You can come here anytime you need some quiet, too." She fiddles with the stuffy, keeping her eyes low.

"Thank you. And so you know, you don't have to call me Miss. It can just be Alice."

"Okay," she says as a tiny smile pulls at the corners of her lips. "And one day I'll get to call you Tia, too, since you also found your pickle." I don't understand what she means, but Charlie seems to, as she clears her throat next to me. Cece's brows furrow as she continues, "I'm not sure if Tio Arthur knows he's your pickle yet. He seems sad today He's talking to Vô in the living room now, and they both sounded not happy. That's why I came here." Her words have me instantly pushing to my feet, and I look at Charlie. I need to move quickly, but I hate to leave Cece like this.

"Go. I've got this." Charlie sends me off with a nod, and I take off running toward the house. When I reach the kitchen, everyone is there, quietly setting the table or preparing something, while elevated voices come from the next room. I can't make out the words, but the tone isn't friendly.

"You shouldn't be here, Arthur." This time, Ivan's voice is crystal clear, even through the wall.

I look around, wondering if anyone is going to do something, and when they don't, I don't ask for permission. I leave the kitchen and walk into the living room.

I hardly recognize the man I've come to know so intimately. He's practically curling in on himself, making himself smaller and smaller with every word his father says.

I can't stand here and do nothing.

I promised to support him, so that's exactly what I'm about to do.

you do not deserve that woman

Arthur

"Arthur?" Alice's sweet voice breaks the awful silence that took up all the air in the room after my dad told me I shouldn't be here. Maybe he's right. I know everyone out there can hear us. I'm sure it's why Alice is here now.

Her small hand slides into mine, holding on tightly. Keeping my eyes on the floor, I can hardly bring myself to squeeze her hand back. "Maybe we should go," I whisper so low, I'm not sure she hears me.

"No," she responds clearly. "No, I don't think we should go. I definitely don't think *you* should go, Arthur." She adjusts her stance, like she's readying herself for battle. "Mr. Machado, it's not my intention to disrespect you in your home, but I need to say this. You're wrong. Arthur *should* be here. Cecilia asked for him to come, and despite the hours he's spent second-guessing his decision, he's here for her. Because she's family. I'm no expert on what a loving family looks like, believe me, but I can give you plenty of examples of a crummy one, if you need them."

She pauses, taking a breath before lifting her head higher, meeting my dad's eyes. "I don't know you, but I've been lucky enough to get to know your son. He's a good man. You must know that because you raised him. He's loyal and kind, he's hardworking and honest. I've lived and worked with him for weeks, and I have yet to find any fault with him. I don't know what happened between the you of two, but is it worth all of this? Is forgiveness harder than not having Arthur present at family events, Mr. Machado?"

She twists to face me, and I wait with rapt attention for whatever is coming next. "And you. Is the pain you're putting yourself through worth it? Are you going to carry all of this guilt around with you forever and let people believe what they want. Or are you going to let them see who you really are? Because I see you, Arthur Ivan Machado. I see you, and I know you're made of pure, solid gold. Regardless of your past."

She takes my face in her hands, those amber eyes I fell hard for on day one, grounding me in a way I've never known before her, and that I don't think I'll find after her, either. "Show him who you are. Talk from a place of love, not of guilt or shame or stubbornness. Don't let this drive a permanent wedge between you, Arthur. You have a family, and it's a really good one. Don't let that go to waste, because people like me wish we had even an ounce of what you've got here. Okay?" Her words are whispered softly, but they hit me like a freight train. She seals her words with a kiss, then walks out of the room.

I chance a look at my dad, and he's as awestruck as I am, but he wipes the look away quickly, replacing it with the disappointment I'm so used to seeing.

"I'm sorry," I say lamely, and he scoffs, the sound putting another crack in my heart.

Shaking his head, my father pinches the bridge of his

nose. "I wish I knew where I went wrong with you. I thought we'd done all the right things, showed you we loved you, but then you—" He stops short, as if finishing the sentence causes him physical pain.

"Then what, Pai? I showed you I'm human? I get it, you never planned on having a son addicted to narcotics. I never planned that for my life either, but that was the problem. I planned everything, until it was all I did, and when I needed an escape from it all, my brain wouldn't let me rest." As my voice gets louder, the room starts to feel smaller. "I know I messed up. I've beaten myself up about it for years, but how am I supposed to forgive myself if my own dad won't forgive me?"

"I did that, Arthur!" he yells with more hurt than I've ever seen in his eyes. "I forgave you, and I helped you, and I loved you through all of it." He looks up at the ceiling, closing his eyes and taking a deep breath. When he levels me with his stare again, he doesn't say anything for several never-ending seconds.

Finally, he speaks, his voice low. "You do not deserve that woman."

I nod in agreement. "You don't need to tell me that. I already know I'm not good enough for her."

"Let me finish," he says, walking closer to me like he's approaching a wounded animal, so cautiously. "You don't deserve her like I never deserved your mother. Decades later, I still don't think I'm good enough for her. But you know what makes me feel like I got it right? Like I could do anything, be anything, and even maybe be worthy of her?" He doesn't wait for me to answer. "Her love. The fact that she thinks I hung the moon, even when we both know I've never even come close. That she chose me as her partner. *Me*. And she chooses me every day. The only other thing that makes me feel like I'm doing things right in my life is watching my children thrive and be happy. I failed you, Arthur. I know I did." He hangs his head low, wiping a tear from his cheek.

"You failed me? Pai. Come on. I'm the one who failed. I fucked up. I nearly caused you to lose everything." My voice cracks on that last word, and he looks up at me again.

"No, filho. Losing everything would have been losing *you*. Money is just that. It's just money. We can make more, we can figure it out. But you? If we'd lost you, I—" He breaks off on a sob, and fuck, nothing tears me apart more than seeing my dad cry. "I can't stand the thought of that happening, so when I saw you at that bar, I decided I couldn't watch you do that to yourself again. I wouldn't survive it a second time."

"What bar? What do you mean?"

He's never told me any of this. I thought he was done with me after everything I had put them through with the debt I accrued, thanks to my addiction, and then the cost of rehab. He told me he never wanted me to pay them back, and he never wanted to speak to me again. And that was that.

"Someone told me they saw you at a bar in Ojai some time after you got back from rehab. Bob's, or something? I don't know. And I couldn't believe it, but then I went there and I saw it for myself. It was you sitting at that bar, switching one addiction for another." His face is full of pain. Pain I caused, but pain that's unnecessary if he thinks I switched from drugs to alcohol.

"Pai. I don't drink. I haven't touched alcohol in a very long time. I don't even take over-the-counter painkillers. Beau, the man who owns the bar, he's my sponsor. I go there every Wednesday after my meeting to wind down and collect my thoughts. I've been sober for over three years." I swallow the lump in my throat, making it hard to breathe. We've wasted so much time. "I met Alice there, actually. She doesn't drink either. I thought she did, and I wanted nothing to do with her at first, but anyway, that's another story."

"Doesn't being at a bar tempt you to go back to your old life?" he asks incredulously.

"Nope." My answer is immediate. "Alcohol was never my drug of choice, which is why it was so easy to give it up. Beau runs a tight ship, and while he's an addict himself, he gets that people who aren't addicts sometimes need a place to think, to process, to vent. He gives that to people. You wouldn't know it by looking at him, but that guy is an amazing listener, and he's full of good advice. He's been pushing me to talk to you for a long time, actually, but I've been too scared. I owe a lot to him for being where I am today." I swallow the emotion lodged in my throat. "I owe everything to you and Mãe, but I've been lucky to have friends like Beau and Owen. And I swear to you, Pai, I've been clean for years."

My father's eyes fill with tears he lets spill freely down his cheeks. "All this time?" he asks solemnly, taking slow steps toward me. He lays both hands on my shoulders, looking me in the eyes. "I'm so sorry, filho. Can you forgive me?"

Now it's my tears that fall. "There's nothing to forgive."

"Yes, there is," he argues. "It's my fault you haven't been here. I let my pain blind me. Instead of asking you, instead of talking to you, I chose to believe what I thought I was seeing."

I pull him into a hug, and a part of me I thought I'd lost forever immediately begins to heal. He whispers more apologies, and I hug him tighter. I say the words I didn't think I'd get the chance to say in person ever again. "Te amo, Pai."

"Te amo, meu filho. I never stopped loving you, and I never will. I hope you know that. I hope I can show you that." With my father's strong arms around me, I silently hope I can do the same.

After a few quiet moments, we pull apart, both sniffling. "We should get back out there. I'm sure Cece is going to demand cake and presents any minute now." My dad wipes his face, and all of the anguish there before has, at least, started to dissipate.

"Yeah, I gotta look for Alice."

"Don't let that one go." He squeezes my shoulder once before walking out of the room. I follow him out, all the while hoping I don't have to let Alice go, but knowing if leaving is still what she wants, I will.

I FIND her pacing on the driveway in front of my truck. She must be so deep in her own thoughts that she doesn't even hear me coming. When she spins to pace back toward the house, she sees me and breaks into a full sprint, running right up to me. I pick her up as she wraps her limbs around me.

"I'm sorry. I'm so sorry if I messed it all up, but I couldn't not say anything."

As she continues to ramble on with apologies for literally coming to my rescue, I move us so we're on the other side of my truck, out of sight from any curious eyes. Once her back hits the driver's door, I rear back, moving her hair off her face until she's looking at me. Only then does she stop.

I take in her tear-rimmed eyes. "Don't cry, baby. Everything is fine."

"You two talked?" I nod, swallowing hard as I think of the moment we realized this was all a miscommunication. "You're okay?" She takes my face in her hands again, waiting for my answer.

"More than okay," I say, and she sobs through a wide smile, half laughing, half crying. "We need to talk some more, but we're good, tesouro. Really good. Thanks to you."

She shakes her head, leaning forward to kiss me as her tears soak our faces. "I'm so proud of you," she whispers. It's these little moments with her that are always the quietest to my ears, but the loudest to my heart. It's at this second that I want to shout out that I'm falling inevitably in love with her.

But then I remember she hates it in Ojai, and her goal has always been to leave.

And then I remember she still doesn't know my whole story.

So I stop myself.

Every time.

the most precious, most beautiful thing—no, person—in my life

Alice

After Arthur and Ivan's talk at the birthday party, it felt like everything had changed again. As soon as we went back inside, the air was lighter. Everyone else felt it, too. Arthur promised to be back for a family dinner, and they all insisted I be there, as well, which had me nearly in tears for about the twelfth time that day.

It's been five days since the party, and I haven't slept in my own bed. Arthur insists, and I honestly sleep better next to him, so it's a win-win. I'll deal with going back to sleeping alone when I have to.

As things progress with the clinic, Rosemary has been looking for another occupational therapist to hire, and it seems she's found a potential candidate. It's a load off my shoulders, knowing I won't be leaving them high and dry when I decide it's time to go.

Given the way things are moving along with Gran's house now that Gabriel helped me get connected with a realtor, it seems I'll be able to cross that off my list soon.

And with Gran's worsening condition, I don't know if I can handle staying around much longer. She either remembers who I am and that she despises me, or she has no clue who I am and is nicer than she's ever been to me. Either option hurts like hell, and I don't know how much more of it I can take.

It's a slow Saturday morning, and after letting Luther out, Arthur got back into bed with me. We've been lying here since, dozing in and out of sleep. It's the kind of bliss I've never known before.

But, as tends to happen when I have too much time to think, my brain takes off down a road that is less happy and cozy thoughts, and more doom and gloom.

Arthur smooths the pad of his thumb in the space between my brows. "What's going on in there?" he asks gently.

I could lie and pretend I'm thinking about work, but instead, the full truth comes out. "I want to tell you why I didn't want to come back to Ojai, if that's okay." Some part of me needs him to understand why it's so hard to be here, why I've been so adamant about leaving.

"Of course it's okay. You can tell me anything, tesouro." He kisses the top of my head and goes silent, waiting for me to begin.

"I wasn't supposed to be born. My mom's pregnancy was an accident, and my grandmother begged her to have an abortion. Mom was in her third year of college, on track to get a business degree, and she had an affair with a professor from another faculty. That's how she got pregnant. She thought if she kept the baby, he'd leave his wife and take care of her, but he didn't. He got a job in another state and left. During the entire pregnancy, according to Gran, my mom thought he'd come back for her. Well, he didn't do that, either. My mom dropped out of college. I was born."

I take a breath, smoothing my hand over his chest. "She was heartbroken, and I don't think she ever got over him. She drank a lot, but when I was about six or seven, she started using drugs." He tenses for a moment, and it's so quick I almost wonder if I imagined it. "I don't know what kind, because I was too young, but I remember the change. I don't think Gran ever knew how bad it got, or maybe she didn't want to see it.

"Suddenly, there were always new men in our house. I think Mom was constantly chasing love. It was like that for years, and then one day I came home from school and there were a bunch of people there. Police officers and para-medics. Gran was there. She didn't even pick me up from school early; she let me come home and see the aftermath for myself. The police tape all over the place. The flashing lights. The body bag being wheeled out of our house. Mom had overdosed, and one of her friends found her."

Arthur's grip on me tightens, and his breath hitches. I know if I look at him, I'll lose it, so I keep going. "That was when I went to live with Gran, who blamed me for losing her only daughter. She had been a single mom, too, and she didn't want that for my mom. Every day, I was reminded I'd been a mistake, so when I graduated from high school, I left. I did so intending to never come back.

"Then, all those weeks ago, I got a call from a doctor who told me my grandmother had advanced Alzheimer's, and that I either needed to provide her with twenty-four-seven care myself or find a place that could do that for her. So here I am, trying to figure out how to sell a house full of painful memories and fire damage, in a town that birthed all my worst moments." I chance a look at Arthur then, and find him openly crying, which instantly makes me do the same. "Sorry," I whisper.

Shaking his head, he wipes my tears away. "There's nothing to be sorry for. I—Thank you for telling me."

Reaching up, I touch my lips to his, but he keeps the kiss short. "Alice, I—"

"I don't want to talk anymore right now. Okay?" My fingers trace his jaw, letting the roughness of his stubble on my skin be the feeling I focus on.

"Yeah." He swallows, his eyes still sad. But I don't want to be sad. I want to enjoy the time I have with him because soon, it'll end. At least now he knows why. Now he understands.

I straddle him and begin trailing kisses down his neck, over his chest. He's quiet, but his breathing picks up.

"Tell me about your tattoos," I whisper into his skin. "What do they mean?" I've always wondered about the colorful flowers and birds he has on his skin, and I have never asked.

"The flowers are for my grandmother. They're roses. Her favorites." He moans when I kiss over his abs, running my hand over the waistband of his boxer briefs. "But we're not gonna talk about her right now."

"What about the birds?" I ask, chuckling while I pull on the fabric until he's naked beneath me, hoping none of the other tattoos are for family members, too.

"The sabiá-laranjeira is Brazil's national bird. I remember the first time I heard them singing, there were thousands of them. It was—" He pauses when my lips reach his hip, and I stop moving, waiting for him. "Incredible," he mumbles, groaning when I continue to kiss him lower.

"And the hummingbird?" I ask, my lips hovering over where he's hard for me. He doesn't answer, and when I swirl my tongue over the head of his cock, tasting him with a moan, a strangled sound leaves him. "Arthur, are you going to answer my question?"

He struggles to answer me again, fisting the sheets when I lick him from base to tip.

"Uh, I l-like them. They're a symbol of, um, uh, r-resilience. They—They're, uh delicate, b-but strong." He struggles through the explanation as I continue to tease him with my mouth, and when he finishes, I wrap my lips around him and take him as deeply as I can. "Oh, fuck," he whispers, his breath catching when I hum around him, sucking as I somehow take him even deeper.

Lifting my gaze, I find his eyes already on me, and it makes my core throb to see him watching me with fire in his eyes. I moan, searching for friction as I squeeze my thighs together.

And then, faster than I can fully process in the moment, he's lifting me so I'm straddling him again and pulling my oversized T-shirt over my head, his heated gaze making my core throb.

"You want my cock, baby?" With all the confidence in the world, he puts his hands behind his head and waits.

"Yes," I answer, bracing my hands on his abs until the head of his cock grazes over my clit, making me moan.

"Then take it, tesouro. Take what's yours. Ride me. Soak me." I move my hips, coating him in the proof of what he does to my body.

Finding some confidence of my own, I lift my leg and maneuver myself until I'm straddling him again, but facing the other way. Keeping my eyes low, I use one hand to guide him to my entrance and the other to brace myself on his thigh.

"Goddamn it, how are you real?" The awe in his question only spurs me on more, and I sink down onto him, whimpering at the delicious stretch and pleasure that seems to reach every part of me.

I lift and lower myself until all that exists are our labored breaths and the feel of him, long and so hard inside me. As my movements become more erratic, I know I can't keep this up much longer, and Arthur senses it, as he holds me at the waist. "On your hands and knees, tesouro."

Holy hell, I might come just from his deep, gravelly voice commanding me. I do as he asks, and whine when he slips out of me, only to find myself moaning loudly the next moment when he thrusts fully inside me with a groan.

He fucks like he does everything else—intentionally, flawlessly. He also fucks the way I've always wanted, deep and long, hard and slow at first. His tattooed arm wraps around my middle, pulling me up until my back is flush with his chest. I brace myself with one hand on his thick thigh, the one that made me come the first time, while the other finds his hair.

"Why do you call me goldie?" Maybe it's the wrong time to ask, but it feels like we're running out of it, and I need to know.

"Your eyes," he says into my skin, thrusting into me in a rhythm that's our own.

"And the other one?" I pant, trying to memorize the way he feels inside me. "What does it mean?" The question I've been wanting to ask since day one finally makes itself known.

"What, baby?" He moans as his hand finds my breast. I love that sound. I love that just touching my body makes him do that.

"Tesouro," I clarify.

"Tesouro," he repeats. "Você é o meu tesouro. A coisa —não, a pessoa—mais preciosa, mais linda na minha vida." He peppers my neck with kisses, bringing his other hand to my hip and squeezing.

"Arthur, please," I beg, needing to know what those words mean. Needing to hear him say them again, even if I never understand them.

"It means treasure." He takes my hand in his, moving them both until they're at my core, feeling the place we're most intimately connected. "You're my treasure. The most precious, most beautiful thing—no, person—in my life." With the admission on his lips and his finger on my clit, I come around him, squeezing and pulsing until nothing else exists but this.

Us.

As his arms tighten around me, he whispers my name into my neck, finding his own release.

I hope I never forget how it feels to be held by him, to be loved by him. Because even if he's never said he loves me, he makes me feel loved and cherished, and that's a priceless gift I'll never take for granted.

As we catch our breaths, his hold on me never loosens, as if he's scared to let me go. I'm scared, too. Scared he'll let me leave when the time comes, even though I know if he asked me to stay, I'm not sure I could deny him. I'm not sure I want to anymore.

Finally, we pry our bodies apart, and Arthur picks me up, carrying me out to the hallway and into the bathroom. "I told you, you don't have to ca—"

He silences me with a kiss before setting me on the vanity. "And I told you I'll carry you anywhere. I'd carry you everywhere. Then you'd never be far away from me."

He cleans us both up as he's done before, then moves away from me to turn on the water in the tub, checking the temperature and then pouring in salts I didn't realize he had stashed away. In seconds, the whole room smells like lavender.

He struts back to where I'm sitting, stunned, watching as his muscles move and his hair falls over his forehead, entranced by the magic and beauty that is Arthur Machado.

He reaches behind me then begins to pull my hair delicately to the top of my head, gathering the strands and tying the scrunchie I left on the countertop around it until it's in a messy knot. I watch his face tense in concentration, brows furrowed and his tongue sticking out between his lips.

My gosh, I want to kiss him. Hug him. Hold on to him and never let him go. I want to be with him every moment until forever.

Before my feelings get away from me, his face softens, and he chuckles at his own handiwork. And then he picks me up again, making me giggle.

"You know what's better than the sound of your laugh?" he asks, my favorite smile tugging at his stubbled cheeks. I shake my head as he lowers me into the tub first, then climbs in himself, pulling me back until I'm resting against his chest with his legs on either side of me. "Nothing," he whispers into my hair.

We sit like that, all gentle touches and stolen kisses wherever we can reach—arms and hands for me, head, neck and shoulders for him.

The first night we met, when Arthur held me like this on the bathroom floor, I never could have imagined we'd end up here.

Now I can't imagine being anywhere else.

when everything goes black, that's all there is

Alice

It feels like Arthur has been trying to tell me something since I dumped all my childhood trauma on him the other day, but I either haven't had the energy for whatever that conversation will bring, or I've been with Gran. Her health's taken a major nosedive, and while Arthur has offered to come keep me company or help me, there's not much he can do. There's barely anything *I* can do, other than be there, so I've spared him the unnecessary additional stress.

Between the challenges at work with preparing for the horses starting to arrive soon and his final testing coming up, we've been preoccupied. In the evenings, we pretty much fall into bed, seeking comfort in one another's warmth. The elephant in the room remains, being ignored. Every time I kiss him feels like it could be the last, and I think he knows.

As I step into the quiet farmhouse, absolutely exhausted, I'm reminded of those first few days here, when

I felt so out of place, when I thought I'd live here for a few days and then find somewhere else to live close by. I never could have seen this coming.

Him. This life.

Coworkers who have become best friends. A dog I can't imagine not seeing every day. A man who can settle my nerves with nothing but a touch, and who truly cares for me.

Nothing about being here was planned, yet some days it's as if someone coordinated all of this perfectly. I moved back to a town I thought I hated, only to fall in love with it again. Only to fall in love.

My phone rings loudly, the tone I set for Gran's care facility stealing all of the peace and comfort I've come to find in this house. And when the voice on the other end calmly tells me I need to rush to see Gran, I do just that.

Amid the chaotic blur of doctors, nurses, and paperwork to be signed, I call Arthur no less than twelve times. Once it became clear I'd be finalizing end-of-life decisions today, and provisions would have to be made for Gran's body, I knew I wanted him here. I only wanted him here. I needed him. *Need* him. But he's not picking up, and no one at the ranch knows where he is, so I've done it all alone. Like I've done just about everything else in my life.

After endless hours, my bones are weary, my head is starting to pound, and my eyes are bloodshot. I try Arthur one last time before I start my Jeep.

Nothing.

I drive in silence, unsure of where to drive to, but also knowing there's only one place I *can* go. My mind wanders between where Arthur could be and whether or not I should start packing as soon as I get back. I wonder what I'll write in my resignation letter and how much notice I'll give. Probably no time at all, because the thought of having to live and work with Arthur with a fixed end date makes my heart ache to the point that it's hard to breathe.

In between every thought, though, there are the same recurring words:

I don't want to go. I want to stay. I want to stay with him. Arthur.

And when a car runs a red light, there's no time to react.

When everything goes black, he's all there is.

Arthur.

my promises might be well-intentioned, but they can be broken

Arthur

Every day, it feels like she's about to tell me this is her last day here. Every morning, I wake up half expecting she'll be gone. And every night, I wrap myself up in her, thankful for one more chance to keep her close, shoving the reminders that I haven't given her my truth yet as far away as I can.

Except today, I couldn't.

I tried to push those thoughts aside, tried to pretend like it hasn't been eating me alive to know she lost someone —no, not someone, her mom—to addiction, and she's been living with, sleeping with, an addict.

So I called an emergency meeting with Beau, who was more than willing to meet and let me sit in silence for a solid hour before I told him anything. Once I started, there was no stopping. I told him what Alice told me. It didn't feel wrong because I know Beau won't share that information with anyone, not even Josie. I told him what I've been feeling lately, that there's this vise around my chest that won't loosen, and I can't take any more, and it makes me want to do something to forget about it all. Something I know I'd regret. Something I promised myself I'd never do again. But I'm an addict, and my promises might be well-intentioned, but they can be broken, especially if I don't check-in at meetings and talk to my sponsor when I start to feel like this.

"It fucking sucks. I've never been this happy, but I know happiness has an expiration date, yet I can't bring myself to be the one to end it. It's no different than being high. You always know at some point, it'll end. It can't last forever, but it feels so fucking good you chase that feeling over and over and over. I know she's going to leave, and I don't care. I want to pretend it's not happening, but that's unhealthy as hell." I shove my hands into my hair, pulling on the ends like it'll somehow pull the answers to my problems out of my brain. "And she has no idea. I'm lying to her by omission. I'm intentionally keeping this massive secret from her because I'm an asshole."

"Try again," Beau offers in his deep voice.

"Because I'm fucking terrified." My voice cracks, the fear seeping into my bloodstream making it hard to breathe. "I know I can't keep her, but this will drive her away faster. I know it will."

"No, you don't. You *think* it will." He's so calm, it's almost infuriating.

"I'm pretty fucking certain. How could it not? And she's been so stressed with her grandmother and things at work. I don't want to add to her load. I can't do that to her."

I won't.

I won't cause her any more stress. Not now.

"You're scared to lose her. You're scared to cause her pain. But let me tell you something, Art, even if you're lucky enough to keep her, that'll never change. And you're going to have to figure out how to live with that." He levels me with a look I know damn well because I saw it a lot when he first became my sponsor.

"I'm still scared Josie will leave my sorry ass. Scared I'll be the cause of any more sleepless nights for her. But I have to trust her love, and I have to trust myself. She chose me through the worst of it, and she chooses me every day. So do I. I choose myself, too, because I want to be here for her. Because I choose life with her above life any other way." He scratches his chin, and I know he's about to really hit me with something now.

"Remember what I told you when I met you? You have to shift from 'you are the problem' to 'you *have* a problem.' I think you sometimes still get stuck thinking you're the problem. You're not. Everyone has baggage. Did you want to walk away from her when she told you about her mom and grandma? No. I know you didn't because you're here. I know you didn't because if anything, her opening up to you made you fall even more in love with her."

The man doesn't falter. He doesn't waver. He puts me firmly in my place after I've spent hours of his time talking about how I've been running in circles.

"Everything she does makes me fall more in love with her, Beau. Since she first looked at me with those golden eyes, I've known she was a treasure I couldn't ever be worthy of." I close my eyes for a few seconds, picturing her perfect face. "I know there's nothing I could do to deserve her, Beau. I know that."

"You could be honest with her. You could let her see *you*. You could let her decide for herself whether or not she can handle what you share. You could ask her to stay. You could go with her." His brows furrow then, and it's the first sight of emotion he's shown, even if his words are full of them. "You have options, Art. And if you don't ask for what you want, you're far less likely to get it."

"You really think it's that easy? Be honest and ask for what I want? Which, by the way, is to be wherever she is. Sure, it'd be nice to be close to my family now that my dad and I are mending things, but he'd understand. They all would." That truth knocks into me hard and fast. My family would be sad to not have me close; they'd be sad not to have her close, too, but they'd understand. I know they would. And how fucking lucky am I that I get to have that.

"I never said it'd be easy, but yeah, it is. If you know she's the one, then you either live with regret or you live knowing you did everything you could." For the first time since we sat in his empty bar, he reaches for his phone. "Sorry, this is the fifth call from this number. Hello?" he says, lifting the phone to his ear. I know it's not Josie because she has her own ringtone. "Yeah. Understood."

There is zero indication of what his conversation is about until he blows out a slow breath and swears. My skin prickles because Beau doesn't react to things. "Give me fifteen minutes. " He hangs up, looping his car keys onto his fingers as he stands. "We gotta go."

I follow him out, knowing whatever is happening is bigger than me right now. Plus, I know what to do. Beau, as usual, is right. I have to tell her everything. About my addiction, about being in love with her, all of it.

After we've driven in silence for a few minutes, it's obvious we're on the way to the hospital. Beau knows a lot of people, so I don't bother guessing who it could be we're going to see. I just don't get why I'm with him.

"I'm gonna tell you what's going on, and you need to accept that this is all I know. We'll find out more when we get there, all right?" He turns to me briefly, catching my nod. "It was Alice. She was in a car accident. Gabriel called me after he couldn't reach you. He doesn't have all the details, but on the scene they assumed at least a couple of broken ribs and likely a pretty bad concussion."

My stomach instantly starts to turn thinking about the pain she must be in. I reach for my phone, which I had turned off when I got to Beau's. When it lights up, there are over twenty missed calls from Alice, Gabe, and Owen. "Gabriel is going to try to get some more information from the hospital, but that's all he knows so far. She's okay, Arthur. She's alive."

Several responses come to mind, and none of them make it out of my mouth. I can't form words, not when guilt is eating me up from inside.

After a few more minutes of silence, Beau looks over at me again. My skin feels tight and my jaw is clenched so hard it's starting to hurt, but I manage to say what I've been thinking. "She needed me, and I wasn't there."

"You were taking care of yourself so you could take care of her. You're going to be there in a few minutes, and that matters, too." Beau stops the car at the emergency door. "I'll be right in." I rush into the hospital, not registering any of the details around me. My body is moving, but I'm not sure how. I'm on autopilot. I need to get to her.

I expect to rush to a desk and beg for them to let me see her, but when I walk in, Rosemary, Gabriel, and Rafael are all there. They spot me at the same time, running over to me, talking at once. Ro shushes my brothers and grabs me by the shoulder. "She's all right. We can't see her yet because they're doing a few more tests and scans, but she's alive. Did you hear me, Arthur? She's all right. I need you to take a breath now, kid."

In the next second, a heavy set of arms is embracing me, and when I feel my brother's chest expand against mine, I start to relax. After a few seconds, my breathing matches his, and I suck in a lungful of air, clearing the haze in my brain. "That's it, brother. You're doing great." Rafael's voice brings me back, and when I look up, Gabriel's concerned eyes are boring into me. "You got this. We're here, and we're not leaving you or her." Raf loosens his hold on me, and Gabriel nods, agreeing with what he's saying.

"Th—" I clear my throat of all the emotion there, the fear lodged so deep it's practically another organ inside me. "Thank you," I manage as I straighten, giving Raf's arm a squeeze. "What do we do now?"

"Now we wait," Gabriel answers.

"Together," Rafael finishes for him.

"You guys don't have to—" I start.

"We're not leaving you, Arthur," Raf repeats. His normally jovial face is serious in a way most people think him incapable of.

"And we're not leaving Alice, either." My mother's voice comes from behind me, and when I see my dad standing next to her, it's all I need to let my tears fall.

taking care of you is also taking care of her right now

Arthur

"Sir, are you family?" the nurse asks me when I request information about Alice.

"No, I'm not, but I'm her roommate, I live with her, and—"

"Unless she asks for you specifically or you're listed as her emergency contact, we can't give you any updates. I'm sorry." She's kind enough about the whole thing, but I'm frustrated, and I need to know if she's okay.

"Art, I got through to the care facility." Gabriel approaches me carefully, giving Raf a quick look before he continues, "Alice's grandmother passed away earlier today."

All the air leaves my lungs. She called me so many times, and I didn't pick up. She needed me, and I wasn't there.

Pushing past my brother, I head back to the nurse's station. "Please, I need you to tell me what's happening with Alice Preece." I'm becoming agitated, and the person in front of me can clearly sense it.

"What's your name?" the nurse asks. I tell them, and after a few seconds of looking at a computer screen, I get a pitying look. "I don't see you listed as her contact. Are you family?"

"No!" I answer more forcefully than necessary. "She doesn't *have* any family! I'm the person she lives with, doesn't that count for anything? Does being in love with someone mean nothing?" I'm practically shouting, and then there's a firm hand on my shoulder.

"Come on." My dad's gentle voice settles my emotions enough for me to stop my tirade. "I'm sorry. We know there's nothing you can do," he says as he guides me back to where my family has been sitting with me.

When I sit, I drop my head into my hands. "She's all alone. She's been all alone and I should have been there. I should be there now."

Several hands hold, pat, and embrace as I stay in my crouched position, beating myself up for how badly I messed up today.

I don't know how much time has passed when a deep voice asks, "Is one of you Arthur?" I look up for the first time, and stand, nodding. "Alice is asking for you. She's asleep now, but she's asked for you several times. If you'd like, I can take you to her."

No sound comes out of my mouth, but the desperation must be evident on my face as the man nods at me and leads me through a set of double doors.

As we walk through the maze of bright white hallways with multicolored arrows on the floor, he explains she's had several tests done. They've confirmed a moderate concussion, two bruised ribs, and that the impact of the accident has caused some neck trauma, which has set off her cervicogenic headaches. Basically, she's in a ton of pain.

When I step into the room, I find it difficult to take a full breath, seeing her sitting slightly up, pillows propping her arms and a brace round her neck. She looks small and fragile, her eyes closed, and her expression free of any sign of distress. A machine beeps somewhere, and my eyes snag on the IV drip responsible for her peaceful features. My breath catches, and the door opens behind me as a doctor enters the room.

"Hi there. I'm Dr. Marishka. Are you Arthur?" The short, dark-haired woman next to me doesn't smile, doesn't try to placate me with niceties.

"I am, yes. Nice to meet you." I shake her hand, so distracted I don't even register what she looks like.

She smiles kindly, and I attempt the same, but I'm not sure my face is capable of it right now. I look at Alice, unable to focus on much else now that I'm here.

"Alice is doing all right," she starts, walking closer to the bed and setting her tablet on a table. "We're going to keep her on morphine for a little bit until the pain lessens. We'll switch her to hydrocodone or oxycodone once she's able to take them orally." I flinch at her words, my muscles instantly tensing as the doctor continues talking, unaware. "She also needs the rest due to the concussion, so you might not see her awake for more than a couple of hours a day, and only a few minutes at a time for the next couple of days. Since she asked for you directly, you're welcome to stay here during visiting hours." She points to the chair that looks about as comfortable as a boulder.

"Thank you. Is there anything else I should know? Anything I can do?" Alice's face and arms are bruised, and her hair is matted. I want her to be as comfortable as possible now, but also when she wakes up.

"If there's anything from home you know would bring her comfort, you can check with the nurses to see if you are allowed to bring it into the room. But for now, there's nothing else. We're going to keep a close eye on her for a little while, and we'll keep you updated." She looks at the IV, then at some of the machines next to the bed, taking a few notes, then nods and leaves the room.

I'm completely helpless. I stand there, staring at her, watching as she breathes, looking at the slow drip in her IV bag and the numbers and lines that make no sense to me on the small screens.

There's a bathroom in the room, which is a semi-private space, but given the size of this hospital, I'm not surprised she has it to herself. Rather than going in, I walk out into the hallway and ask a nurse to direct me to a restroom nearby. I check for anyone else inside, then I call Beau. He picks up on the second ring.

"Everything okay?" His voice is full of concern—probably for both me and Alice.

"Yeah. No. They let me in to see Alice since she asked for me when she was awake, but she's on morphine. They're talking about giving her oxy once she's awake. I want to be here for her, Beau, but can I? Should I?" I honestly don't know. I never imagined myself in this situation, where I would be ready to put someone else's needs ahead of my own so easily. Yet I'm unsure whether that's the right thing to do because of my addiction.

"You should absolutely be there for her, but Arthur, that doesn't mean you need to be in the room." He pauses, likely thinking over his next words. "I know you want to be there with her, but you can step away if you need to, if you feel yourself going to a place that's not healthy for you, because that's still taking care of her and doing what's best. Taking care of you is also taking care of her right now. You can also talk to the nurses. Tell them you want to know when they're administering any medication, and you'd rather not be there for that. Start there, and call me whenever you need to." That's all he needs to say, really, because he understands.

"Okay. Thank you. I should go update my family, but thank you, Beau." We say a quick goodbye and I hang up, feeling better that someone knows what I'm up against here.

Once I update Gabriel and Raf, asking them to go home, I sit in the chair the doctor pointed to and wait.

Hope. *Pray?*

I don't even know.

I sit there, watching Alice, letting all the thoughts of the day run through my mind. I pull the chair closer to her bed and lean back. At some point, I fall asleep, because the next thing I know, a nurse is tapping me on the shoulder, telling me visiting hours are over.

SHE WOKE up last night asking for me.

I wasn't there for her.

Again.

The nurse this morning told me she was agitated, mumbling, and trying to move, but with her brace and her rib injuries, they worried she'd hurt herself more, so she had to be sedated again.

Now I'm here, somewhere between hopeless and guilt-ridden. The only time I leave the room is every four hours when they need to push more morphine into her line, or when they're talking about it. It's hard to come to terms with the fact that the thing that nearly killed me is what's keeping her comfortable. It's harder knowing she still has no idea.

After hours of sitting by her bed, her eyes open, squinting at the light. "No, no, no," she says, her voice raspy, rough, and filled with anguish. "Not again. No."

"Shhh. Baby, hey, it's okay." I stand, and when her eyes meet mine, they're unfocused and dull, filling with tears. When she begins to sob, one of the machines starts to beep louder, and a nurse comes into the room.

"Alice? You're all right. If you move too much, you might hurt your ribs or your neck, so I need you to try to calm down, okay?" She takes Alice's other hand, but Alice's eyes don't leave mine as she continues to cry.

Seconds later, the nurse is fidgeting with something, and I turn away, knowing Alice can see me doing so, knowing the nurse is giving her something to calm her down.

like a feather floating down, only to land like an atomic bomb

Alice

Everything hurts. I want to look and find out the source of the pain, but I can't seem to convince my eyes to comply. There's an annoying beeping sound coming from close by.

I want it to stop.

I know I'm in a hospital. Every time I've opened my eyes, I've been greeted with bright lights, nurses, and doctors, all telling me to stay still. Just like when I was little.

The memory causes panic to rise inside me, but I try to keep calm this time, reminding myself I'm not a child who's going to wake up scared and alone in a hospital room. Arthur was here. He at least came to see me. And even though the last thing I remember is him turning away from me, he was here.

He came.

I shift, trying to gauge the extent of the pain. My head. My neck. My chest. Fortunately, the brace around my neck is soft, yet it grates my skin simply because I know what it is and what it's for.

When I wiggle my fingers, trying to feel something other than unbearable ache, my right hand catches on something soft, and when I move it, there's a roughness that reminds me of Arthur's cheeks when he doesn't shave for a few days.

Reaching my fingers toward the softness again, I squeeze my eyes, keeping them shut, imagining it's Arthur's hair and I'm back in his bed. That we're happy together.

I tighten my grip, and the meds I'm on must be strong, because I swear I feel movement, hear his voice, smell his shampoo.

"Alice, baby, are you awake?" I'd know that deep, gentle tone anywhere, but is it real?

I pry my eyes open, prepared to wince at the lights, but they're dimmed. My hands are no longer tangled in hair, so I must have imagined it. As I scan the room, there are flowers on the windowsill, a stuffed pickle propped against one of the vases, and a stack of books. As I continue, I note the balloons swaying in the corner and the cards propped up on the table with a cookie tin next to them. Finally, I meet a set of deep brown eyes I wasn't sure I'd see ever again, eyes filled with unshed tears, looking weary and tired.

The relief that he's here, that he stayed, washes over me like a wave on the beach, clearing away all of the markings left behind on the sand.

"I'm so sorry," Arthur whispers, sniffling. "I'm sorry I wasn't there."

And then that relief is gone, replaced with the knowledge, the memory of being alone. Of having called him, and my calls going unanswered. That hurt might be worse than the physical pain my body is in.

"Why?" I whisper, my voice hoarse. The dryness in my throat becomes impossible to ignore, and I wince when I swallow. Arthur sighs, his face tense and hard, so I prepare myself for the worst.

He reaches for something, and then there's a straw at my lips. "Here." He holds the cup as I drink, not meeting my eyes.

When I stop, he puts the cup back where he got it from. "I was with Beau. I needed an emergency meeting with him because I was having a hard time. He's my NA sponsor."

The words settle slowly, like a feather floating down, only to land like an atomic bomb. The damage is instantaneous.

He has a sponsor.

He's an addict.

I fell in love with an addict.

"I've been sober for over three years. I go to weekly meetings on Wednesdays and meet with Beau at least every other week. Being an addict is why I don't drink. I didn't want to replace one substance with another." He reaches for me, likely to wipe the tears streaming down my face, but he pulls his hand back at the last moment. "I'm so sorry, Alice. I was always going to tell you. I wanted to tell you as soon as you told me about your mom, but the more time passed, the more scared I got that you'd hate me, that you'd leave." He sniffles, but I can't bring myself to look at him again.

I thought I was tired before, when there was nothing but the physical pain and knowledge that I was officially all alone in this world, but now the exhaustion is quickly taking me under.

I close my eyes, hoping that when I open them again, this is all a bad dream.

BUT NO.

When I come to, Dr. Marishka is quietly speaking to a nurse at the foot of my bed. She notices my movement and finishes her sentence quickly, turning to face me. "Good morning, Alice. How are you feeling?"

"Probably as great as I look." I try for a smile, but I'm not sure it's successful as she gives me a sad look.

"The good news is we can try taking off your neck brace today, and I don't think you need to be on morphine anymore." With those pieces of good news, I attempt to turn my neck a bit, finding there isn't as much pain as there once was. Too bad I can't say the same about my ribs. Who knew bruising your ribs could hurt so much? I sure am glad they didn't break.

"We can move you to taking oxycodone orally." The blood in my veins freezes with that word.

She continues to talk, saying something about how I won't be as sleepy and will be able to stay awake longer, but without pain, but all I can focus on is that she's planning on putting me on a drug that's highly addictive.

I don't know what my mom was on when she died. I don't know what Arthur chose when he was using, but I know this is a problematic drug when it comes to addiction.

When she finally stops talking, I look at her, my mind made up. "I don't want to take that. I don't want anything I could become addicted to or dependent on."

"Alice, you have a moderate concussion, severely bruised ribs, and your existing neck condition has flared up significantly." She steps closer to the bed, where I don't have to strain as much to look at her. "You're going to be in considerable pain for the next two-to-four weeks. I strongly recommend you take oxycodone or hydrocodone for the next five-to-seven days, then transition to over-the-counter—."

"No. I'm sorry, but I'm not going to budge on this. My mother was an addict, and she died of an overdose when I was a child. I just found out the man I love is in NA and has been sober for more than three years. I won't do anything to jeopardize his recovery. I can't." Despite the dryness in my throat, my voice is steady and firm. I don't need time to consider this. It's not something I'm willing to budge on. If having a mother as an addict weren't enough to set me on this path, being in love with one sure is.

"I understand," she says, looking at the nurse who is taking notes. "We could try amitriptyline for the nerve pain from your neck, high-dose anti-inflammatories, and muscle relaxants. We could also give you a couple of intercostal nerve blocks while you're here, but I have to warn you, the injections themselves are painful. We can administer the first one later today, then another before you're discharged tomorrow. They'll relieve your pain for up to twelve hours, and if it becomes unbearable once you're home, you could come back."

"Okay. Yeah. I appreciate that." My eyes fill with tears. I'm so grateful for her understanding.

The doctor nods. "The reality is, rib injuries hurt. A lot. Even bruised ribs can be quite painful for weeks. I don't want you suffering unnecessarily, but I also respect you're considering your home environment. We can start with the non-opioid route and reassess if you're not managing well." I wince at her words. I don't want to have to reassess. "Either way, you'll need someone to help you at home for at least a week. No lifting or driving, and you'll need help with daily activities."

That thought has my chest tightening. I don't want to put my burdens on Arthur. I don't want to put them on anyone. But if these last couple of months have taught me anything, it's that the people around me will want to help. As I look around the room, I see it already—the helping hands, the cooked meals, the check-ins.

I don't want to ever experience the addictions my mother did, but I think I could become addicted to this feeling. To being cared for and loved.

It's one more way I don't want to be like Gran or my mom—I don't want to be alone, pushing away the people who love me.

Now that I've found them, now that I've found Arthur, I don't want to go through life on my own anymore, and I'm certain I won't have to.

my home, my safe place, my love

Arthur

She didn't say anything. A single tear rolled down her cheek, and she closed her eyes, eventually falling back asleep as the grogginess of the meds took her under again. But she didn't say anything after I told her about being an addict, about where I was when she needed me.

I stood, frozen next to the chair I'd become very well-acquainted with, watching her chest rise and fall with every careful breath. The silence felt like a black hole, like it could swallow everything.

My confession hung in the air like smoke. Three years clean, Narcotics Anonymous, the shame I've carried—all of it now between us.

Alice's tears replayed in my mind on a loop. Were they disappointment? Relief? Hurt that I'd hidden this from her?

I couldn't know, yet I stayed, studying her sleeping face for clues that weren't there.

This has been the worst part. Not the confession itself,

but this liminal space where I don't know if I've just lost everything or if we're about to start over with honesty surrounding us. I wanted to wake her up, demand an answer. I wanted to run. Instead, I sat vigil, watching over the woman who now knows my worst truth.

IT'S BEEN three days since the car accident, and today is supposed to be when they stop her morphine and start her on oral opioids. Just thinking about it makes my skin crawl and my stomach turn.

On top of the weight of how things were left yesterday, there's this crushing realization that *I* need to be her strength. I'm going to help her manage pain medication schedules, support her through recovery, and be the steady presence she needs. But I can feel my own foundation starting to shake. I haven't called Beau yet today. Every instinct in my recovery toolkit is screaming at me to remove myself from a situation saturated with the very substances that nearly killed me.

But I can't leave her. *Won't* leave her. So instead I'm supposed to somehow compartmentalize watching the woman I love take pills that look exactly like the ones I used to crush and snort, supposed to hand her medication and not think about how easy it would be to palm a few for myself. I'm supposed to be her rock while standing on quicksand.

The irony isn't lost on me that loving Alice might be the thing that threatens my sobriety, and losing my sobriety would mean losing her anyway. I'm caught in a trap where helping her heal could destroy the person she has fallen in love with. *Hopefully* has fallen in love with.

I've been pacing in front of her room for ten minutes, and the nurses are giving me strange looks. I didn't get here as early as I wanted to—as early as I should have. I don't even know if she wants to see me.

Dr. Marishka comes around the corner and I nearly bump into her. "Arthur, hi." She smiles, and I can't return one with my thoughts waging war inside my brain. "Alice will be happy to see you." That gets my attention.

"She's awake?" Fuck. That means she'll probably be asleep again soon. I should have been in there.

Dr. Marishka clearly senses my anxiety as she steps closer. "She'll be awake for a little while now. We've stopped the morphine as of this morning." I rub a hand down my face as she continues, "Alice has declined our standard pain-management protocol in favor of non-opioid alternatives. It's going to be more challenging for her recovery, but she was very clear about her decision."

I pull in a sharp breath.

What is she talking about?

My shock must be written all over my face because the doctor's expression softens. "Why don't you go on in and talk to her?"

"Yeah. Thank you."

As she walks away, I take three deep breaths before knocking gently on Alice's door. Her raspy "Come in," reaches my ears, and I push the door open to see her sitting up. She has color returning to her cheeks, but her eyes are sad and distant until I walk into her line of sight and she looks at me.

My gorgeous girl with her golden eyes is looking at me, not with the pity or disdain I have been expecting and rightfully deserve, but with the same warmth she's gifted me with since the very first moment we locked eyes.

"Hi," she whispers. "You came back." The surprise in her tone breaks my heart.

Did she really think I wouldn't?

What does it say about me that she'd think that? No, what does it say about the people who *should* have been there for her before?

"I only leave this hospital because they make me, tesouro, or I'd never leave you." Stepping closer to the bed, I tentatively reach for her hand, and she lets me take it. The relief that washes over me is instant.

"Your family came, too." She looks around at the flowers and cards in the room. She pauses on the stuffed pickle Cece insisted on giving her.

"They did. Beau and Josie, too. Elaina, Charlie, Maeve. Everyone from the ranch." Even the nurse from her grandmother's facility asked about her when I went there yesterday to pick up her belongings. I don't think she realizes how much the people who know her care about her.

"Wow," she whispers as her eyes fill with tears. "I—I didn't mean to worry so many people." Her voice cracks, and so does my heart. She thinks she's such a burden, when the reality couldn't be further from the truth.

"They came because they care about you, Alice."

She shakes her head, blinking back her tears. She might not believe my words, but the proof of them is all over this room.

"I want to tell you everything. About my past, about my recovery." I swallow the giant lump in my throat, knowing this could be the beginning of the end for us.

"No, Arthur. You don't have to, I—"

"I want to. I *need* to. I need you to know this part of me." And I do. I need her to know all the parts of me so she can decide for certain if this, me, is what she really wants.

With a nod, she looks down at our joined hands, squeezing a little tighter.

"I didn't go to college right after high school. I stayed

at home to help my parents until my dad begged me to get a degree so I could take over Machado Grove. I was studying business management. I'd moved nearly three hours away to go to one of the best schools that focused on agricultural studies. I knew it wasn't what I wanted, but he did. He wanted it so badly." I pause as the details of a story I haven't thought about for a long time come back to me. "My dad started working at that grove when he moved here from Brazil as a seasonal worker. He went back for three years before he got hired on full-time. He worked his way up, learned the business inside and out and lived on the property with my mom. They got married there. That little house is where I spent my first few years, before we moved to the main house when the previous owner decided to retire and sell the grove to my parents. They'd been saving for ages, and it still took my dad nearly twenty years to pay it all off. I'd been told since I was a little kid that one day, the grove would be mine. I thought I could learn to like it, but when I was at school, it was so hard. I hated it. I was older than everyone else, and I felt like such a loser. I was stressed out all the time, feeling this pressure to do something expected of me for so long. It felt like it was too late to tell them I didn't want to do it."

I blow out a heavy breath, and Alice's grip on my hand tightens, her thumb drawing soothing circles on my skin.

"People partied hard at school. Everyone felt a lot of pressure to do well, and most of my classmates came from families who had owned farms for multiple generations. I always said no to drugs because I thought doing shit like cocaine seemed too dangerous. Then one night in my third year there, I was offered a pill. They said it was a prescription medication, so it was safe, just to take the edge off. And it did. Suddenly, everything felt manageable. I started taking them before tests, phone calls with my parents, anything that caused stress. It helped so much. I didn't feel high, I felt like I could actually do all the shit that felt so hard before. But then my tolerance built up, and I needed more."

I lower my eyes to our hands, still connected. I can't stand to watch the disappointment that I'm sure is about to be on Alice's face. I'm too much of a coward to witness it.

"Six months in, I was starting to miss morning classes because the withdrawal symptoms were so brutal. I couldn't remember things as easily. My grades dropped from B's to C's to D's. I was on academic probation. I spent the money for textbooks and rent on more pills. Eventually, I spent tuition money, too, until I was kicked out. That's when my family found out what was happening.

"My parents paid to send me to a rehab not too far away. It was a reputable facility. Expensive. Between my debts and rehab, I nearly bankrupted them. They could have chosen one further away, but they wanted to be close enough to support me. That was what they did. They loved and supported me, and I was such an ungrateful piece of shit. I didn't stop using after rehab. It wasn't as bad, and I kept it hidden, so I pushed my family away. It was my lowest low. I didn't have my family, didn't have friends, and I hated myself. That's when Raf introduced me to Owen. Eventually, I met Beau and started going to meetings. I was just starting to consider making amends with my parents when my dad told me he wanted nothing to do with me. I thought they'd all be better off with as little contact as possible from me, so I focused on the ranch and my recovery, and here we are. Now you know everything. Now you have every reason to hate me, to be disgusted by me, because this is who I am and I chose to keep it from you." I haven't wanted to cry until this very moment, when the realization that my actions are about to push the woman I love away hits me.

This might be the last time I see her, so I let my gaze meet hers, finding those golden eyes shining with tears.

"I could never feel those things about you, Arthur. I won't. Ever. How could I? You're the strongest person I know. The kindest, bravest, best person I've *ever* known." Her grip loosens, but only so she can wrap her fingers around my wrist to pull me closer to her. "I'm sorry I didn't let you tell me all of this sooner. I'm sorry I made you feel like you couldn't." I open my mouth to deny it, but she tips her head to the side, shaking it. "I did. I was so caught up feeling like *my* life would be too much for *you*, like my burden would be too much for you to carry, that I didn't give you the chance to share your own. I didn't trust that when I fell, you'd be there to catch me, because no one has ever been. But you were. You *are*. I didn't trust that when I fell in love with you, you might fall in love with me, too."

"I did," I say quickly. "You didn't fall alone, Alice. It was when *we* fell, not just you. I started falling in love with you the moment we locked eyes, but I didn't trust it then either. I didn't believe it could be real."

"And now?" she asks as another tear falls down her perfect cheek. I reach out to catch it, wipe it away.

"Loving you is the realest thing I've ever felt, tesouro. I've never believed in anything, trusted anything, the way I believe in this. Us." I keep my hand on her cheek, and she nuzzles into it, a small smile tipping her lips up.

"I came here with every intention of leaving and never coming back. I wanted to leave and find a place that felt like home, where I felt safe and loved. But I found it here. You're my home, my safe place, my love." She reaches up with her free hand, wiping away my tears like I did hers. "I love you, Arthur," she whispers with eyes still locked on mine.

A sob that should make me embarrassed leaves me then, and I inch closer to Alice, bringing our foreheads together.

"I love you," she repeats as we hold on to one another.

"I love you," I say, kissing her tears away. I repeat those three words until her tears are dry and a giggle escapes her. I've never felt so light, so free, as I do in this moment.

you wanna teach me to ride, baby?

Alice

It's been a week since the accident, three days since I came back to the farmhouse, and I don't think I've been alone for more than thirty minutes.

Arthur even keeps me company when I shower or take a bath. He's kept a close eye on my painkiller schedule, and despite the pain sometimes being near unbearable, I haven't needed to take anything stronger than the over-the-counter medicine the doctor sent me home with.

I'm pretty sure every member of Arthur's family has been here, even if it was just to drop something off. I haven't driven anywhere, haven't cooked anything, haven't been allowed to do more than go on slow, gentle walks.

Someone is always here to help me sit or stand. Fortunately, they leave me alone when I go into the bathroom, but Arthur's mom did offer to help me in there once. I nearly died of embarrassment, but she assured me that after giving birth as many times as she had, she's needed help in more ways than she thought possible. I thanked her, but we didn't cross that line.

Arthur has taken to sleeping in the guest room, which I hate, but he's worried he'll try to cuddle me in his sleep and hurt me. The thought does terrify me. He's hardly touched me because even hugs hurt these days. Not being able to touch me hasn't stopped him from doing everything he can to show me he loves me, though. He took care of everything at Gran's care facility. Sam and Paige finished cleaning out her house while I was still in the hospital. Gabriel's been super helpful with the realtor since they're friends.

I've tried to resist the help a few times, have felt guilty for taking it, but only due to my own issues, because no one has made me feel like I'm a burden.

It'll take some getting used to, but I've accepted that this is my life now. It all happened so fast, but nothing's ever felt as right as being in Ojai, and that's not something I ever could have anticipated or planned for. This town and its people have surprised me in all the best ways.

IT'S BEEN NEARLY four weeks of recovery, and I'm officially pain-free—something I've been trying to convince Arthur of since I met with Dr. Marishka.

I snuck into the barn to see the horses, and I know he's eventually going to find out and give me that concerned look he seems to wear permanently. I'm starting to hate it now that I'm finally feeling like myself again.

Just as I expected, there's a shuffling of boots behind me. "It's him, isn't it, Moose?" The giant horse nuzzles into me in a movement that feels like a nod, and it makes me laugh.

When I turn, Arthur is breathing heavily, like he just ran here. When he sees my riding boots, he pinches the bridge of his nose, closing his eyes. "Jesus, woman. You're going to give me gray hairs if you keep doing shit like this."

I giggle, moving close enough that I can reach up and touch the hair peeking out beneath his backward cap, where he already has a few grays that I absolutely adore. He hasn't had a haircut in weeks, and I love that I can so easily touch his hair even when he's wearing a hat. "Aww, my love, it's too late for that."

He moves his hand to my waist, keeping his eyes closed as he breathes through the frustration I'm clearly causing.

"Are you going to be a helicopter dad when you have kids?" His eyes pop open, but I don't stop. "Protect them from every little thing? Because you can't, you know? Kids get hurt. And I'm not a kid. I'm fine, Arthur. I've healed." I lower my hand to rest on my hip, waiting for him to argue with me.

"You want kids, tesouro?" His eyes soften, his hand pulling me closer.

"Um—I—Do you?" Oh gosh, what have I done? I just brought up him being a dad, like the true dummy that I am. It's too much. Too fast. Yes, we've admitted our feelings and we live together, but this is too far, isn't it?

"With you? Hell yeah, but I asked if *you* want kids. Do you?" His other hand travels from my hip to my lower back, causing my arm to fall limply at my side.

"I do," I whisper with my heart threatening to beat its way out of my ribcage. It's not a thought I've ever allowed myself to have out loud, but despite my own upbringing,

I've always dreamed of giving kids the childhood I didn't have.

Arthur's smile is blinding, his deep brown eyes crinkling at the corners as he studies me. "Good. When *we* have kids, yeah, I'm gonna do everything I can to protect them. You can keep me in line when I hover too much, okay?" He pulls me closer until our bodies are flush. "Breathe, baby. We have time. We're not having kids right now, it's all right." He chuckles because, of course, my panicked expression gives me away.

I take a breath, then and force a straight face as I say, "Well, no, we'd have to have sex for that to happen, wouldn't we?" My smug smile breaks free, knowing I've hit a nerve when he squints his eyes. "You do know that's how babies are made, right? If you want kids, you're gonna have to fuck me, Arthur." Desperate times call for desperate measures. I've been begging him to get naked with me for days, ever since the doctor gave me the all clear.

I arch into him, and he hisses in a breath. "You're a brat, you know that?" His fingers tighten at my back as he keeps me close.

I shrug, still smiling. "Just want to make sure you make good on your promises. I mean, I'm pretty sure you said you wanted me to teach you to ride English, but that has yet to happen…" I keep playing with his hair, twirling the ends that have grown and curl under his hat as I sigh, pouting for good measure.

"You wanna teach me to ride, baby?" Still pouting, I nod. "And you think you're ready for riding?" He pushes his hardness into me, and I gasp, my nod becoming frantic as my lips part. He lowers his hand to my butt, and I hope and pray he's about to carry me to the tack room and fuck me senseless. But no. He smacks me lightly and steps back.

"Let's go." He keeps walking backward, away from me with a devilish smile. His wink is followed by a laugh as he turns around and heads into the tack room.

I stand there, mouth agape and in disbelief that he just did that. I watch as he preps Scout with an English saddle and then does the same to Moose. My shock turns into excitement when it hits me that we're about to ride together, and I beam with hope that this means I also get to ride *him* tonight.

I KEEP my eyes locked on Arthur's butt, doing my best not to laugh. "Okay, now rise with the trot—"

"Rise? I thought the point was to stay in the saddle!" The exasperation in his voice is clear, and Moose is probably not super impressed with what's happening right now.

"You're posting, not ejecting. And stop looking for the horn!" I easily move around him as he reaches yet again for the non-existent horn in front of him. I've watched Arthur while he's riding. Many times. He's relaxed and confident on a Western saddle, but this… this is equal parts hilarious and adorable to watch because he's so far out of his comfort zone.

"How do you steer this thing?" He lifts a hand, nearly falling off Scout, and I bite back a laugh, but I can't help my smile.

"With both hands on your reins. Use your legs and seat. And stop dropping your hand!" I get into his line of sight again, trying to demonstrate what he needs to do, but it's no use.

"This feels like the horse is trying to buck me off in slow motion." He bounces awkwardly, and I let out a giggle. He's trying so hard.

After twenty minutes of watching Arthur flail around

like a rag doll, I can't stay in the saddle anymore—I'm laughing too hard. I slip off Moose and bend over, clutching my stomach as tears blur my vision.

Meanwhile, Arthur remains determinedly mounted on Scout, his dignity hanging on by a thread. "Oh you think this is funny, do you? We'll see what's funny when I fuck you tonight in our bed and the only things bouncing around are your perfect tits." He turns and rides back toward the barn while I'm left with my jaw on the floor for the second time in an hour.

As I get back on Moose and follow Arthur, his words replay again and again like my favorite song.

When I fuck you tonight.

Our bed.

Promises, promises…

WHEN WE GOT BACK to the barn after his disastrous lesson, Arthur claimed he had some work to do, despite the fact that it's Sunday. I reminded him about family dinner, and secretly hoped he'd make good on his words from earlier before we had to leave, but nope. No sex for me. Yet.

Instead, here we are, sitting in his truck, about to arrive at his parents' house. I've had to endure the entire twenty-minute drive with a freshly showered and shaved Arthur, smelling good and looking even better. I watch as the muscles on his tattooed forearm flex, putting the truck into park.

He reaches over and wipes at a spot on the corner of my lip. "You had some drool right there." When I respond with a glare that I'm sure does nothing to make him believe I'm angry, he chuckles, opening his door and rounding the truck to get mine. I let him because I have a tray of desserts on my lap that I know I'll drop if I so much as touch the handle myself.

I don't make eye contact as I climb out, and I don't say thank you when he helps me. But that feels wrong. I'm frustrated, but I'm still obsessively in love with the man. "Thank you," I murmur.

The only indication that he heard me is the kiss he leaves on the top of my head as he breathes me in. "I'll make the wait worthwhile, baby."

I repeat my thoughts from earlier. "Promises, promises…" His response is a deep chuckle that makes me smile, as I look up at him. He laughs so easily these days. Smiles more. So do I.

As we walk into the already bustling kitchen, Rafael greets us with a wide smile. He's got an apron on that says, "This guy rubs his own meat," and I chuckle. Ana Maria always makes him wear these whenever he insists on helping in the kitchen. I set the tray of cookies that we'll be making into ice cream sandwiches later on the counter and greet Vó with a kiss on each cheek before making my way to do the same with all of the Machado family members congregating here.

When I get to Charlie, I take in the bright yellow apron she's wearing with the words, "My boyfriend's sausage is bigger than yours," in bright red letters. My hand flies to my mouth as I try to hold in my laughter, and my eyes dart to Rafael, expecting to see a proud, smug smile on his face.

"You don't like the apron, Raf?" Arthur asks, squeezing his brother's shoulder.

"Not particularly, no. It should say fiancé, not boyfriend." He winks at Charlie, and all eyes dart to where she's standing, left hand proudly held up in the air and the biggest smile I've ever seen on her face.

The room erupts into cheers and tears. Before we know it, there's a song playing and everyone is partnering up, dancing around the kitchen. I've never seen Charlie look happier, and when I look up into Arthur's eyes, I notice the same is true about him.

He brings his lips to my ears so only I can hear his next words. "You okay with this chaos for the rest of your life, tesouro?"

My stomach flutters, thinking about him wanting me forever. I've been sure about Arthur since before the accident, my feelings only solidified once he shared the remaining pieces of himself he'd kept hidden for too long. But knowing he's sure too is overwhelming.

Somehow I find the words, running my fingers over his smooth cheek and meeting his eyes as I nod. "It's better than anything I've ever imagined or hoped for."

We seal our promise of forever with a kiss as whistles sound off next to us, no doubt from Arthur's rowdy brothers.

And it's perfect.

Epilogue

A year later.

Arthur

"Gabriel?" I call out as we walk into his house through the side door carrying more candy than anyone should. It's Halloween, and for the first time, Cece has decided she wants to go out. Gabe's stressed as hell, so me and Alice have offered to come hand out candy while he takes her around the neighborhood.

"Weird. His truck is here," Alice says as she starts to fill a bowl with chocolates, clearly unfazed by the lack of people in the house. We've been here often lately, helping Gabriel with Cece as he continues to struggle to find a nanny or even a reliable babysitter.

I'm about to reach for my phone to call him when the front door opens and then slams closed.

"Gabe?" I try again, hoping it's him, though the door

slamming seems weird for my normally cool-and-collected brother.

"Yeah," he says a little too loudly. As he walks into the kitchen, he's tugging at his hair. "Hey. Sorry about that. The fucking neighbor is driving me insane."

"Maggi?" Alice asks, popping a candy into her mouth. Gabriel nods, his nostrils flaring at the mention of the woman's name. "She's so sweet!"

"She is the furthest thing from sweet. That woman is a *menace*, and she's everywhere. I asked her if she could tone down the scary decorations in front of her house because I didn't want my daughter being scared. Do you know what she said?" We both shrug, afraid to answer my now very agitated brother. "No." He scoffs, pulling at his hair again. "That's it. Just no. And when I asked her to elaborate, she said it again! No. Because, according to her, 'no is a full sentence, asshole.' Those were her words. Can you believe this shit?" He paces around the kitchen, taking a few deep breaths.

"Well, she's not wrong," Alice murmurs. I shoot her a sideways glance, trying not to laugh at the situation. We've been hearing about Gabe's neighbor for weeks now, and she doesn't seem to be going away.

We're saved from further tales of the "awful" woman when the side door opens.

"Daddy, look!" Cece comes blasting in, hardly noticing us standing there. "Look what Miss Noli did today!" She's more excited than I've ever seen her before, and that's been happening more and more since this artist started volunteering at her school.

Gabriel's face blanches, and he looks from Cece's face to my parents, who are standing at the door, and back down to her face. I can't see anything, and Alice is trying to twist until she can, but she doesn't have any luck. I look to my dad for a hint, but he shrugs, putting his hands up in surrender.

Cece turns around to show us when her dad doesn't react, and Alice gasps next to me, immediately breathing out a "Wow!"

My niece walks up to her with hopeful eyes, or at least I think her eyes are hopeful. It's hard to tell with all the makeup on her face. "Do you like it, Tia Alice?" I clutch my chest because the Tia thing is new and I fucking love it.

"Oh, Cece, I love it. It looks so real! You're like a real zombie, aren't you?" Alice inspects her face, oohing and aahing at every new angle.

"Well, zombies don't exist, so, no," Cece answers in a serious tone. "Miss Noli painted it today. I told her I wanted to look *really* scary, but she said that might not be a good idea at school because the little kids might get scared." She rolls her eyes, like she's not seven years old. "So she stayed until after school, and Vô and Vó waited while she painted my zombie face." She points to where there's a too-realistic scar on her normally sweet face. "Cool, right?"

"Ye—" Alice starts, then clears her throat as she takes in Gabriel's scowl. "You should get dressed, kiddo. It's almost time to head out."

With that, Cece runs up the stairs. Gabriel pinches the bridge of his nose, mumbling a string of swear words, and my mother laughs.

"She loves it, filho. Let her have her fun." Mom waves a hand in front of her like this is no big deal. I mean, it isn't, so I'm not sure what's up Gabe's ass.

He huffs out a breath. "Thank you for picking her up. And feeding her dinner."

"Anytime. Tchau, meus amores!" Mom calls out, blowing each of us a kiss as she disappears through the door they just came in from. My dad mouths an apology to Gabriel before giving us a wave and following his wife.

"Just fucking great," Gabriel huffs.

AN HOUR LATER, it's just me and Alice in the house, taking turns answering the door as trick-or-treaters ring the bell. The neighbor Gabriel is determined to hate, and who shares a wall with him, has been playing some spooky music and turned some colorful lights on outside. She even has a smoke machine. It's pretty cool, but I'm not going to tell my brother that when he gets back with Cece.

Alice has changed into her witch costume, and I'm having a very hard time keeping it together every time she bends over to toss some candy into the kids' bags. The black skirt she has on rides high enough to show off her toned thighs, and she has fishnet stockings on. When she first came down, wearing her big black hat and matching lipstick, I thought she looked cute, but now? Now I'm struggling not to turn off the lights and ignore the doorbell as I lift her skirt to find out exactly what she has on underneath.

And it's that train of thought that has me reaching for her as soon as she shuts the door. With my chest flush against her back, I reach for the bowl and set it on the nearby table. "Arthur, what—" She gasps when I press my already hard dick against her ass. "Oh," she breathes out.

"This fucking skirt is driving me crazy, baby. Tell me what you have on underneath." Running my hand up her thigh, I lift her skirt higher and higher, but not high enough to answer my own question. I want to hear it from her mouth.

"Um, th-that black lacy thong you like," she pants out, and as my hand travels up, I find that her stockings are thigh-highs, so my fingertips meet her smooth skin. Her head whips back to rest on my shoulder when I run a finger from her entrance to her clit over the already soaked material.

The doorbell rings, and she straightens as if the kids can see her through the solid wood door.

Fuck.

If it's not my dog trying to cock block me, it's other people's kids? Doesn't seem fair.

Alice

When Gabriel got back with a sleeping Cecilia in his arms, he seemed to be in a far better mood, though he did grind his teeth when a man's booming laughter came from next door.

Arthur and I rushed out of there, both because we didn't want to get in the middle of whatever mood Gabe's in and because we really, *really* needed to get home. And naked.

He makes the twenty-minute drive in fifteen and rushes to let Luther out into his dog run while I run upstairs to wash off my black lipstick. I whip my shirt off as soon as I get into our bedroom, about to push my skirt down when his voice stops me.

"Don't you dare." His dark gaze is locked on my hands at my waist. "Leave that skirt on. You're going to give me your first orgasm while you're still wearing it."

I whimper, and in three long strides he's standing in front of me, his own shirt coming off in a swift, one-handed move. He didn't have a costume tonight. He's saving it for the Halloween party we're going to at Beau's tomorrow. His pants and underwear come off next, and then he's standing in front of me completely naked. It's a sight I'll never tire of.

"Sit on the bed for me, baby." His voice is equal parts gentle and commanding, and I waste no time doing as he says, "Bra off." My hands move of their own accord. He kneels in front of me, pushing my knees apart. "Lay back."

Like he did earlier, he smooths his hands along my thighs, pushing up my skirt. He hums his approval, no doubt seeing how wet I already am. Have been. The ripping sound registers at the same time as cool air hits my slick center. *He tore my thong.*

"Hey," I protest. "I liked tho—oh. Oh!"

I lose all train of thought when he flicks my clit with his tongue, then sucks it into his mouth. Hard. He chuckles, and the sound with the vibrations have me nearly coming already. His answering hum as I push myself against his mouth makes me arch my back, my hands finding my hardened nipples.

"That's it, tesouro. Play with those perfect tits and come for me." He sucks my clit again, three times in quick succession, and I free-fall right off the cliff I've been on the edge of since he touched me earlier tonight.

As I'm coming down, still panting, there's another rip as he obliterates my thong and tosses it across the room. I groan, and he lifts me until my head lands gently on my pillow. When he kisses me, and I taste myself on his lips, I tug on his hair, pulling him impossibly closer to me and kissing him with everything I have.

We pull away, breathless, and his eyes meet mine. "Do you want soft and slow, or hard and fast?"

"Yes," I whimper in response as the tip of his cock meets my still-sensitive clit.

He lines himself up and thrusts inside in one slow, methodical movement that has me gasping for air. Again and again, he repeats the measured movement, eyes never leaving mine.

"I love you," he whispers so low I almost don't hear it. But I do. I always hear him because his I love you's are in every touch, every kiss, every single thing he does.

"I love you," I answer on a moan. And that's enough for him to give me what he knows I want. He pushes in hard, keeping his thrusts long and deep, and it takes no more than a minute before I'm screaming his name, my nails digging into the skin of his shoulders.

With his eyes locked with mine, he comes on a groan so deep, I feel it in every bone in my body. Then he releases his weight onto me, letting me have all of it with his face buried in the crook of my neck, and I run my nails up and down his back.

"Fuck, baby. I wanted you to come one more time, but the way your pussy grips me is so fucking good I couldn't hold back." At his words, I swivel my hips, still somehow so turned on and ready for more. This is what he does to me. What him talking to me like this does. Or it's the hormones. I'm not sure. "You wanna come again, Alice?"

The "yes" that comes out too loudly is entirely involuntary.

"Good," he says, lifting himself off me before pulling out and making me whimper. But then his fingers are there, pushing inside. "Fuck, I love the way my cum looks dripping out of your pussy." I clench around his fingers just before he pulls them out, gathering his release and pushing it back inside me. "One day soon, we're gonna make a baby, and I can't wait to—"

"We already did," I pant, mentally cussing myself out for not waiting for a better moment. But then again, this is what he's always done to me. He makes me lose all sense, all thought. I just found out this morning, and it's been so hard to keep it from him. After I came off birth control a few months ago, we promised not to put any pressure on ourselves, but every month I've taken a test. And finally, today, I saw the little plus sign.

"What did you say?" He pauses, fingers still inside me.

"We made a baby. I'm pregnant." I make sure to look into his eyes when I say it, and when I do, he curls his fingers, causing me to moan.

"Say it again," he whispers, shifting until we're nose-to-nose. I repeat everything, word for word, and he groans. "You're pregnant?"

"Yes," I say, our lips brushing.

"Will you marry me?"

"Yes," I answer, and with a final, perfect curl of his fingers, I come, and his lips latch onto mine, catching every moan, every needy sound.

When my limbs turn to Jello, and every muscle in my body is spent, Arthur leaves one more tender kiss on my lips before kissing my nose and my forehead. Only then does he slip his fingers out of me.

"Are we getting married?" I ask, and his lips turn up into a brilliant smile.

He nods. "And having a baby." His soft laugh is almost disbelieving, like the truth of it is sinking in. "I have your ring in my sock drawer. I've had it since you stopped birth control. I wanted to ask you when you told me, but tesouro, I just didn't expect you to tell me when I was pushing my cum back inside you."

I bring my hands up to my face, covering up my heated cheeks. "I'm sorry. It was terrible timing, I know—"

"None of that," he tells me, pulling her my hands away one by one and kissing my cheeks. "It was perfect timing. Just like everything else about our story." Of course he would be so calm about this.

"No, I ruined it. We can't tell anyone this story now. People are going to ask how I told you and how you asked me. I can't say, 'Oh he was pushing his cum back inside my pussy after sex, and I was so brain dead from multiple orgasms that I told him, and then he asked me to marry him, and I said yes, and then I came again.'" I roll my eyes at the ridiculousness of it all, only to find Arthur with his lips turned down, brows high, nodding.

"Sounds like a pretty awesome way to propose and announce a pregnancy to me, goldie." When I smack his chest, he laughs, and the sound inevitably makes me smile. "What would you rather tell them? We can make up any story you want."

"No, we can't!" I'm exasperated and annoyed with myself. This isn't the story we're going to tell our child. Or anyone. Ever! "You know I can't lie, Arthur. Everyone would know if I tried to tell a different story."

"Then let's create a different story. Ready?" He shifts so we're lying side-by-side with his legs intertwined with mine, the way we do most nights when we talk before snuggling up to fall asleep. I'm confused, so he continues with whatever he's doing, letting out a long breath. "Alice Margaret Preece, you are the love of my life. You're my best friend and my favorite person in the whole world. You've gifted me more love and happiness than I ever thought possible, and I'm going to spend every single day of my life showing you, telling you, how much I love you."

He pushes a stray curl off my cheek, tucking it behind my ear before catching the tear on the bridge of my nose. "I think your name would sound really good if it was Alice

Margaret Machado, but I'm completely okay with becoming Arthur Ivan Preece, too, if you'll say yes to marrying me. What do you think, tesouro? Want to be my wife?"

"Yes," I whisper, unable to find much volume when there are so many emotions clogging up my throat. "I want that more than anything." With my still-strangled voice, I continue, "I'm pregnant."

Saying the words has tears instantly pooling on my pillowcase and my nose, but then I hear my favorite sound. Arthur is laughing, and it's the happiest, most amazing sound in the world. It coaxes my own laughter out of me, and before I know it, we're all tangled up in one another, smiling and laughing from the joy that can't be contained inside our bodies.

"How's that for a story?" he asks once my head is on his shoulder and he's gently brushing his fingers through my curls.

"I think they're both pretty perfect." I pause, tensing before adding, "But you're still never allowed to tell a soul the first version."

His chuckle is deep and quiet. "I promise. That one is just for us."

"Just for us," I say before closing my eyes and falling asleep in the arms of my future husband, the father of my child, and my one true love.

THE END

Want more of Cristina's books?

First of all, if you liked *When We Fell*, please consider leaving a review. Seriously, those things are world-changing for authors and help so, SO much!

Now, if you're ready for more of love stories, you're in luck!

LOVE IN LA SERIES

Book 1: Lost Love Found (Adam + Elaina)

- friends to lovers

- fake dating

- love after loss

Book 2: Sparks Still Fly (Owen + Maeve)

- second chance

- best friend's brother

- accidental marriage

Book 3: Out of Focus (Rafael + Charlie)

- frenemies to lovers

- intimacy lessons

- ADHD, Autism + Dyslexia rep

BALSAM BAY SERIES

BOOK 1: FROM AWAY (LEO + NEVE)

- workplace romance

- small, coastal town

- social anxiety + endometriosis rep

BOOK 2: TBA (DARCY + BILLIE)

- one night stand

- just one (more) time

- healing together

MACHADO FAMILY SERIES

BOOK 1: WHEN WE FELL

- workplace romance

- forced proximity

- age gap (8 years)

BOOK 2: TBA (GABRIEL + MAGNOLIA)

If you want more of the Machado Family Series, Gabriel and Magnolia's book is next! Want to know when their story will be here, get the title reveal, cover and more?

Sign up for Cristina's newsletter

https://csauthor.substack.com/

cristinasantosauthor.com

Acknowledgments

No book is possible without the best partner in the world, who encourages me to write, asks how many words I got in, and whether I say five or five thousand, celebrates me just the same. Thank you forever, my love. And thank you to my little boys who ask questions, sneak into my office trying to read what I'm writing (yikes!), and are constantly in awe of how many words I've written. If you are their school teacher and you've been gifted this book, I'm so sorry. They absolutely insist that their teachers want my books, and I don't have the heart to tell them no when they're so proud of their mama. Great. Now I'm crying.

Megan McSpadden, these characters wouldn't exist without you. I'm so glad Alice has a little piece of you in her. Thank you for endlessly putting up with my voice notes as I brainstormed and processed out loud. Thank you for being my sounding board, my safe place to vent, celebrate, cry, laugh—sometimes all in the same message. You embossed only heart permanently!

Maggi, you changed my writing career with an email. How lucky am I that because of that I get to give you real life hugs, name a character after you, and celebrate your wins with you? The luckiest.

Megan, Meg, Julie (alphas who read my messiest, shittiest words and love me anyway), Amanda, Camille, Jessica, Joana, Kari, Katie, Maggi, Melanie and Nicole (the bestest betas): thank you for helping me make sense of things when I veer off in weird directions, write the runniest run-on sentences known to humanity, and inevitably get a name wrong somewhere in the story. You are a key part of making these books what they are, and I couldn't do this without you. I certainly wouldn't want to! Thank you forever and ever!

Kristen, thank you for telling me when I'm telling too much and not showing enough. Thank you for being a fact-checking expert. Thank you for putting up with my unfinished manuscripts!

Katie, No book would be the same without your voice notes telling me when I've made you cry. I'm so thankful for your expertise, your advice, your words of encouragement and your friendship!

Cami, your Monday morning check-ins are forever my favourite thing. Your support means everything, and I'm so lucky I get to work with you *and* have your friendship. Thank you for everything these last two years.

Gatinhas (that's you, street team), thank you for celebrating these characters with me, for giving me feedback on everything from cover design to character art to the playlist. Having you in my corner is such a highlight of my days!

Anyone who's given this book a chance, whether it's as an ARC reader or years after this book is released—thank you! All I've ever wanted is for my stories to make people feel seen, to help them to believe in themselves and believe that the reality that being loved for exactly who you are, as you are, is not only possible, but that you deserve it.

With all my love,

xoxo,
Cristina

About the Author

Cristina Santos is a mom of two little boys who hopefully will never read this book. She is married to the man of her dreams and lives lakeside with all her wild boys (pup included) in Nova Scotia, Canada. She loves a good sunset and will forever and ever and ever believe in the power of playlists, 90's romantic comedies and love stories.

This is Cristina's fifth book.

cristinasantosauthor.com

Want more Machado brothers?

Book 3 in the Love in LA Series is Rafael's story.

Flip the page for the first chapter!

1 / Ouch. That's going to leave a mark.

Charlie

Now

"Stop calling me, Robert. I'm not your girlfriend. I never was. You made that perfectly clear." I breathe in a lungful of the warm Los Angeles air and immediately regret it. I came outside to clear my head. To go for a walk and forget about London and Robert for a bit. And now, I'm acutely aware of everything around me yet again.

What is that smell? And why does the bottom of my shoe feel sticky?

"You said you needed space. How much more space could you need? We're on opposite sides of the planet!" His words instantly make my temples throb.

"You know that's not what I meant. We agreed that you would give me time." I huff out a breath, unsure of how many more ways I can find to tell him that I need him to leave me alone.

"Charlotte, stop acting like a petulant child. Come home."

A few weeks ago, I would have.

I would have said I was a shoo-in for CFO at the company Robert and I work for. Worked for? I haven't formally quit, but the thought has crossed my mind more than a handful of times in the seven months since my last visit to LA. I've earned this hypothetical promotion, though, and that's why I haven't handed in my resignation. As their VP of Finance, I helped Robert Thorpe, the current CFO, and voice at the end of the line, reduce costs and address operational inefficiencies. A job he has proven to be completely inept at. Now, Robert's father is stepping down as CEO, and he's gunning for the job. Instead of staying and fighting for my place as the company's first female with a C-level executive position in its seventy-three-year lifespan, I asked for a leave of absence. Effective immediately. And then I got on a plane to LA. Again.

"Charlotte? Are you even listening to me?" Ugh. I hate that he keeps calling me by my full name. My mother calls me that. Well, my mother *and* Robert, who refuses to be called anything else. The Thorpes only do full names or obnoxious nicknames. There's no in-between. My thoughts are slipping away again, so I know what the answer to his question is.

Nope. So not listening.

Squinting against the harsh sunlight, I realize that I forgot my sunglasses yet again on my way out the door. The sunglasses that are sitting on the kitchen counter, next to my to-do list, which includes a reminder to change my phone plan while I'm here because, this time, I am staying. This won't be like last time when I only stayed for a few days before running back to Robert and whatever emergency he was feigning.

I wonder how much this call is costing me. And did I close the balcony door before I left?

I take a breath and decide that it's fine. I'll tackle the list later, and it's okay if the door was left open. The flat is on the seventh floor, so it's not like anyone can break in, and it rarely rains here, anyway.

Despite the circumstances, I couldn't have come to LA at a better time. It's been two weeks since I told my twin, Maeve, that I was finally ready for the change I claimed to need all those months ago. Last time I was here, she had just accidentally married the love of her life and then decided to officially adopt the baby who had been placed in her husband's care. Owen's gone through a lot, and a drunken Vegas wedding was apparently what they both needed to start their lives together.

Since then, both Maeve and our best friend Elaina announced pregnancies just weeks apart. Elaina and Adam had their baby girl on New Year's Day, just two years and a day after they met. I've missed so much over the years, and it feels good to be here and witness all of the joy in Maeve and Elaina's lives. They're the two most important people in my world, and while they've been falling in love and growing babies, I've been living a monotonous routine of work, takeout, and a standing three-night-a-week date with my vibrator. I'm not jealous of what they have because I'm truly so happy they have found such joy, but I'm tired of hearing about everything over phone calls while I feel stuck living a life that isn't exciting anymore. I want more for myself, and I know I deserve it.

Between our mum's latest man drama and the announcement at the firm, I was being suffocated in London. I've always loved the city, but lately, everything there has felt wrong. Including Robert. Maybe, especially him. And that's why I'm here. I need space, clarity, and to make sense of my life.

Thanks to my twin's endless connections in Los Angeles, I was able to sublet a furnished place as soon as I got here. Maeve and Elaina have lived in LA since we graduated from NYU eight years ago. They asked me to come then, too, but the thought of living in another strange city just four years after moving from London to New York was completely overwhelming to me. Once I got the scholarship to Oxford for my master's degree, it was time to head back to England and eventually back to London after I graduated.

LA made sense for them. They were pursuing jobs in Hollywood, and they've both made names for themselves in their respective careers. I'm immensely proud of them. I suppose I've done the same, just in London and in a career I'm not entirely sure suits me anymore. A career I picked because it seemed like the right thing to do. It was safe. Predictable, yet challenging. It seemed so perfect. And I'm so damn good at my job, but is all of that enough?

I must make some sort of noise because Robert sighs and continues. "Oh, good. You're still there. Charlotte, you've got to come back. My father won't step down until I prove I've settled down. We've talked about this. We're the dream team. CEO and CFO power couple. Please, Lottie." He's the one sounding like a petulant child now. A spoiled rich boy who's always gotten his way, and that has unfortunately included with me as well. Right down to the fact that I let him call me that ridiculous nickname, which he reserves for when he wants something from me.

He latched on to me the moment I started impressing our professors at Oxford. I caught his attention, intriguing him with my brain. My mistake was thinking he'd be interested in other parts of my body, but all he's ever done is allude to the fact that he's not ready to take that step yet. He loves to tell me how someday we'll be the ultimate power couple, married and running the company his great-grandfather founded. Once he's done enjoying being a bachelor, that is, because he'd hate to resent the woman he spends his life with. And I've understood it.

We met at twenty-two, and I didn't want to get married then, either. I wanted to focus on school and my career. So when Robert said he wanted to wait until we were both ready for that final commitment, it made sense to me. And it made me feel like I had a safety net ready to catch me. I figured marrying the right man was worth the wait. And despite his many faults, Robert mostly understands me and accepts me as I am.

We decided years ago that an open relationship was the best thing for us. We knew we wanted to eventually fully commit to one another. Robert wanted to make sure we both got dating other people well out of our systems before we became exclusive.

Maeve doesn't understand it, but for me, it always made perfect sense. I got the security of knowing I'd found my person, and I could choose to date other people if and when I wanted to. Though for the past couple of years, I haven't wanted to, and Robert and I have spent almost no time together as a couple.

"Lottie. Babe. I'm ready now. What do I have to say to make you believe me?" His whiny voice cuts through the noise, and I shake my head, attempting to focus.

"Nothing. I've already told you I need a break. That's why I'm taking this leave of absence. I need you to respect that this time." My voice is firm, even if inside, I'm completely falling apart. "Two months ago you said that we're not in a relationship. Now you want me to commit to being with you permanently because your dad is giving you an ultimatum?" My heart is racing, and my nerves are completely shot. Have I just left behind my one chance at the two things I've always wanted? A top position in my field and a husband. Those are the next goals to be achieved.

A husband.

Something both my best friend and sister have now. Well, Elaina will soon. She's been engaged to Adam for over a year, but her pregnancy was so rough on her that she couldn't bring herself to plan a wedding at the same time.

"Well, yes, Charlotte. I'm ready now because the CEO position is ready now. We both said we wanted to meet career goals before committing. We both agreed. We've waited years for this, and you know you're the only one I could ever marry." This fact is what had kept me going. Kept me waiting. I always thought Robert was a good guy for not pressuring me into a relationship when I wasn't ready. He once told me that he knew the first time I smiled at him that I was the one. I don't even remember the moment. Don't remember the smile since it was probably fake. Likely because I was trying so hard to look like I belonged in the room, rather than fighting off the urge to put on headphones or leave and quiet my mind with a book or a walk. I had my mask on when I gave him that smile, but he doesn't know that. Most people don't.

"How long?" Robert's voice barely registers among all the noise. In my head. Out here. I need to find somewhere quiet.

"What?" I ask, not even sure what he's going on about.

"How long do you need?" His tone's changed from cajoling to slightly annoyed.

"I'm not sure. Perhaps until Lainey and Adam are married? Once Maeve gives birth? I don't know. I need space, Robert. I need space from *you*." There. I said it. It might feel as though my heart is about to gallop out of my chest, but I said the words.

Robert clears his throat. "Oh. I didn't realize. All these years, I thought, well, I thought you wanted this. Me."

"I did. I…" I can't force myself to say I do because I'm not sure that's true any longer. "I did. I still might. But I can't figure that out when you tell me we're not together and then two weeks later decide you want to marry me because your dad has a position ready for you. Where am I in all of this? When do my feelings start to count?" I take an exasperated breath. "We made this decision years ago when neither of us were ready, and I'm still not sure that I am. I need to see for myself what the best thing for me is. Personally and professionally. And my sister might need me here. It's a delicate time. There's so much going on. I don't want to miss it all." My temples throb as the words pour out of me.

"I'm trying to understand, Lottie." This time, when I hear the nickname that only he uses, my muscles relax. The familiarity is soothing. This is the conundrum I always find myself in with him. One moment he overwhelms me, and the next, he's the familiar presence I need to calm down. But it never lasts with Robert. One way or the other.

"Thank you. Are you all right?" The words stick in my throat. I know I need to do this, but Robert has been a constant in my life for years. Other than Maeve and Elaina, he's the person who knows me best. Who mostly understands my need to get away; my difficulty with sensory overwhelm. It's hard to simply let a person like that go, especially when I'm not very good at letting people in.

"Yeah. Fine." His voice is a bit harder again, and I'm back on the Robert roller coaster. Is it too much to ask for to simply be understood? Fully? "Is this you trying to get back at me? Because we agreed to an open relationship until we were married, Charlotte. It's not my fault you chose to stop dating other people, and I didn't. But if what you need is for us to be broken up so you can shag some LA boys before you come home to me, then fine. Get it out of your system." He's completely serious, too.

It's never bothered him to think of me with other people. I thought it was sort of progressive, even if it did always feel like a bit of red flag hanging limply between us. Now that red flag is practically glowing, waving aggressively and warning me to stay away.

He's partially right, though. It's not his fault I chose to stop dating, but now, I feel completely unprepared for the possibility of a permanent relationship. With anyone.

"I should go. I'll call you when I'm ready, all right?" I'm about to say goodbye when I hear the telltale sound of the call ending. He hung up. I keep the phone to my ear, embarrassed.

Do the people around me know I was just hung up on? Can they tell? I say goodbye, pretending that didn't happen and willing the burning sensation in my cheeks away.

It doesn't work. The whole interaction throws me off, and I end up pacing back and forth on the sidewalk for several minutes. My phone is clutched to my chest like a security blanket as I dwell on every single word we just said to one another. My heart rate is still accelerated, the whooshing sound loud in my ears. Sweat is trickling down the back of my neck, making me itchy. Tears sting my eyes, but I can't let them fall. There are too many people, and I can sense their eyes on me, so I start walking.

What am I doing here? I should have stayed in London. What if

I go back and they don't want me? I won't have a job. How will I make money?

I should have moved to LA a long time ago. I haven't been happy in London for ages. Have I ever been happy? Why don't I know the answer to that? What is wrong with me?

What if working in finance is my entire purpose, and I've just messed it up? I should go back. But what if I hate it? Do I have to do it for the next several decades?

I owe it to myself to figure this out. That's why I'm here. But what if I don't? Do I have to suffer through living in this limbo forever?

Why am I so indecisive that I can't just pick something and someone and live a happy life? Why am I so stupid and unable to handle simple things like everyone else can?

When I find myself in front of a small park, I spot a woman running, and I remember the reason I left the apartment to begin with: to escape. While the world of finance is where I've always excelled, writing is what brings me home.

On my walks, I often get lost in the characters I'm reading or writing about. What started as a hobby, quickly turned into a hyper-fixation, and has now morphed into an all-consuming, secret side hustle. I write the love stories I wish I lived myself. I write the happy endings I hope everyone gets to have. The one I never saw my mum get because she was so selfish and always seemed to pick unavailable men. I live in both worlds, but this one that I've created, with flawed but beautiful characters, I get to keep to myself. I get to control it.

I tuck my phone into the pocket of my pants and take in my surroundings. The relief is almost immediate as the thoughts fall away, and I focus on my breathing and the movement of my legs.

Soon, my thoughts trail to the characters I'm writing. I get lost in the mental planning of the settings, the mood, and how I want things to feel. I let myself get lost in getting to know these people.

I walk for so long that my legs are almost numb, but I can't stop now. Not when my mind finally clears. I need to hang on to this feeling.

I close my eyes for a second. Just a second. And my body comes in full contact with a wall. Then, the pavement. I open my eyes just in time to feel my elbow hit the sidewalk.

Ouch. That's going to leave a mark.

I lay my head back on the floor and drape one arm over my face to hide from the embarrassment of walking with my eyes closed. I'm acutely aware of the shooting pain in my other elbow and the soreness in my lower back since I landed mostly on it. Words are leaving my mouth, but I couldn't tell you what they are. And is someone talking to me?

"Can you tell me where you're hurt?" The voice is soothing and sounds a little closer now.

"I think it's mostly my ego if I'm honest. I'm so very sorry. I was just getting into this groove, and I closed my eyes for only a second, I swear—"

"So, you *did* have your eyes closed." My whole body tenses. Recognition hits me harder than the pavement beneath me. I know the sass in that tone. I can practically see the arrogant smirk painted on the face of the jerk it belongs to.

Rafael Machado.

You have got to be bloody joking me.

Out of Focus is available on e-book, Kindle Unlimited and paperback.